WHISPER CREEK

WHISPER CREEK
By Valerie Davisson
Copyright © 2021 Valerie Davisson

WHISPER CREEK is a work of fiction. Names, characters, places, and incidents are the product of the author's imagination or are used fictitiously. Any resemblance to actual events, locales, businesses, or persons, living or dead, is coincidental.

Published by Vaughn House Publishing, Depoe Bay, OR
First Edition

Print ISBN - 978-1-7340119-7-5
Ebook ISBN - 978-1-7340119-8-2

Cover and Interior Design by Kimberly Peticolas, www.kimpeticolas.com

Library of Congress Control Number: 2020917232

10 9 8 7 6 5 4 3 2 1

WHISPER CREEK

A Logan McKenna Novel

VALERIE DAVISSON

To John,
True blue, smart, and loving, my rock in swirling waters.
You're my Ben, honey!

Prologue

A light rain misted the highway. The tires hummed.

Alignment, need to get that checked.

But not tonight. Tonight, tire alignment was way down the list of priorities or concerns. And after tonight, such worries would be swept away. Almost there.

Twenty minutes later, a great horned owl, perched high above Whisper Creek, hunched against the slanting rain, taking it all in. The parking lot, the school, the gardens beyond. Large, yellow eyes tracked the solitary figure skirting around the edge of the dining hall, hidden by the shadows of western red cedars and pines.

Family was supposed to show up for the talent show by five. Leaving work early to get here on time could have been tricky, but it wasn't a problem. Most everyone left by two on Fridays anyway.

A frisson of energy and hope shot through the driver's body, ending with a tingling at the fingertips. Soon. Very soon. Freedom was within reach now. Tonight, the bitch would die—and not a nanosecond too soon.

No rush, though. No reason not to enjoy the evening. Parents and faculty were arriving. Gravel crunched, warm, golden light exuded from the dining hall's open doors, welcoming everyone. Cheerful chatter floated out into the forest. A staff talent show. What a great way to kick off the year—and a great cover for whatever sounds might otherwise break through.

Ahh . . . there she was. Stepping out of her Lexus. All red stiletto heels, form-fitting suit, and that waterfall of perfectly smooth, blonde hair.

Bitch.

She had no idea these steps, these last few hours of flirting and manipulating and controlling were her last. All her conniving would end. Tonight. In just a few hours, they'd all be free. She just had to be coaxed to leave the company of other humans and venture into the night. Into the dark. Where she belonged.

That wouldn't be difficult. Not when you knew her. Not when you knew all she wanted was whatever she wanted, whenever she wanted it—*her* needs met, no matter how many people she hurt. The woman was nothing if not predictable.

Almost an hour later, night fell and the rain softened to a drizzle. Landing silently on a thin branch high in the trees, the owl neatly dispatched a small vole by swallowing it head-first. This was his third foray over the field. The gibbous moon made for a productive night.

On the ground, far below, another nocturnal predator pulled out a phone. Twenty-two keystrokes later, it was done. A slow smile stretched across a satisfied face.

Sure enough, the woman almost immediately emerged from the dining hall, slipping out quietly, golden light and strains of classical guitar music and applause trailing behind her until the door clicked shut.

Head down, intent on her phone, she trotted down the stairs, tapping on her screen as she went. When she reached the garden, she strode into the night, until all that could be seen were the backs of her blood red heels, her pale, yellow hair lit ghostly white.

The owl ignored her. Not for him to interrupt another predator's hunt.

And in the dark, the woman neither saw nor heard the figure that followed, nor the soft, murmured warnings of Whisper Creek.

1

For most of the afternoon, a muted rain fell, leaving behind a freshly washed, pearl-gray sky from which emerged the ghostly trunks and branches of evergreens and alders. Now and then, a few lingering raindrops answered the call of gravity, rolling to the end of a graceful cedar's fingertips, creating a symphony of singular notes as they plopped heavily onto different surfaces—the solid, wooden deck, the soft, dark soil in the planter boxes, or the conical, metal hat of the space heater that made sitting outside in January possible.

Listening to the varying notes, Logan stepped out onto the deck. C-E-G-A-flat? She made a mental note. She'd pick her violin, Bella, up later and see if it fit with the new piece she'd been working on. She always did her best composing at night.

For now, she just wanted to be.

The kids came up for the holidays and loved all the work she and Ben had done on the house since they had bought it as a vacation home last year. Everyone had just left. She missed them all already, but it was nice to have some time alone before flying back home to SoCal. Actually, she was beginning to think of this place as much like home as her beach house in Jasper.

Before sitting down on one of the deck chairs, Logan tapped the thermometer Ben had mounted just outside the sliding glass doors before he left. Forty and rapidly falling. The weather channel said it might dip below freezing tonight. Perfect as far as Logan was concerned.

Born a Southern Californian, she was surprised at how quickly her body had acclimated to the cooler climate here on the Oregon coast. She zipped up her jacket, adjusted the flame on the heater, and snugged into her favorite chair, a sturdy teak number that sloughed off the rain with ease. Tonight, it was dry due to the overhang Ben had installed over the deck. It allowed them to stay out of the rain while still leaving the sides open to let in the fresh air.

Although she loved the view of the ocean down and across the highway from the front of the house, Logan found herself more often drawn to the back deck, immersing herself in the calming company of the trees. Her whole life she'd been rushing—raising Amy, running the business with Jack, then, after the car accident, picking up the remnants of her life, rebuilding, and creating and running her seminal Music/Math program, Fractals.

She'd pulled Bella out from the back of her closet and had been rediscovering her music, learning to love and trust again. In just the last three years, her fairly simple life had expanded to include not only a significant other, a son-in-law, a grandson, the mother she'd been estranged from for most of her life, but also a half-sister she didn't know she had. It was all good, but a little overwhelming at times.

Almost completely dark now, Logan could only see a few feet into the forest. The house, built on the eastern edge of the small coastal town of Depoe Bay, Oregon, backed onto a large tract of forestry land extending she didn't know how many miles east. She just knew it was a selling point for her. She liked quiet and didn't want to live in cheek-and-jowl suburbia or watch anyone brushing their teeth in the morning across ten inches of manicured lawn.

As the space heater softly hissed and occasionally crackled beside her, the trees became silhouettes in varying shades of charcoal and ash. Cedar boughs nodded sleepily—the whole scene fading slowly into a watercolor wash in gradients from slate gray to obsidian.

Just as her eyelids began to lower to half mast, a distinctive shape in the gloaming caught Logan's attention. Leaning forward, she peered into the forest. High in an alder, perched absolutely still on a slender branch, sat what must be an owl. But it wasn't like any owl Logan had ever seen. For one thing, it was huge! And no ear tufts. Just a very rounded head—like a Russian nesting doll. But in every other way, it sure looked like an owl. She watched it sitting there, in perfect possession of itself and its realm, wondering how the weight of so large a bird could be supported by the spindly branches in the upper-most reaches of the tree.

Moving her arm as quietly as she could, she reached for her phone and looked up 'Oregon owls,' then 'large owls on the central Oregon coast.' Too many results. When she added 'mixed conifer forest' to her search request, Google presented her with a couple of possibilities, including the snowy owl and the great horned owl, but that one had prominent ear tufts sticking up. She looked up again to see if she'd missed them somehow, but it was gone. The dark cutout where the shape had been was again a smooth and empty space—as if she'd only imagined its visit.

The phone she'd forgotten on her lap rang in her hand. She almost dropped it but managed to keep it from clattering onto the deck just in time. She glanced at the screen to see who was calling. It was Bonnie, her best friend from home.

"Hi, Bonnie."

Logan always enjoyed catching up on all things Jasper. Bonnie knew everything and everybody and wasn't afraid to share.

"Logan! Are you sitting down?? Do you have your phone? Of course, you do . . . arrrgghhhh! Go to YouTube! Right now!"

She'd never heard her bubbly friend this excited, and that was saying something. Bonnie was always gushing about something.

"Okay, okay," Logan said, pulling up the internet on her phone. "What am I looking for?"

"*You*! Your video's gone viral!"

"What video?"

2

"*Your* video," Bonnie shouted into the phone. "You have your own channel!"

"My own channel?" Logan said.

She felt stupid just repeating everything Bonnie said, but she had no idea what she was talking about.

"Just go to YouTube and type in 'Logan's Laments,'" she said, "You're huge!"

With some measure of disbelief, Logan did as instructed. What she saw left her speechless.

As an extension of her Fractals program, she'd done some recording with a couple of her high school students off and on last summer, and often sat in with some friends of hers in her old bluegrass band, but . . . she couldn't imagine any of that being on YouTube, and she certainly would know if she had a YouTube channel, but there it was. Larger than life.

"Oh, my God!" Logan said.

"Well, I don't think God did this, but whoever did, did a damn good job!" Bonnie laughed.

Logan watched in shock as the professionally-produced video rolled, rotating through several different backgrounds and songs, some she recognized, others she'd never seen before. In the first song, a sweeping, overhead shot looked like she was playing on top of a wild, windswept hill in the Scottish Highlands, fields of heather unrolling at her feet. In another, a plaintive lullaby she'd played for Amy when she was a baby—the only one she'd go to sleep to—was more intimate. Somehow, a camera was positioned looking over her left shoulder from the back. Soft light glinted off Logan's lush, copper waves and Bella's golden finish as she played, pulling the rich, rounded notes from the violin, letting the music flow across the room.

On hearing the first notes and seeing the sleeping infant under the soft, pink blanket—where they found footage of a sleeping baby girl she had no idea—a surge of emotion welled up in Logan's chest, bringing tears to her eyes and a flood of memories of Amy as a baby. Amy was twenty-six now, with a child of her own—Ian, Logan's grandson.

Logan tried to place where and how these songs could have been recorded. She remembered several sessions where they used her new arrangements of these traditional ballads and lullabies. They'd even recorded a few of her original pieces she'd written when she began composing again and some of her student, Brandon's, too.

Often, when they'd finished in the studio for the day, even though the sound couldn't be controlled as well, they hauled the equipment up onto the roof of her house, which was located just a few yards away. Ben had converted her single-car, free standing garage into a studio and built a second story for her office so she could work from home when she wasn't visiting the schools.

"Wow," Logan said, her brain quickly compiling this new information. "Looks like someone pieced together different recordings, cleaned them up, put in some new backgrounds, and voila! But why? And who would want to take the time to do all this?"

"Your students," Bonnie said. "It has to be! Brandon's dad does all that video stuff. He could get his hands on the mixing equipment or video editing or whatever you call it."

Logan couldn't think of anyone else, either. She'd have to give Brandon a call. If he was capable of doing this level of work, he sure as hell didn't need her tutoring anymore. And while it was flattering, the why of it still nagged. She looked at the time. It was a school night and Brandon's folks were pretty strict. They always let him hit the beach in the morning before school—Brandon and his brothers were die-hard surfers—but all the kids were home hitting the books at night.

"I'll call you back," Logan said.

"Okay."

***

Out of respect for his parents, Logan always called their land-line. Brandon's mom caught Logan up on small talk, then before calling her son to the phone, she added, "We're just proud as punch about the video. Brandon made us all keep it a secret! Let me go get him."

"Brandon! Ms. McKenna's on the phone!" she said.

"We only put it up a couple of weeks ago," Brandon bubbled when he came on the line. "We were going to wait until it did something to let you know. Isn't it awesome?! You've got over 2 million views already! Someone in South Korea found it and when it hit Germany . . . it just exploded!"

After reassuring Brandon that she was suitably impressed and genuinely in awe of his technical and creative abilities, she asked her question, "But why? Don't get me wrong, I think it's great, but whatever possessed you to do this?"

"Well, it just kind of snowballed. Remember the song you wrote for Jeff?"

Several years ago, a talented young teenager in the Fractals program—and Brandon's best friend—lost his life trying to defend Amy from a desperate killer.

"Jeff. I started out wanting to do a great version of Jeff's song—you know, the one you wrote and played at his memorial," he said. "And then, my dad saw all the other clips we had and said we needed to put something together to get those out there."

"I don't know what to say, Brandon," she said, still trying to process everything.

"And it wasn't all unselfish," he added, "I used this whole album as part of my portfolio. They wanted to see recent work. I applied to Berkeley and I just got my letter! I'm in!"

"That's wonderful, Brandon!" Logan said, "I'm so happy for you! Your mom must be over the moon!"

Brandon's mom was a Berkeley graduate and a musician in her own right. She still taught harp lessons in her living room and had the back and arm muscles to prove it. She had to do special chest exercises to keep the front and back of her body balanced.

"Oh, and it's not just about getting a lot of fans," Brandon said, "it's about making money. The first day it caught on, you got over a 150 million views!"

"What does that mean?" Logan asked.

Launching into a rambling explanation of how many thousands of fans you need to monetize your creative work, kinds of viewership, clicks, subscriptions, ads, and more . . . Sensing he was losing his audience, Brandon summed it up, "A LOT! Ms. McKenna . . . a LOT!"

3

At this point, Brandon's father, Mark, got on the phone.

"Putting it in simple terms, Ms. McKenna, music videos average about $2,000 per million views," he said, "depending on a variety of factors. In the first hour after it went viral, you made $300,000.00. I have no idea what it's at now."

"But this is Brandon's project," she objected. "It was all his idea. He should earn the money, not me."

"For right now, it's all going into a business account we set up for Brandon. We'll send you all those statements for your records and get your share of the money into your own account. I'm sure we can come up with a formula that will be fair, but it's you playing and your songs that are the meat of the thing. Your copyright," he said. "No matter how we split it, you're going to get a chunk of change, Ms. McKenna. I can put you in touch with my asset manager. She is also a tax specialist, which you'll need so you don't wind up giving it all to the government."

When Logan didn't respond right away, he added, "I'm sure you need some time to adjust to this news, and you'll probably want to talk with your own people. Let's talk in the next few days."

Finding her voice, but still stunned from the news, Logan agreed. She'd be happy to consult with her own 'people'—if she had any! He'd mentioned attorneys and agents, none of which she currently possessed.

After promising to talk soon, Logan just sat there, staring into the deepening dark of the forest. How could her world have shifted so suddenly? She wanted to call Ben, but first . . . she needed a few minutes. She needed to think how this fit in with her other big news. This sure was turning into an eventful week.

Logan looked down at her left hand, adjusting the ring on her finger with her thumb, making the beautifully cut square emerald in the center catch the light from the heater's flames just right, making it glow from within. Set in platinum, flanked on each side with two small diamonds, it was beautiful.

Ben had proposed New Year's Day. He'd packed a picnic breakfast, built a bonfire at Beverly Beach, timing the tides just right so they wouldn't get cut off from the path that led back to their car. Oregon beaches in the winter were mostly empty and stretched for miles. Other than a few seagulls, they had the place to themselves. Flames from the bonfire popped and crackled and the ocean's winter waves boomed on the distant rocks.

While sitting as close to the fire as they could, wrapped in several wool blankets against the piercing cold, Ben popped the question—handing her a traditional velvet box containing his grandmother's ring along with a modest pair of emerald studs he'd had made to match.

For a split second, she'd panicked. Her new life, her independence—all flashed before her eyes, but then she relaxed. She knew in her bones Ben respected that part of her and had no desire to commandeer her life. His steady patience and consistent love over the last seven years also had finally convinced her that not all men were unfaithful like Jack had been. Ben was the real deal. Loving and being loved by Ben felt natural and right. She wished her father could have met him and lived to see her so happy.

But now, with money in the mix, how would Ben feel? He'd once rejected the whole world of wealth and power the law represented, and much to the chagrin of his attorney father, chose to take over and run his grandfather's landscaping business instead. He'd done well, but lived a modest, middle-class life as she did.

Without really discussing it, they already acted like a married couple. As far as she knew, until now, they both earned roughly the same amount of money. They'd gone in fifty-fifty on the house and repairs of this place, too. Everything was going so well. Would her having more money change things? How traditional was Ben? Would this rock their smooth-sailing boat?

Why couldn't life ever just stay the same?

4

Logan got through the phone call with Ben, sharing the news, but significantly downplaying the amount of money Brandon said the video was generating. It was probably a one-time thing, anyway—a fluke. They joked about upgrading their honeymoon, but that was about it. Logan left it at that.

As expected, Ben was mostly just happy for her that her music was getting out there. He had always told her how good she was, how much he loved to hear her play—particularly her original compositions, but he kind of had to say that, being her boyfriend . . . uh . . . fiancé. That sounded so weird.

If Mark's formula was accurate and there really was a substantial amount of money coming in that would keep coming in for the foreseeable future, this was a conversation she and Ben needed to have in person, not over the phone. And not until she could verify everything and had all the facts.

In the meantime, she had work to do. She was heading out to The New School in the morning for a few days—her regular January trip. Work always soothed. It was concrete, manageable, and one of the few things in life within her control.

Tilly kept Fractals running back in Jasper without much help from her these days, but Logan still managed the satellite program at The New School, just outside of Portland. Tilly also kept Lola, Logan's '58 sapphire-blue convertible Corvette in fighting shape, getting her detailed often and taking her out on long drives down the coast to visit her kids in San Diego. A graduation gift from her father, who had since passed away, Logan sure missed that car, but Lola was better off in Southern California. You didn't see too many convertibles up here on the rainy, central-Oregon coast. What was the saying she saw on a t-shirt recently? 'Oregonians don't tan, we rust.'

The New School was funded largely by grants and tuition was on a sliding scale, creating a vibrant, diverse student body ranging from kindergarten through high school. Rita Wolfe, the director, an Amelia Earhart look-alike with white hair, tried to recruit Logan to come work there full-time, but when that didn't work, Rita finally convinced her to bring Fractals north at least part-time, by squeezing extra funding from her beleaguered donors. A tireless fund raiser, Rita always got her way.

Logan worked with their resident tech guru, Huey Le, on these trips. He ran the computer lab and over the last few years, had become a good friend. Huey was set to show her his latest updates in MuMu, an animated math training program featuring a cute dolphin that was based on some of the latest developments in brain research she'd shared with him on their last visit. Studies were showing how early math and music training complimented each other and that kids learned best when they were having fun. These concepts provided the foundation of her program, Fractals.

Now that she and Ben had the house up here in Oregon, Logan looked forward to going out there more often. She believed in Rita's mission for The New School. It felt good to be working with people who shared an ideal of what education should and could be for kids—creative, holistic, and not aimed solely at test scores. A true education. Kids from all walks of life built things, kept chickens, and worked in the community garden. In fact, most of the food the kids ate in the cafeteria was grown and cooked right on the premises.

Another reason Logan looked forward to these visits—the food was amazing! Nick, the chef, could make even kale taste good. His main mission was to make healthy breakfasts and lunches kids actually wanted to eat, which he was very successful in doing, but he really pulled out all the stops for the staff's evening meals, after the students went home for the day. Logan's mouth was watering already. And the man knew his wines. Logan knew red and white, but his selections were always better than hers. She never remembered the names when she got to the store, so she'd started taking pictures of the labels of ones she liked with her phone to pull up later. Much easier.

Realizing how late it was, Logan turned off the heater and put her phone back in her pocket. Her fingers touched the velvet box.

Absentmindedly, she ran her thumb over the soft surface. Stepping over to the railing, Logan let her eyes adjust to the dark. A muted dusting of stars could be seen through the gap in the trees and with the hissing of the heater silenced, the night settled around her. Gentle breaths of cold air rustled the branches softly above her. The chirps and chatters of pine squirrels and all the other bustling, quick movements and daytime sounds were quiet. But somewhere in the night, one denizen was awake.

Hoo-Hoo-HOO-Hoo-Hoo.

Thinking of tomorrow's trip, Logan slipped the ring off her finger and tucked it back into the box, snapping the lid shut. She absolutely wanted to marry Ben, but she just wasn't ready to tell the world about it, yet.

5

Checking the weather report one last time, Logan decided she didn't need to leave water running or take any other precautions against freezing pipes before heading out. She wasn't going to be gone that long and temperatures, even in January, were generally mild along the coast. It wasn't supposed to drop below the mid-forties for the next few days. Besides, she still had Clay's number on speed dial. Clay Soren was the taciturn and talented handyman who'd managed the remodel, bringing 354 Barber Road back to its prime and the cozy family home it was built to be. When he was done, the raccoons were banished, the wood floors gleamed, the fireplace drew properly, and both windows and roof were tight against the rain.

Clay always kept an eye on the place when she was out of town. Whenever she offered to pay him, he just shrugged his shoulders and said he was usually working nearby anyway. No trouble at all. Since she and Ben bought the place, he considered them neighbors and that's just what neighbors did.

Making sure she had all her chargers and technology tucked into her roller bag, she securely stowed it in the back seat of Rita's Rav4. Rita insisted she could borrow the Rav anytime, but now that she was here more often, Logan didn't want to impose. She needed to buy a car for up here. Just one more thing on her to-do list.

Logan backed out of her gravel drive and zigzagged two streets down to Collins before turning north onto Highway 101. She'd filled up yesterday, so wouldn't have to stop for gas. That gave her enough time to swing by Pirate's and pick up coffee and a snack for the road.

A rush of warm air, laden with aromas of roasted coffee beans and cinnamon enveloped her as soon as she pulled open the heavy door and stepped inside. Locals in the know stopped by to fill their thermoses on their way to work, but it was the lull after the morning rush, so Logan walked right up to the counter and put in her usual order, a large coffee and since she hadn't eaten yet, a breakfast burrito to go. A frosted snickerdoodle called her name, so she had them add one—well, two—to her order.

It was an hour and a half drive to The New School. A girl has to keep her strength up.

Logan paid, polished off one of the cookies on the way to the car, buckled in, did a u-turn and got on the road. Twenty minutes later she arrived in Lincoln City. A popular tourist destination, it often had bumper-to-bumper traffic, but today she sailed through without any delays, turning east onto Highway 18 at the north end of town.

Logan settled in for the drive. She and Ben always tried to see how many hawks they could count on the way to the Port-land airport. The most so far was fourteen. She allowed her mind to drift and her body to go into a sort of autopilot fugue.

Coastal forest gave way to open, rolling fields. Before she knew it, she was in McMinnville, then turning left up into the hills.

Within minutes, the scenery changed again. The town

quickly fell away as thick brush and tall trees lined the narrow road, blocking much of the sun, blanketing everything in shade. Whisper Creek babbled contentedly beside the meandering road, disappearing for stretches, then reappearing on the other side. As Logan slowed down for one of the sharper turns, she smiled at the memory of Glenda taking that same turn in her new Tesla.

A retired school nurse from Jasper and an accomplished herbalist, Glenda wrote a book called The Herb Bible, which had paid for said Tesla. She had been recruited by Rita to come to The New School and she, in turn, had sung Logan's praises to Rita and dragged Logan up here to meet her a few years ago. All's well that ends well, but Logan sometimes wondered how she'd survived that first trip into the hills. A speed demon at heart, Glenda did *not* take turns slowly!

She pressed the gas pedal just a little more. She really needed this break. Time to get her thoughts together about the video. Time to adjust to being engaged. Just the luxury of getting to spend time with friends.

If she played her cards right, she'd make it in time for lunch.

On the other side of Whisper Creek, perfectly camouflaged against the rough bark of an old hemlock, perched a small western screech owl. Blinking once, he sat perfectly still, gazing intently, rotating his head—almost imperceptibly—his yellow eyes following Logan's taillights until they disappeared.

6

Fifteen minutes later, Logan left the paved road and drove under the graceful, wrought iron arch that announced the entrance to The New School. A low rock wall curved around both sides of the property until it petered out somewhere back in the forest behind the classrooms. She knew it didn't go all the way around because Whisper Creek ran back there and there was only a foot bridge leading to the staff cabins. Glenda had one of the original cabins and Logan always stayed with her.

Pulling into the parking area as far left as she could, leaving space in front for parents to circle through and pick up their kids later, Logan glanced at her dashboard clock. 11:45 a.m. Her stomach growled. After all, it'd been at least an hour since she polished off the last cookie and the breakfast burrito was ancient history.

Lifting her bag up over the wide porch steps, she set it down and pulled up the handle, then rolled it behind her through the open double doors. A gangly, dark-haired boy with a bad case of acne manned Carla's desk. His nametag read Ethan.

Carla was the wonder woman who ran the front office. Her apple-cheeked, smiling face was the first thing students saw when they arrived each morning and the last person they waved to as their parents picked them up each afternoon. A bundle of love armed with gigantic, chocolate chip cookies she kept in a large jar on her desk . . . all the students adored her. Originally homeless and married to a dark, macho grouch named Robert, Carla had really blossomed since getting her job at The New School and kicking that loser to the curb.

Juniors and seniors all had to log service hours. This must be Ethan's. Junior, Logan guessed.

He looked up at the sound of her footsteps on the wide-planked wood floor. He already had a dark dusting of facial hair on his upper lip, but the eyes of an innocent child still delighted by a new Lego set on Christmas morning.

In a surprisingly deep voice, Adam's apple bobbing, he asked, "Hi, are you Logan?"

When Logan said yes, she was, he pointed out the open back door across the quad to the dining hall, "Ms. Morgan's expecting you. She said to tell you they're saving you a seat in there."

Logan thanked him, and on her way out asked, "What's for lunch?"

"Beef stroganoff or green curry," he said, already turning back to his work.

"What did you have?" she asked.

"Stroganoff," he answered, as if the vegetarian option were even a remote possibility.

Logan liked both, so she'd just have to make up her mind when she got there.

Nick and his crew opened the doors to students at noon sharp. The staff got first dibs at 11:45. Logan had learned that it was wise to arrive promptly, because after the students went through the salad bar, it looked like a bomb went off in it.

She entered just as the students were going in, so joined the line and waved at Rita and Carla, who pointed to the empty seat next to her. They were already tucking into their meals. Logan always enjoyed the buzz and energy of being around kids. So much potential, adolescent anguish, and sweet innocence, all wrapped up in each package.

When she got to the window, Nick waved a serving spoon in an enthusiastic welcome. At six foot three Nick towered over all the kitchen staff, even his wife, Brittany, who was a respectable five foot eleven herself. An accomplished nutritionist and no slouch in the kitchen either, Brittany—a Scandinavian blonde—was in charge of the organic garden program. She and Nick had a precocious set of soon to be one-year-old twins. They'd sent Logan a 'Save-the-Date' Birthday Party invitation, but she couldn't remember when it was.

"Hey, Lo!" he said, over the clatter and din of the lunch rush. "Glad you could make it!"

"Me, too," Logan said.

Just then, Brittany came up behind Nick and squeezed him around the waist.

"Hi, Logan! You coming tonight?" she asked.

"What's happening tonight?" Logan asked. "How are the girls?"

Named Rosemary and Thyme, Nick and Brittany's twin girls reflected their parents' latent hippie genes.

"The first ever New School Annual Staff Talent Show!" she said, releasing her husband in order to grab an empty tray. "You have to come! Nick and I have a *surprise* talent . . ."

At this, Nick rolled his eyes, but looked pleased, all the same.

"Okay, then!" Logan said, "Of course, I'll be there. Wouldn't miss it!"

"There's a flyer on the door. Carla knows all the details,"

Brittany said over her shoulder as she retreated back into the kitchen to refill the curry pan, which had been surprisingly popular with the kids. "See you later!"

Deciding on the stroganoff, Nick gave her a generous portion and Logan loaded up her tray with extra sour cream, some green beans almondine, iced tea, and a chocolate fudge brownie with whipped cream.

No one even commented when she got to the table. Everyone was used to Logan's appetite.

"What's this I hear about a talent show?" Logan asked as she sat down and began to eat.

"It was Carla's idea," Rita said. "Thought it might be fun for the staff, and the kids always enjoy watching us make fools of ourselves."

Rita emptied the last of her iced tea, gathered her dishes and stood up to go.

"I won't be able to be here tonight," she added, "I'm meeting with some donors in Portland, but Carla's got it all organized. They're taping it, so I'll get to see you all make fools of yourselves when I get back."

Carla turned to Logan, "So, did you bring Bella?"

Carla had asked her to bring her violin—now Logan knew why.

"Yeeeessss," Logan said. "It's up at the office with my bag. Ethan's keeping an eye on them for me."

"Good," Carla said, "Ethan's such a great kid. He's helping with the show tonight, doing lights and sound."

Student pick-up was between 4:30 and 5:00 p.m., but Ethan's parents said he could stay. They were leaving work early so they could see the show. They had their own engineering company, Quantum, Inc, up in Portland.

"Oh," Carla added, "and you're going on right before the

finale, right after Nicole. And don't worry, you can play whatever you want!"

Logan smiled and started mentally going through her playlist. Carla had a knack for sweeping everyone up into her plans with her enthusiasm and getting them to agree to whatever she wanted them to do. Including last minute performances.

7

After lunch, Logan made her way across the quad and found Huey in the lab, frowning at a disemboweled computer on the table in front of him, screwdriver in hand. Not wanting to break his concentration, she waited patiently for him to look up before announcing her presence.

As always, Huey was dressed comfortably, but neatly. Ivory button-down shirt, V-necked sweater, and charcoal gray slacks topped softly buffed brogues. No one had ever seen him in jeans. His thinning hair was always neatly trimmed and combed to the side. She knew it was thinning because Huey wasn't much taller than some of the fifth graders. At five foot eight, Logan could see right over the top of his head.

Huey's Vietnamese name was Le Hai Hieu, but nobody could pronounce it. Sensing her presence, he straightened up and stretched his back.

"Hi, Logan!" he said, looking at his watch. "Did I miss lunch again?"

Feeling guilty he'd been working while she was eating, Logan handed him the extra chocolate brownie she's swiped on her way out, which she'd looked forward to enjoying later with a hot cup of Glenda's special blend Nighty Night herbal tea. Whatever she put in that stuff knocked Logan out like a light.

Dispatching the brownie neatly, without getting a single crumb on his sweater, Huey sat down in his chair and rolled over to one of the intact student computers.

"Take a seat. Let me show you what we've got. We've added a new level in square roots that uses music patterns as clues."

For the next few hours, they worked together companionably. Around four, Glenda leaned in, knocking on the open-door frame. She had Logan's roller bag in one hand and her violin case tucked under her arm.

"I'm heading back to the cabin," she said. "Thought you might want to settle in before dinner."

Huey told her to go ahead, he had some emails to answer and he needed to wait for Ethan anyway. He was coming by to pick up some extension cords and one of the mics that had been in for repair. They would join them later in the dining hall.

On their way, they walked past the garden area. Glenda pointed out the new raised beds, currently being tended by Brittany and a cohort of students—one in a wheelchair. The raised beds allowed him to participate with the other kids. They waved. Just then, a familiar figure rounded the corner, pushing a wheelbarrow loaded with dirt. He was accompanied by another thinner, younger man, carrying two shovels.

"Hi, Joe!" Logan said, walking over.

"Hey, Logan," he said, putting the wheelbarrow down to give her a hug.

A Vietnam vet, formerly a homeless alcoholic living on the streets in Portland, Joseph Maynard, known to everyone as G.I. Joe, barely resembled the man Logan first met.

He'd arrived at The New School—still shaky and shy—several

years ago as part of a program Rita had designed with a homeless shelter called Blanchett House to help the recently clean and sober stay that way.

Appropriate candidates were first screened by Blanchett. Those who also managed to survive Rita's no-bullshit interview were offered a chance to come out to The New School, away from their old environment. They worked in the garden, kitchen, or grounds in exchange for free room and board and a little cash. It was an opportunity to break old habits, learn some new skills, and save money for whatever they decided to do next. The rules were strict, but fair.

The man at Joe's side turned out to be the most recent arrival. Joe introduced him as Carson. The back and sides of his head were closely shaved, leaving a thick mop of tightly wound, sandy brown curls on top, springing from his head in every direction. Slate-blue eyes looked shyly out at them from under thick, straight brows. An aquiline nose ended in a small, pink mouth with cupid's bow lips.

Glenda later told Logan that Carson, a former meth addict, had gone through the same rigorous detox and rehab program as G.I. Joe had at Blanchett House. He'd been here about a month. He helped Joe in the garden most of the day, but also parked himself in front of a computer in the lab several hours a day. He was getting his GED online. If he stuck with it and passed all his tests, he'd be able to attend college next fall.

They were all pulling for him. So many young people just like him—but without the support of a program like this one—were lost forever in the revolving door of detox centers and shelters. Most drifted back to their former lives on the streets and whatever drugs or alcohol helped them get through the day.

Clean and sober seven years and forty-two days, G.I. Joe was one of Blanchett and Rita's success stories. Even though he was older and had been on the streets longer than most—written off by family and forgotten by everyone else—the man had an inner core of strength, long hidden in the haze of alcohol he used to dull the pain from memories of what he'd been through in the war and all he'd lost when he returned.

Joe was still quiet and kept to himself, but he'd gone from a broken shell of a man to a confident human being who took pride in his work and used his newfound strength to mentor others. He'd filled out and had a beautiful laugh. It came out rusty at first, but was now effortless, melodious. She never tired of hearing it.

Logan peered into the wheelbarrow at the rich, dark soil. "Is that some more of your famous Joe's Gold?"

Joe only nodded, but you could tell he appreciated the compliment. "Just prepping the new beds," he said. "Spring will be here before you know it."

With the temperature hovering around 40 degrees, Logan couldn't exactly agree with him, but she supposed it was all in your perspective.

After visiting for another few minutes, the two women let Joe and Carson get back to work and made their way to the footbridge and crossed over into the forest. The dirt paths were well worn and Logan had little trouble wheeling her bag the rest of the way. After admiring the pop-out, mini-greenhouse Joe had built for Glenda off the kitchen window, complete with several new varieties of ginger, Logan went to change and run a comb through her hair before dinner.

Because everyone needed to get ready for the talent show, Nick had informed them tonight's dinner was going to be early and simple. Logan didn't care if he was serving peanut butter on stale soda crackers, she didn't want to miss it. She was already starving!

8

Dinner was a far cry from Nick's usual spread, but better than advertised. A variety of overstuffed sandwiches were heaped onto a platter next to the hot soup station. Tonight's selections were vegetable beef or chili with all the fixin's. Desserts, coffee, and tea would be served at intermission. Logan selected a turkey and swiss cheese on pretzel bread and ladled up as much of the chili as would fit in her bowl, then piled it high with sour cream, onions, and grated cheddar cheese.

Huey and Ethan jogged down the short set of stairs on the right side of the stage and after getting their own dinner, joined them at the table. Both wore black. Typical stage-hand attire, psychologically rendering them invisible to the audience for prop changes onstage. Huey's hair was neatly combed, and his shoes were dry, even though it had started to rain. How did the man do it?

Everyone's outerwear was hung on pegs that ran along the back wall off each side of the entrance. Small puddles had formed under some of them. The dining hall smelled of soup, onions, and wet things. Occasionally, a whiff of fresh, pine-tinged air rushed in whenever someone opened the door.

Surprisingly, there were quite a few people Logan didn't recognize. Glenda explained that since most of the staff were in the show, Carla and Rita had invited spouses, some of the vendors, and, of course, the parents of any students who were helping out tonight.

Pointing with her spoon between bites, Glenda filled her in on the people she knew.

"That's Duncan and Monica, Ethan's folks," she said, pointing to a couple at the end of the food line.

A tall, dark-haired man, dressed simply in a fisherman's sweater and jeans, was easily identifiable as Ethan's dad. He looked just like him but filled out and with clear skin—the man his son would grow into someday. Probably gave the boy hope. He was ladling a bowl of soup for his wife, putting it on her tray. A smooth cascade of expertly highlighted blonde hair skimmed her shoulders. Armor-clad in a severe, off-black suit, her put-together-Portland-business-woman look ended in a pair of bright-red, pointy-toed, strappy stilettos.

Why? Why did women do that to themselves?

Logan couldn't remember the last time she'd stuffed her feet into a pair of shoes like that.

Never . . . the closest she'd come was for Bonnie's wedding. As maid of honor, she'd managed to wobble down the aisle in heels, but almost lost it at the turn. If one of the bridesmaids hadn't discretely grabbed her elbow, she would have gone down for sure. As it was, she'd nursed a twisted ankle with a bag of frozen peas throughout the reception.

She watched as the couple walked toward them, Monica in the lead—definitely *not* wobbling. Logan had to admit, the stilettos didn't seem to be giving the woman any trouble. She confidently strode across the floor and every man in the place took note.

Huey, however, looked slightly alarmed when he saw her

coming and began shoveling in the last of his sandwich, wiping his mouth, and gathering up his cutlery. But before he could make his escape, they arrived.

Glenda made introductions. Monica nodded briefly at Logan, then beamed a sparkling smile at Huey.

"We just wanted to thank you again for giving our Ethan here this opportunity, Huey," she gushed, patting her stepson's shoulder with a slender hand. Manicured nails, recently done.

Even though Huey didn't respond, she continued, "It's such good experience! He's learning so *much* from you!"

Keeping his eyes on his bowl of chili, Ethan shrank almost imperceptibly from his stepmother's touch. Logan didn't blame him. It was as if he knew he was being used as a prop.

Huey mumbled something and said he and Ethan needed to get going. The show started in a few minutes, and they still needed to do a last-minute equipment check. Ethan looked grateful to have a reason to escape, too.

Her audience gone, Monica took a few spoonfuls of her soup and looked listlessly around the room, as if she didn't want to be there and couldn't wait to get away. Soon the lights were dimming, and Carla announced the show would begin in fifteen minutes. People started drifting over to the folding chairs set up in front of the stage.

Duncan reached for his wife's tray, but after a quick glance over her shoulder, in a fawning, fifties housewife move, she said something about him working hard all day, and insisted on taking both of them back herself.

A couple of minutes later, under the table, Glenda tapped Logan's leg to get her attention and gave a meaningful nod toward the back of the room, by the dish trays. It looked like Monica had Nick cornered. She wasn't touching him, but through some invisible force, she kept him pinned against the back wall. Feet planted, shoulders squared, chin tilted up, she was letting him have it. Nick, fists clenched and his face darkened into a scowl Logan had never seen before, said something slowly and carefully in return, but the clatter of dishes, chairs scraping the floor, and people talking, made whatever they were arguing about impossible to hear. No one else seemed to have noticed what was going on.

Just as Monica turned and stalked off, flipping her hair over her shoulder, Brittany materialized at Nick's side. Smoothly linking her arm through his, she propelled him back into the kitchen.

Logan glanced at Duncan, but he was watching the stage, oblivious. By the time she arrived back at the table, Monica had composed herself. She smiled winningly at her husband and they went to find some seats. Logan and Glenda followed suit.

Logan raised her eyebrows questioningly, and Glenda shrugged her shoulders. They'd definitely have something to talk about over Nighty Night tea, later.

9

About fifty or so folding chairs had been set up in front of the stage, two blocks of five abreast, with an aisle down the middle. The curtains were closed and a mic awaited Carla, who was emceeing, to start the show. House lights were on and people were still straggling in.

Glenda and Logan found a couple of seats on the outside edge on the right, so Logan could slip out the side doors quietly just before it was her turn to go on. The backstage door was right around the corner. She wasn't up 'til after intermission, so she settled in to relax and enjoy the first half. After securing Bella under her chair, Logan sat back to indulge in one of her favorite activities—people watching. She liked to think of herself as intellectually curious—and she was, but she long ago admitted to herself she was also just plain nosy. Every face had a story behind it and she wanted to know what all of them were.

Ethan's parents sat a few rows in front of them. While Monica arranged her legs to their best advantage and scanned the room, Duncan went up to talk with his son, who was untangling a mic cord. Whatever he said must have been positive, because Ethan's face lit up with a smile. They had an easy rapport. It was obvious he was closer to his dad than his mom. Stepmom as Glenda had just informed her. News at eleven . . . back in the cabin. Logan couldn't wait to hear the scoop on this woman.

G.I. Joe and Carson, the new guy they'd met this morning in the garden, came in with a blast of cold air along with a few more late arrivals. Hurriedly wiping their shoes on the large mat, they shook off their wet coats before finding pegs to hang them on. Both men cleaned up pretty well, Logan noted. She'd only ever seen G.I. Joe in his work clothes.

The kitchen quieted down and the house lights dimmed. Thick, velvet stage curtains stirred briefly before settling down.

Carla walked onto the stage.

"Welcome, everyone, to the First Annual New School Staff Talent Show!"

She waited for the round of applause. No one was expecting much, but they were an enthusiastic and supportive crowd. It would be a fun night.

"Fair warning, this is our first performance," Carla said, "sort of a dress rehearsal before strutting our stuff next week for a much tougher audience—our students! So be gentle!"

Scattered laughter.

"Before we begin, just a quick note for anyone new to our campus. Bathrooms are in the back, cell phones stay off during the performance and for anyone who missed dinner, coffee and dessert will be served during intermission. And now, without further ado . . ."

A drum roll could be heard from the wings . . .

"Please help me welcome to the stage, fresh off their hugely successful, multi-million-dollar international tour, the magical team of Nick and Brit!"

WHISPER CREEK

When Nick came out dressed in drag, everybody roared. The fishnet stockings showed off his hairy legs to great effect. Nick made a great magician's assistant to Brittany's top-hat-and-tux, crimson-caped, magician get up. She sawed him in half, had him disappear and reappear with bunny ears in the audience, and did a few card tricks, which he humorously sabotaged. They were actually pretty good. She had no idea Brittany knew magic.

Next up was Gaby from the Art Barn, who was a pretty good mime. One of the English teachers recited Jabberwocky—twice—while juggling, keeping three plastic busts of famous literary figures in the air: William Shakespeare, Thoreau, and Edgar Allen Poe. Glenda even got in the act. She and the science teacher, a young woman from Chicago, dressed like two girls sitting on a stoop steps outside a brownstone, did a complicated hand clap and jump rope routine. Glenda was over sixty, so she let the science teacher do the jump rope bit. Logan didn't blame her, after wrenching her knee a few times the last couple of years, she'd probably take a pass, too.

Logan glanced at her program. Only one act before intermission. The invisible stage hand, Ethan, slid the faux stoop away and set up a single stool in the center of the stage. The stage went dark, then a single spotlight focused everyone's attention on the man in the center, one leg hitched up, holding his guitar like an old friend.

Keeping his eyes closed, nothing moving but his fingers, G.I. Joe sent the first notes floating out into the audience. Logan instantly recognized *Tahitian Skies*, an old Chet Atkins tune. From the first note to the last, G.I. Joe held everyone's attention. He was really good! She had no idea he could even play the guitar, let alone that well. After completing the medley, including *Wildflower* and John Lennon's *Imagine*, he shyly acknowledged the enthusiastic applause and exited stage left.

The house lights went up and Carla announced a ten-minute intermission, directing people to help themselves to the coffee, tea, and dessert on the table in the back. A few smokers went out onto the deck. Although he tried to sneak out, G.I. Joe was soon surrounded by fans.

Nick and Brittany, still in costume and character, were in the back, keeping the cookie platters and coffee urns full, so Logan located the remaining performers and complimented them on their acts.

The second half of the show went quickly. Logan was enjoying Nicole's Chopin piece so much, she forgot she was on next, until Glenda elbowed her in the ribs. She grabbed her violin case and slipped out the back doors.

The rain had stopped, but the temperature had really plummeted. Glad she had her coat, Logan hustled around the corner and let herself in the back door to wait until she went on. Out of the corner of her eye, she saw Monica picking her way across the uneven ground in the garden, hurrying as quickly as she could in those heels, head down, texting on her phone, sans coat. Was she nuts? Where was she going this time of night? It was dark out there.

To each her own. Not my problem.

10

Sitting in the darkened auditorium, watching the show, Duncan's excitement grew. He ran through the actions he'd taken to prepare for this night but could detect no flaws in his plan.

It wasn't his original plan, but she'd left him no choice. She'd gotten too greedy. She'd already spent half of Ethan's college fund. If he divorced her, she'd take everything. He didn't care as much for himself, as for Ethan. Inwardly, he cringed at the thought of how he had allowed this greedy, selfish woman into their lives, into their home. How had he been so blind? How could he not have seen Monica for what she was?

He'd tried to think of another way. He'd consulted the company attorney and the best divorce lawyer in town. They both said the same thing. He'd been an idiot not to have a prenup. The minute he filed those papers, he could kiss his company and half his assets goodbye. More than half if you counted the damage she could do to his reputation with his clients.

She knew enough about the business to make her lies believable, so they wouldn't doubt it if she told them he'd taken a shortcut here, a bribe there. Portland was in many ways a small town. All the major players knew each other. He had always enjoyed a well-deserved spotless

reputation in his field. Any hint of disreputable behavior could ruin him.

He wouldn't care so much for himself. He'd been the fool who'd followed her cute butt to disaster. He deserved whatever he got, but Ethan shouldn't have to pay for his mistakes. Ethan had already lost his mother, then the safety and comfort of his home. After his mother died, Ethan had to come live with them full time. It was hard for him, and Monica hadn't made it any easier—changing everything, pulling them apart, making Ethan's life miserable. And right under his nose! He realized now that he had only seen what he wanted to see.

Reaching his hand into his inside pocket to make sure the papers were there, he straightened up in his seat. All that stopped tonight. She'd sign. He'd make her sign. Then he'd be free! He'd make it up to Ethan. Take a trip—they could go camping or to Europe—wherever Ethan wanted to go. Things would be different.

Duncan glanced at his watch. The Tig Heuer, a dive watch given to him by one of his clients, had too many dials and complicated features for his taste, but Ethan thought it was cool. The next time his client invited him to go on a dive trip to Malaysia or Australia, he'd have to say yes. Ethan would probably love to go.

The African dance and drum act ended and Ethan, doing his stage-hand thing, unobtrusively removed the folding chairs and adjusted the mic. Ethan was such a good kid. And smart. He couldn't wait to spend more time with him. In another year, Ethan would be in college and then he could bring him into the business. Things were going to be great.

As long as everything went smoothly tonight.

The house lights went down, then one of the women who had been seated at their table, Logan something—a music teacher, he thought—took her place at center stage. Just her and an old violin. Everyone got quiet.

Her long, auburn hair gleamed under the single spotlight. When she lifted the violin, which glowed the same warm tones as her hair, she looked briefly out into the darkened audience, then closed her eyes, seated her instrument firmly under her chin, and began to play.

For a moment, he forgot where he was. The music was haunting, captivating everyone in the room. But then he remembered. Where he needed to go. What he needed to do.

Careful not to make any noise, while everyone else was mesmerized by the performance, he rose from his seat and stepped into the even darker area outside the block of folding chairs which had been set up for the audience.

A few minutes earlier, Monica had slipped out the side door. Smoke break. Right on time. Monica couldn't go more than an hour without a cigarette. This was his chance.

Quickly, but quietly, he made his way toward the back of the room. Nick and his wife, done with their work for now, were seated out front, watching the show. The kitchen was dark. Good. He hadn't been sure about that. That was the only possible glitch in his plan. If they'd been in the kitchen, he would have had to wait.

Making sure no one observed his movements, he slipped into the unisex bathroom in the back. The room had two access doors, from the auditorium and the kitchen, so anyone working in the kitchen wouldn't have to exit and walk all the way around to use the bathroom. He entered from the dining hall and then, without using the facilities, exited into the kitchen hallway, carefully closing the door behind him so it wouldn't click or thunk as it shut.

He couldn't believe he was really doing this.

Looking down the short hallway which lead to the back door and out into the garden area, he saw the only other door, opposite where he stood and just a few feet away. He closed the distance and walked in. He'd watched a YouTube video on picking locks and had a kit with him—amazingly, Walmart carried them. He'd paid cash and walked out with it in less than ten minutes, but luckily, didn't need to use it. The door was unlocked. Nick was probably planning on locking up when they were done. They still had coffee and cookies set up from intermission. They'd need to bring those back in at some point.

Crossing the small room—no more than a closet, really— careful not to bump into the mops and brooms on the left or the shelves of canned goods and supplies, he went to the desk. Scanning the narrow shelf directly above it, he reached up and lifted down a smallish, black, metal box. It also was unlocked.

And empty . . .

11

arla walked to center stage and announced the last act of the evening would be something of a surprise. A hush settled over the audience. She gave a slight gesture with her left hand and a glossy-coated Golden Retriever came trotting out and sat neatly by her side, looking up at her adoringly.

"Allow me to introduce Freya, the Wonder Dog!" Carla said.

For the next ten minutes, Freya did a number of cool, but predictable doggie tricks on stage, but then Carla had her display her true talent. Holding a leather glove out for her to sniff, Carla pointed out into the audience and said, "Freya, Search!"

Delighted murmurs rippled through the audience as Freya trotted down the stairs and dutifully began weaving in and out of the rows, her nose leading the way. When she got to Logan, she abruptly stopped, her butt hit the floor. Holding herself perfectly still, her beautiful, brown eyes laser-focused on Logan's violin case.

"Good, Freya!" Carla said, rubbing her ears and giving her treats.

With a twinkle in her eye, she opened Bella's case and took out the matching glove, holding it up for everyone to see.

"I snuck it in there after you finished playing, Logan," she whispered, as everyone applauded. "I hope you don't mind."

Logan didn't. It was a cool trick. Freya made it look simple but Logan knew from her brother, Rick, a K-9 cop in Southern California, how many hours of training it took to bring a dog to that level of skill—and keep them there. His K-9 partner of the last four years, Charlie, a female German Shepherd from Austria, was an amazing animal.

Taking the golden retriever with her back up on stage, Carla explained to the audience that, Freya, a three-year old rescue dog she'd only had for six months, had been doing scent training, working toward becoming a search and rescue dog. Working with the Newberg-Dundee Police Department K-9 team, she'd taken to nose work like a champ. It would be a while before she could do actual tracking, but Carla said eventually she could be called upon to help find lost hikers and the like. Just as a volunteer.

Carla wrapped up the show, thanked everyone for coming, and then, in typical mom mode, reminded them to be careful walking to their cars and to drive safely.

"Black ice is no joke, people!" she said.

Released from her 'job,' Freya was free to be petted and oohed and awed over by everyone. She didn't play favorites but accepted all her fans' adoration with equal grace. No one was rushing to their cars. Everyone wanted to give Freya a pet first.

Huey, Ethan, and Ethan's dad, Duncan, began putting the folding chairs away, so Logan went to find Carla to see what else needed to be done. She also wanted an excuse to pet Freya. She found Carla by the front entrance, deep in conversation with a pushy parent. Something about the Science teacher not being willing to budge on the due date of to their child's big end-of-the-year science project. Yes, their child had had all year to gather data and complete the project, but they had been on a family vacation to Europe, which was educational in itself, didn't she agree? Carla said she'd be happy to schedule an appointment with the director, but encouraged them to meet with the teacher first to try to resolve the issue.

It didn't sound like the parent was giving up, so Logan was about to leave when Carla turned and handed her Freya's leash.

"Would you mind, Logan?" she asked. "Freya needs a potty break."

She dug into her pocket. "Here's a poop bag. You can just take her out back. Walk around and be boring, she'll go pretty quick." She looked down at Freya. Speaking in a higher tone, she said, "No walkies, Freya, just potty, okay?"

Logan didn't know what she was supposed to do with the poop bag when it was filled-there were special doggie stations back home in Jasper and she hadn't seen any of those here, but there was a trash can outside the stage door entrance. That would have to do. Freya, unconcerned with these human issues, trotted easily by her side.

The rain clouds had moved on, revealing a scrap of navy sky packed with stars. While she breathed in the cold, clean air and allowed her mind to go blank, Freya walked a few feet into the brush, sniffed a bit, found her spot and did her business. Piece of cake.

Logan was tying off the top of the bag, her arm loosely looped through the leash handle, when Freya bolted, almost pulling her over.

"Freya!" she yelled, "Come back here!"

Was that even a command? She didn't think so.

She tried to grab the end of the leash, which had whipped out of her hands, but it quickly disappeared, along with Freya, into the garden area across the path. The last she saw of either of them was Freya's flag tail, high and waving, disappearing into the maze of raised garden beds.

Damn!

Using the flashlight Glenda had given her, Logan threaded her way in and around the beds, looking for the runaway. Maybe a lone rabbit had come to munch on some winter greens. That would get any dog's attention, even a well-trained one.

Nope, not there.

Then she heard something over to her right, at the far edge of the garden. Squinting, she could make out Freya's form, nervously pacing back and forth, sniffing and whining along the front edge of the chicken coop.

Several chickens milled around on the inside of the front half, but from what she could see through the open wire mesh, none of them were injured. The door used to enter this area was latched shut. No chickens got out as far as she could tell.

The back half of the structure was enclosed to give the hens a quiet, dark place to sleep and lay their eggs—she remembered Brittany calling it a nesting box.

From here, Logan could see the small ramp that gave chickens access to the nests, which lined the side walls. Egg collection was done through a clever, pop out opening on the side, and when humans did need to enter, there was a human size door in the back. Both sides of the structure were tall enough to stand up in.

So, what were the chickens doing up and running around in the middle of night? Shouldn't they be sleeping? Something must have gotten in.

Coyotes? Raccoons? Whatever scared the hens out of their avian slumber might still be in there. Logan listened intently but couldn't hear anything. Peeking around the corner, she saw the back door was wide open.

Not good.

She had her flashlight. She could just take a quick peek to make sure the marauding poultry thief wasn't still in there, then shut the door so the chickens didn't escape.

But she resisted the urge. Her first responsibility was to Carla's dog. She'd get Freya back safely, then bring Nick or Brittany out here to check it out and re-secure the door. But before she could grab her leash, Freya wandered off. She found her standing in front of the open door in back, hackles raised and a low growl rumbling in her throat.

Logan walked cautiously forward, looking for the end of the leash, staying as far away from the open door as possible. It would not do to have Carla's dog torn up by a coyote. She assumed the wild animal would win in a dog fight.

Bending down, she gathered the leash a few inches away from Freya's collar and straightened up, letting the leather slide through her hands until she got to the handle at the end.

"It's okay, girl," Logan said. "Come on . . . let's go see mom . . ."

Leash firmly in her grip, she turned to go, but couldn't resist one quick look through the darkened doorway to see if she could see anything moving inside.

What she saw wasn't moving at all.

12

Caught in the beam of her flashlight was a stark red leather stiletto, bright and hard against the soft, wooden floor. Farther in, the dull sheen of something dark and viscous glowed next to an outflung arm.

OMG . . .

Unlike in the movies, Logan did not let out a blood curdling scream which made everyone come running. She couldn't make a sound even if she had wanted to.

For a split second, she couldn't move, then wrapping Freya's leash around the door handle, her lifeguard training from years ago kicked in. She stepped over the blood as best she could and leaned down to check for a pulse. Trying not to look at the large, dark splotches on Monica's white blouse, she placed two fingers on her neck, to the side of her windpipe over the carotid artery.

Nothing.

She forced herself to look at her face. Monica's hair still looked perfectly styled and the expression on her face looked merely surprised, but her eyes staring straight up into nothing were unsettling. Her skin was a lifeless gray.

Backing out the way she'd entered, careful not to step in the blood, Logan grabbed Freya and ran back to the dining hall. Juggling leash, phone, and flashlight, she dialed 911.

***

Police and fire were on the scene faster than Logan would have expected. Tucked up into the hills, The New School felt remote, but was in reality only fifteen minutes up from Dundee and less than an hour away from Portland. She heard one of the officers say the Deputy Medical Examiner was en route. In the meantime, the dining hall had become a very busy place. At least six officers and two police detectives were taking statements and crime scene techs were already at work from there to the chicken coop.

Logan could see them from the porch step, where she had gone to sit and wait. Nick had turned on the outside lights, so she could see all the way to Whisper Creek pretty clearly. They were positioning bright red, numbered mini cones here and there, and placing invisible things in baggies with tweezers. Someone had called Rita and she was on her way.

This alone made Logan feel better. Rita would take charge. If you were ever in a wreck at sea, Rita's the one you'd want in your lifeboat.

It was freezing out here, but better than being in the stuffy dining hall. Too many upset people in there. Everything was taped off and one of the patrol cars had been placed across the gravel road at the entrance to The New School. No one was going anywhere, at least not until the police said so.

Carla came out to wait with her.

"How's Ethan?" Logan asked. "His dad still with him?"

When she first burst into the dining hall and everyone heard the news, Ethan froze in place and looked stunned, but

Duncan let out an unearthly wail and ran out to the chicken coop before anyone could stop him. The distraught man tried to pick up his wife's body and carry her back to get help. Huey and another teacher managed to pry him away and convince him his wife was beyond help now and to go back to wait for the police.

They calmed him down by telling him he needed to take care of his son, then had them sit in a relatively comfortable and private area on the stage steps. When Logan saw them last, that's where they huddled. Duncan's arm around his son's shoulders. His shirt still bloody from picking up his wife's body.

"Yeah," Carla said. "Glenda got them some blankets from the health office. They're both still in shock, I think. I'm not sure who's comforting whom, but they're together, anyway."

"That's good," Logan said. "I can't imagine what they must be feeling right now."

Logan knew the police would probably separate father and son to take their statements, but didn't say so. Someone had shot or stabbed that woman—there was so much blood she couldn't tell—and it was always the husband, wasn't it? Monica was not a likeable person, but no one deserves to be murdered. Divorce her or leave her, but don't kill her.

But she couldn't imagine him being guilty. Duncan had seemed so nice, so attentive to his wife. She'd sensed no under-current of anger or resentment in the man. Could he have killed her? He didn't even seem to realize she was flirting with Huey or embroiled in a dark argument with Nick. He struck her as more of a geeky engineer with his head in the clouds. Could you tell by looking at someone if they were capable of murder?

Logan shook her head to clear it of her spinning thoughts. She didn't know these people. Let the police figure it out. She had planned on staying a couple more days, but now . . . she should just leave early and come back when all this was over and things were back to normal.

Forcing her attention back to Carla, she asked, "How's Freya?"

"She's fine," she said, "Thanks for asking. And thanks for taking such good care of her. One of the officers in there is from the Newberg-Dundee police department. He's with the K-9 training unit we've been working with. He had one of the officers walk us back to the cabin, so I could put her in her crate and keep her calm. She'll be okay. That's her happy place."

"How are *you* doing?" Carla asked. "Can I get you anything? Nick and Brittany made more coffee and pulled out some cookies I made for tomorrow. He said they'd make sandwiches if all this goes on much longer."

"I'm okay," Logan said. "I mean, it was awful, finding her like that, but I didn't know her. I just met her. It's not like discovering someone close to you."

She hoped this was true. Seeing the murdered woman up close like that—all the blood—it was not something she would ever forget.

"Well, you're lucky you didn't know her," Carla said. "I hate to speak ill of the dead, but Monica was a piece of work."

13

Logan was about to ask for clarification when they were called back in. A sandy-haired man, somewhere in his forties, about her height, stood at the open door, waiting for them. Plain clothes, but he had cop written all over him.

"Detective Wright, Newberg-Dundee police department," he said, offering a brief, but firm, handshake before leading them to some tables where quite a few officers, some in uniform, some not, were already taking people's statements. Everyone else was seated near the stage, waiting their turn to be interviewed. He put Carla at one table and took Logan to another.

Logan noticed a few creases across his forehead, but mainly, he just looked tired. Probably already put in a full day. And then this.

"You want anything before we start?" he asked as they passed by the coffee station Nick and Brittany had set up.

"No, I'm good," she said.

"Suit yourself," he said, stopping to fill a large cup from a carafe—not decaf—stirring in enough sugar to make him a diabetic by fifty.

"Let me know if you change your mind," he said, tossing his stir stick neatly into the trash.

"Two points," Logan said.

He either didn't hear or chose not to respond.

"Do you mind if I get my violin?" Logan asked, pointing back to where someone had picked her case up off the floor and put it on the stage.

"Sure, go ahead," he said, pulling out a fresh field interview card.

FI cards, as they were called, were used to gather basic information and establish timelines. More detailed, follow-up interviews—or interrogations if they were lucky enough to land a suspect—would be held at the station as needed.

Bella safely stored under her chair, Logan got comfortable—as comfortable as one could get on a folding, metal chair about to be questioned by the police. Unfortunately, she'd been through this before. At least this time she wasn't a suspect. She'd just found the dead body, not created it. Not that she had last time either, they just thought she might have.

After getting her full name and explaining her relationship to the deceased—didn't have one, just met her—he had Logan relay the events of the evening, starting with her arrival, up until chasing Freya to the chicken coop and making the gruesome discovery.

"So, at what time did you see Mrs. LeGrange alive and walking toward the garden?"

"I'm not sure exactly, someone else may know. I was the second to the last act," she said. "Intermission started at 6:45, according to the clock," Logan pointed to a large schoolhouse clock on the wall behind the Detective. "Intermission was about ten, fifteen minutes, then the show started again. Carla would have a better idea. She was emceeing the show."

"Are you sure it was Mrs. LeGrange you saw?" he asked. "Was anyone else out there? Could anyone else have seen her?"

"I didn't see anyone else around, but I was only out there for a few seconds, on my way to the backstage door. Yes, it was definitely her. I saw her clearly before she got too far away. She was walking like she was in a hurry to get somewhere, from the dining hall into the garden. It was dark, but her hair—it stood out—it's very light blonde . . . and it's hard to miss those heels," she added.

"Did you hear anything? Did she say anything?" he asked.

"No, I didn't hear anything, I don't think she was talking to anyone. She was looking down, texting, I think," Logan said. "Like I said, I only saw her for a few seconds."

He went through everything again and asked a few more questions, but none that made Logan feel she had to share her negative first impressions of the woman or divulge the argument she observed Monica having with Nick after dinner. It was probably nothing, anyway. She didn't want the police chasing after Nick.

Handing her his card, Detective Wright asked her to call if she thought of anything else and asked for her contact information in case they needed to reach her.

"I'll be outside if you think of anything else," he said, nodding toward the bright lights in the garden. "For now, you're free to go."

Somewhere during the interviews, the Deputy Medical Examiner must have arrived, done his or her business, and left—with the body. Out of respect for the husband and son, Logan assumed they must have carried the deceased around the dining hall rather than through it. Which was just fine as far as Logan was concerned. Even zipped in a body bag, she didn't want to be anywhere near Monica LeGrange's body—or any other dead body, for as long as she lived.

After talking with Ethan and his dad—separately as Logan had expected—and collecting their fingerprints, for elimination purposes she assumed, Detective Wright thanked everyone for their cooperation and released them to return to their homes—or in the case of The New School staff, back to their cabins. He asked them not to leave town without notifying them. They all had his card, or if interviewed by any of the other officers, the number of the station. All calls regarding this case would be referred to him.

He warned everyone that they would continue processing the scene and the entire area would be off limits until they were done. It was going to be a long night.

Brittany asked and was given permission to relocate the chickens to a temporary enclosure, under supervision, of course. Since all the chickens had run down the ramp to the front area and none were in the enclosed section where the body had been found, they weren't worried about her contaminating the scene.

As Logan had hoped, when Rita arrived, she took charge of the staff. Even Detective Wright seemed a little intimidated by her commanding energy. She could have taken charge of the investigation if he'd let her.

Logan stayed and helped Huey, Nick, and G.I. Joe clean up the dining hall and put away the chairs. Carson would have helped, but he had gone back to the main house early. G.I. Joe said the poor guy was running a fever and needed to be near a bathroom, so one of the officers had taken his presumably very short statement in his room.

School would be cancelled for the rest of the week, and even though Nick said he and Brittany could put something together, Rita insisted everyone was on their own tomorrow for breakfast. All the cabins had full kitchens and most people kept snack food if nothing else.

"You've all handled this very well," she said, "let's leave the police to their work and get some rest. We can tackle all this in the morning."

Nicole slipped her arm around Rita's waist and gave her a squeeze. The two of them started walking back to the main house.

"And remember," Rita added on her way out, "for now, the garden is off limits and no talking to the press. If anyone tries to contact you, it's 'no comment.' Just refer them to me or Carla. Hopefully, the police will find out what happened here, soon. Until then, we will fully cooperate. If you think of anything—any detail, no matter how small, call that Detective . . . Wright—you all have the number. The faster they find out who did this, the sooner we can put that poor woman's body to rest."

14

Exhausted and wrung out, Logan and Glenda finally got back to the cabin around one-thirty.

She'd called Ben earlier and told him what was going on but hadn't gone into much detail. Really, there wasn't much to tell. She didn't know anything. Other than finding Monica's body, she didn't know who had killed her or why. They hadn't even been told exactly how she died, although given the blood on her chest Logan assumed she'd been stabbed or shot, but she hadn't seen a gun or knife. Of course, she hadn't been looking, either.

When they got back to the cabin, Glenda filled her in over a cup of Nighty Night tea, augmented with a shot of Elijah Craig. The burning combo was just what she needed to scrape away the image in her mind of finding Monica dead.

According to Glenda, Monica flirted with anything with a Y chromosome, from delivery men to CEOs. Huey was her latest focus, but she'd gone after just about every other male at the school, too, including Nick.

Logan wondered if that's what she and Nick had been arguing about when she saw them. She'd never seen Nick's face so full of anger. But why would he be angry? If Monica was coming on to him, couldn't he just ignore her like Huey did? His dark fury seemed out of proportion to just being inappropriately pursued.

"Didn't Duncan notice?" Logan asked. "I mean, was he totally oblivious?"

"That or he just didn't care," Glenda said. "Presumably, this isn't new behavior. Leopards don't change their spots."

Logan considered this and took another sip of tea. The tendons in her neck began to unravel as the fiery concoction slid down her throat.

"What was all that with Nick about?" she asked.

"Ahh . . ." Glenda said. "I'm not positive," she said. "But I'm pretty sure they had a thing a while back."

"Nick?" Logan said. "No way! I always thought he and Brittany were so happy—solid—with the twins and they're so good together."

"I don't think he was still seeing her—I mean, not now," Glenda said, "but there was a time—right after Nick and Brittany got engaged—you were down in Jasper then—they had a huge fight. Brittany went to her mother's place in Vancouver, Nick stayed here.

"For the rest of that summer, Monica managed to find excuses to come out here a lot. Checking on Ethan, bringing things she said he forgot at home, picking him up for doctor's appointments, then saying she got the wrong day—like that. Always winding up in the dining room, ostensibly for a cup of coffee or whatever."

"What was Nick's reaction?" Logan asked.

"One afternoon she said her car was on the fritz. Rita put her up in the spare bedroom downstairs at the front office— the one Carson's in now. That's where the new guys from Blanchett House stay, but it was empty. With the kids and all,

Rita's really picky about which candidates she allows in that program.

"Anyway, the next morning, I was coming back from an early wild mushroom foray, around five-thirty. I saw Nick sneaking into the kitchen.

"Doesn't he always open the kitchen about that time, to get breakfast ready?" Logan asked, not wanting to think of Nick as having an affair, broken up with Brittany or not.

"Yes, but he was coming from the *front*, from the main house," she said. "Nick and Brittany's cabin is back here, not far from mine."

Logan let that information whirl around in her brain for a minute. Then she asked the question she didn't want an answer to.

"Did you say anything to the police?" she said, wondering now if she should have, too.

Glenda looked up at a spot on the ceiling for a minute before answering.

"No, I don't think they're related," she said. "It's not going on now. After that night, Monica stopped dropping in. Nick took a week off and got his head straight, I guess. He and Brittany got back together, got married and now they have the girls. As far as I know, even if he did use bad judgement and sleep with Monica once, what would be the point in telling the police? Of course, Nick wouldn't kill anyone, and what would be his motive? A one-night stand? I don't think he ever saw her after that."

Glenda shook her head, dismissing the idea.

Logan was relieved.

Still, they'd been arguing about something. Until Brittany steered him away. Why was Nick so upset, and how much did Brittany know?

***

By ten the next morning, the police had completed much of their work and cleared the chicken coop and dining hall. Logan and Glenda stopped for a minute and watched a few officers, including one of the K-9 teams, finishing their search in the field just beyond the computer lab for the murder weapon. They learned from Carla's connection that Monica had been shot. They wouldn't know what caliber until after the autopsy.

Carla said so far no one had found the gun. Except for the search going on in the field, one cop car in the parking lot, and a few remnants of yellow crime-scene tape peeking out of a trash can, you wouldn't know a woman had been murdered here just hours ago.

She said G.I. Joe had already started cleaning up the chicken coop. Logan's mind flashed back to when she discovered the body lying there in all that blood. There had been so much of it. Logan wondered if they could just scrub everything down, or if floorboards would have to be replaced before new straw could be spread in and around the nesting boxes and the chickens could be let back in. Would animals sense the violence that had happened here? Would the smell of cleaning disinfectant or blood upset them? She realized she didn't even know if chickens had a strong sense of smell or not.

When Logan got to the office, Carla said Nick had helped and between the two of them, he and G.I. Joe had gotten the worst of it. Carson wanted to help, but Rita told him to stay in his room. She wanted him to wait until his fever went down to make sure they didn't have a breakout of the flu at the school on top of everything else.

15

Even though classes had been cancelled for the rest of the week, Carla was stuck in the office, fielding calls from the press and concerned parents, so Logan offered to take Carson some breakfast.

"Yes," Carla told the parents, "School would start back up on Monday," and "No comment," she told the press. She didn't know anything and wasn't authorized to tell them if she did.

Brittany was in the kitchen, prepping a scaled-back lunch for the staff, but stopped to give Logan some oatmeal, ginger ale, and soda crackers on a tray for her charge.

"Sorry it's not much, but he probably won't feel like eating, anyway," she said. "Tell him we're making chicken soup for lunch. Best thing for what ails you, my grandma used to say."

Logan wouldn't know. She'd never got to meet hers. She lived somewhere in New York and hadn't even come to her son's funeral. Logan's Appalachian great-grandmother, though, her dad said was a great woman, full of love. She wished her great-grandmother had lived long enough for them to meet, but Logan had inherited her love of music—and Bella.

When Logan got to the office, carefully balancing the tray,

Carla, still taking phone calls, pointed across the reception area to a short hallway and did a charade of knocking on the first door on her left. Her hands occupied with the tray, Logan used the tip of her right boot to tap on the bottom of the door. Hopefully, Carson would hear that.

"Come in," he said.

She managed to open the door with her elbow and looked for a place to set the tray. The room was spartan, but neat, except for a pile of crumpled clothes the young man had worn the night before. What with the rain, they didn't look nearly as neat and nice as they had when he and G.I. Joe came into the dining hall last night. And something smelled! Jeez, no wonder he was sick.

The mom in her wanted to do his laundry—something in this room smelled—and scrape the muddy clumps of straw off his nice shoes, but she resisted. Carson was a grown man and could take care of himself. He probably wouldn't appreciate her butting in.

He seemed embarrassed to be caught in bed, but thanked her for the food delivery. He was feeling much better and yes, he could eat something. Logan found room on a window seat for the tray, said she hoped he'd be up and about soon, and made her exit.

Next stop was the computer lab. Huey was already there, and the police had cleared the crime scene, so Logan decided to stay and finish their work together before heading back to Depoe Bay.

When she'd talked to Ben last night, he'd expressed concern that whoever shot Monica might still be around and in a murderous mood. He wanted Logan home—yesterday—but she reasoned with him that it was unlikely a random stranger had wandered off the highway to hold up a chicken coop.

Whoever shot Monica must have known her—had lured her

there, presumably. Or she was luring someone else there. Why else would she have been there in the middle of the night? To collect eggs for breakfast? Hardly.

Talked off the ledge for now, Ben begrudgingly agreed that she could stay. Logan stifled a laugh. As if she needed his permission! Knowing when to choose her battles, Logan kept her thoughts to herself. She still had some issues to work out with this whole 'someone-loves-me-and-wants-to-protect-me' thing.

16

Bright sunlight forced its way into the room through a gap in the shutters, slashing across Ethan's face, dredging him up from the depths of a dreamless sleep. They'd gotten home about midnight last night. He'd barely been able to drag himself up the stairs and fall into bed. He hadn't even bothered to change clothes. He'd just kicked off his shoes and crawled under the covers.

Not wanting to fully wake, he lay there, eyes closed, listening to the silent house. And then a lovely thought drifted to the surface of his mind. He smiled.

The Wicked Witch was dead!

He felt a short stab of guilt, but quickly dismissed it. One minute, she had been there, ruining his life, the next—Poof! She was gone!

Throwing off his covers, Ethan jumped out of bed and looked around the room. A sudden urge to purge came over him. With more energy than he'd had in months, he flung open the doors to his closet and started yanking things out.

No more 'appropriate' clothing. No more button-down Oxford shirts and cashmere sweaters! No more Ferragamo loafers! After emptying his closet of almost everything in it, he started in on the dresser. When he'd amassed a decent pile of new and almost new clothing, most with the tags still on, Ethan raised both arms in the air, fists clenched in a silent cheer of triumph.

"Yes!" he whispered fiercely to himself so as not to wake his dad, "No more *Monica*!"

Monica hated his jeans and hoodies. When he'd moved in, she'd said that now that he lived with them fulltime, he needed decent clothes to wear when they went out. His old clothes—the ones his mom had given him, the normal ones all his friends wore—were frowned upon at first, and then gradually outright banned. She'd even come in one day while he was at school and taken a bunch of his stuff to Goodwill. What gave her the right?! That may have been the day he began to hate her.

His dad had said it was Monica's way of building a relationship with him after his mom died, showing she cared. He'd said Ethan should be appreciative and thank her for going out of her way to do nice things for him, and that he knew it was hard, but Ethan was going to be here full time now. They were a family. He'd said Ethan needed to make an effort.

He'd tried. For his dad's sake, he'd tried, but he knew phony when he saw it. He felt her resentment. And when Dad wasn't around, Monica didn't bother to hide it. It seethed out of her.

She'd really started in when Dad bought the house out here in Middleton—in the middle of *nowhere*—according to her. That's when Dad had finally started to see Monica's true colors. But even though he'd heard them fight over the move, Dad still defended her. Maybe it was just easier to go along with her. Things seemed to calm down after that. Sometimes too calm, like something churning just beneath the surface. And what was that all about last night? His dad had acted like he was so upset that Monica was dead. He hadn't liked Monica for a long time, now.

He'd never understand adults.

Waiting to go downstairs to get a trash bag for the clothes until his dad got up, Ethan quietly pushed open the exterior shutters and looked down into the yard. He liked it here. Maybe now he could get a dog. The Wicked Witch had said she had allergies, but his dad said they would get one of those doodle dogs. They were supposed to be hypoallergenic. He remembered how the Wicked Witch had plastered a smile on her face, said 'Great,' and then left for Pilates. There was no way in hell she was going to let him get a dog.

Now at least he could get whatever kind he wanted. Some of his friends liked rottweilers or pit bulls, but he didn't want a scary dog. Carla's dog was nice. Maybe she'd know where he could get one like hers.

Distant, clanging sounds drifted up the stairs from the kitchen. Dad was making breakfast. Maybe even those breakfast sausage sandwiches with thick slices of cheddar cheese melting out from between two pieces of grilled sourdough bread like he used to make.

Suddenly, Ethan was starving, not just for food, but also for his father's company. Since Monica came into their lives, they'd hardly ever got to spend time alone together. A while back, his dad had mentioned a project he thought they could work on together down at the office—on the weekends—his dad didn't want it to interfere with his schoolwork. He was definitely looking forward to that. Things were looking up.

The air coming in the window was cold, so he pulled a hoodie on and padded downstairs.

17

The Newberg-Dundee police department had thirty-five sworn police officers supporting two Divisions: Patrol and Special Operations. Special Operations encompassed computer forensics, property crimes, person's crimes, and narcotics.

Detective Wright was person's crimes. Normally, it was just him, but when they had a homicide, they pulled out all the stops and called in the Yamhill County Major Crimes Response Team, consisting of a mixture of members of his own department, the Sheriff's Office, the Oregon State Police, and the District Attorney's Office, depending on who was on leave or what special expertise may be required. For this case, Wright was lead.

Even though half these people had been up all night already, working the scene, the department was buzzing with activity, setting up the command center in the larger of the two conference rooms, bringing in computer equipment and whiteboards. As soon as they were settled, he'd bring everyone up to speed.

Anyone who watched crime shows on TV knew that if a case

wasn't solved within the first forty-eight hours, their chances of catching the killer dropped substantially. They were coming up on fifteen hours, maybe more, according to the DME's best estimate last night. The clock was ticking.

*****

9:00 A.M.

INCIDENT COMMAND CENTER

CONFERENCE ROOM 2

NEWBERG-DUNDEE POLICE STATION

Showered and powered by caffeine, Wright waited until everyone was present and got their own coffee. Shermann, a deputy with the Sheriff's Department, was the last one to arrive. He had escorted the body to Clackamas, where the autopsy was scheduled for one o'clock this afternoon. Wright kicked off the meeting with facts most of them already knew.

"Last night at 8:17 p.m. dispatch received a 911 call from a Logan McKenna, reporting a possible homicide at 1427 Whisper Creek Road—that school up in the Dundee Hills."

There were several nods around the table. Most were familiar with the facility. One even had a child who attended The New School. Since it was a private school, some of the locals had the misconception it was only for the rich—an Ivy League prep school.

Wright pulled the whiteboard over, where an enlarged copy of Monica's driver's license photo had been taped at the center. As the investigation progressed, this board would hopefully fill with many more pictures and connections. One of them would be her killer.

He tapped on the photo.

"Monica Grace LeGrange, female, age 42, resided at 83 Peregrine Lane, Middleton, with husband, Duncan LeGrange, and their son—her stepson—seventeen-year-old Ethan. Ethan's a Junior at The New School. That's why the family was there last night—for a school event, a staff talent show. The kid was helping with the lights."

"Sherman," Wright said, "you're up."

Sherman's report was short. There wouldn't be much to share until after the autopsy, but he did have the Deputy Medical Examiner's preliminary assessment at the scene.

"Cause of death—two shots to the chest. From the look of it, a .22 or .25 caliber, no exit wound. No brass. TOD was sometime between 6:00 and 8:00 p.m. No defensive wounds or evidence of other injuries. Whoever it was just walked in and shot her. Must have happened quick, no indication she tried to run or fight back."

"Which brings me to some information we are still trying to verify," Wright said. "If accurate, TOD gets narrowed down to a window sometime after 7:00 p.m. Logan McKenna, the same woman who discovered the body at 8:15 and called 911, said she saw the victim walking toward the chicken coop at approximately 7:15 p.m., texting on her phone."

This was good news. Hopefully when they went through the FI cards, someone else would be able to corroborate.

"And before anyone asks—no phone, no gun," Wright said.

This was *not* good news. Hard to tie a shooting to a killer without a murder weapon. No fingerprints, no ballistics. And without the phone, they'd have to waste precious time waiting for a warrant for the phone records. They'd need those in reconstructing the woman's life and who she was texting that night.

Dale Johnson stood up next. A tall man with deep-set eyes and thick, salt-and-pepper hair, Dale normally handled property crimes but would be partnering with Wright on this one. They'd worked together before and got along well.

Detective Johnson referred to a map on the board and distributed copies to everyone.

"This is all on Google, of course, but you can mark this one up," he said. "On the back is a separate map of the campus itself. The New School is located off Whisper Creek Road, twelve miles from here. The campus and outlying buildings, including the garden and chicken coop where the body was found, only take up a few acres. The rest of the property is undeveloped, except for a few staff cabins scattered in the forest just across Whisper Creek at the back of the property. It's pretty much all trees back there."

"Anyone on either side?" asked one of the patrol officers. "Do we have statements from any neighbors?"

"Forestry land on the north and east, one neighbor with five acres on the west, too far to have seen or heard anything and they weren't home last night. Someone will need to go back out today," he said. "Oh, and west is to the *l-e-f-t* as you're facing the school, Dombrowski," he added with a smile, slowing his speech down as if speaking to someone dimwitted or hard of hearing. Dombrowski was new and last month had shown up at the wrong house looking for a no-show warrant on a DUI and almost arrested the mayor. He knew he'd never live that one down. He took the ribbing in stride.

Johnson continued, serious again, "We're looking, but no sign of anyone accessing the campus on foot, ATV, or other vehicle from across open land, except for the staff tracks to and from their cabins across the creek."

"Which leads us to the staff and others who were on campus for the show last night," Wright said.

He held up a stack of FI cards in his hands. "We've got forty-seven with three unaccounted for. Two vendors and a parent. Left early before it all went down. None of them claim to know our victim, but Meyers and Boston are on their way now to get their statements anyway. Then we'll have an even fifty.

"Now that we've got daylight, we've got a couple of uniforms and a K-9 team combing the surrounding area for the murder weapon, phone, or anything else of interest, but unless they turn up something we missed last night on campus, we're looking at a contained crime scene. Murder on the Orient Express," he said.

He clarified in case anyone missed the reference.

"Barring a random, stray shooter wandering the Dundee Hills, there was only one way in and one way out—through the entrance and gravel road to The New School. It had to be someone already here."

He held up the stack of FI cards.

"Someone in this stack killed Monica LeGrange. The only way we're going to find out who killed this woman is to take her life apart. Who loved her? Who hated her? Did she owe money to anyone? Anyone owe money to her? Affairs. Ongoing disputes with anyone present that night. Anything and everything."

After handing out assignments, including writing a search warrant for her cell phone records, Wright and Johnson drove over to Middleton. Time to pay a visit to the husband, who presumably knew her best. They still had a couple of hours before they needed to be at Birdwell's lab for the autopsy.

They drove to the LeGrange home. Duncan had stayed home with his son instead of going in to the office. After interviewing Duncan and getting his permission to access their financial accounts, their plan was to hopefully pick up

Monica's computer, grab a hamburger to go, and make it to the autopsy by 1:00 p.m.

They took Wright's car. Like two dogs on the hunt, it felt good to be out of the office. They could sleep later.

18

Highway 99 was only a two-lane highway, but mid-morning, traffic wasn't bad. It wouldn't get truly snarled until Beaverton and they were only going as far as Middleton.

An unincorporated area just past Chehalem, Middleton was a mixed bag. No central downtown with cute little shops, and housing was scattered, ranging from manufactured homes to mansions. Although not a mansion, 83 Peregrine Court was closer to that end of the spectrum.

Wright's GPS led them to a small development of about fifteen homes, all on two-acre, nicely landscaped, wooded plots, set back from the road, but still only a few minutes from the highway. Easy commute for people who worked in Portland. The LeGrange house was large, but nothing special, design-wise. White with forest green shutters, tucked into a variety of maples and fir trees, it was just another oversized, boxy suburban home with a three-car garage and a pebbled drive.

It was so quiet they weren't even sure anyone was home, but Wright knocked anyway. Nothing but more silence. Just as they were about to give up and come back later, Ethan, dressed in flannel pajama bottoms, a faded t-shirt, and a hoodie, answered the door. He either hadn't been to bed or hadn't gotten up yet. It was hard to tell. He seemed to have lost the power of speech.

His father stepped in front of his son, opening the door a little wider.

"Hello, detectives," he said.

"I am sorry to bother you at home," Wright said, "but we need to take you and your son's full statements. We thought it might be more convenient for you here, rather than at the station. As I'm sure you understand, time is of the essence. It won't take long."

"Of course," Duncan said, stepping back. "I don't think there is anything I can tell you that will help, and I am in the middle of making funeral arrangements—speaking of that, they said they took the body to the county morgue for an autopsy. Is that absolutely necessary? Some crazy person shot her—it's not like there is any doubt about how she died. Why do they need to . . . to do that to her?"

"In the case of a homicide, an autopsy is routine," Wright said. "We'll just take a few minutes of your time," he added, stepping into the house before Duncan could change his mind.

Ethan had melted back into the foyer.

"We can talk in here," Duncan said, leading the way to a formal front room. He pointed to a navy and ivory striped couch, upholstered in some kind of silk fabric. It was obvious no dog, cat, or even human had ever sat on it before.

Duncan sat on a side chair opposite them but did not relax. He obviously wanted to keep this conversation brief.

Wright began, "We're sorry for your loss. In order to find the person who committed this crime, we need to learn as much as we can about your wife's life, her friends, anyone who may have had a motive to harm her, her recent whereabouts, etc. I know we covered some of this last night, but we need a more detailed picture. It would be helpful to go through your family's movements yesterday."

Rubbing his face with his hands, looking past them out a large picture window into the street, Duncan gathered himself and did as Wright requested.

"After I dropped Ethan off at school, I went into the office. Monica's not a morning person, so she usually arrives in her own car—the Lexus—around ten or so. She does a lot of her work from home, though, emails, Zoom conferences, phone calls . . ."

"Speaking of your wife's phone, do you have it? It hasn't been located," Wright said.

Duncan knitted his brows together.

"Monica always had her phone. It must be there somewhere," he said.

"We're still looking, of course," Wright said, glad he had already requested the warrant be written up.

Next, he asked for a list of Monica's friends and co-workers, which Duncan said he'd have their office manager provide. Wright thought it was odd that he didn't know who his wife's friends were, but said nothing.

"What about neighbors? Was she close to any of the neighbors, here?" he asked.

"Not really, Monica was a city girl, most of her friends are in Portland," he said. "And we haven't been here long. We used to live downtown. We moved to Middleton when Ethan came to live with us full time. We've only been in the house for about a year."

"Why the change?" Johnson asked.

"Ethan is my son from my first marriage. His mother had

primary custody, but she got ovarian cancer a couple of years ago. When she passed away, Ethan came to live with us full time. That's when I bought this place. Thought it would be good for Ethan. It was close to The New School and has, you know, fresh air and trees. We were thinking about getting him a dog."

"How long had you and Monica been married?" Wright asked.

Duncan looked up sharply.

"She didn't break up my first marriage if that's what you're implying. I met her about six months after Virginia left," he said.

"I'm not implying anything, Mr. LeGrange," Wright said. "How was your relationship with your wife—with Monica? Any trouble at home?"

"No, everything was great. Monica was beautiful, and smart. She fit right into my life. When I met her, she didn't know anything about engineering, but when we started seeing each other, she jumped right in and learned the business. Amazing, really, for someone without an engineering background. I did the engineering—Monica was more of a people person."

Wright threw a question in from left field.

"Do you own a firearm, Mr. LeGrange?" he said.

"What?" he said. "No, of course not. I'm an engineer, not a hunter."

"Thank you for your cooperation, Mr. LeGrange. Just a standard question we have to ask everyone."

He flipped a page over on his notepad.

"We need to speak with Ethan, also," he said. "Oh, and we need Monica's computer and any iPads or other electronics she may have had. We will give you property receipts and return everything as soon as possible."

"Monica didn't have an iPad, just her phone. Her computer crashed last week. She just had the one she took back and forth from work. The IT guy tried to salvage it, but it was a total loss. Spilled coffee on it—absolutely fried the CPU. Totally irretrievable. I believe Adrienne, our office manager, ordered her a new one. MacBook Air. I'm an IBM/Android guy, but she preferred Apple."

"If you could call and ask your office manager to hold onto it for us, we can stop by and pick it up later. We just need to speak with Ethan and then we'll be on our way," Wright said.

"I'll get him," Duncan said. "But please try to keep it short. This is very upsetting for him."

The detectives exchanged looks as Duncan went to the bottom of the stairs and called his son down.

Johnson didn't have kids, but Wright did. Wright understood the father's protective stance, but this was his job. They couldn't afford to tiptoe around people's feelings when it came to murder. Everyone who knew Monica LeGrange was going to have to answer some questions. Ethan may not know anything—it didn't sound like his stepmother had been in his life very long or that they spent much time together, but it was a box to be checked and he was going to check it.

19

When Duncan returned, Ethan in tow, he sat in the same chair and Ethan sat in the one next to him, opposite the couch. Duncan nodded. Wright introduced themselves to the seventeen-year-old and they got started. He'd jump in as needed, but he let Johnson take the lead.

Maybe it was the gray hair, or the weight of what the soft-spoken detective had witnessed over the years that had settled behind his eyes, but kids trusted him. Without trying, Johnson commanded a quiet respect. Interviews with teenagers were his specialty. After they got Ethan's name, rank, and serial number, and the specifics of his whereabouts yesterday, Johnson continued.

"So, you were helping out with the lights and sound for the staff talent show last night," he said. "That's a big responsibility. Have you helped out with other events there? They must trust you with all that expensive equipment."

"Yeah, I guess. I help Mr. Le out whenever they have a holiday show or the drama team puts on a play or something," Ethan said.

"Mr. Huey Le?"

"Yeah."

"Ethan has designed quite a few entire sets with working parts," Duncan interrupted. "And the flying apparatus for Peter Pan—that was all Ethan."

"Impressive," Johnson said. "I can't nail two boards together. If anything's broken at our house, I have my wife fix it. I'd electrocute myself if I tried to change a lightbulb. With the kinds of skills you're learning, are you planning on going into the family business someday?"

"Sure, probably. I don't know yet," Ethan mumbled, looking at his dad, who spoke at the same time.

"Of course! He's a natural," Duncan said. "He used to come down and work with me at the office, right, Ethan?"

"Your stepmother worked at Quantum Engineering, didn't she?" Johnson said, ignoring Duncan. "Did you work on any projects with her?"

"No," Ethan said.

"Why not?" Johnson asked. "It's a small company."

Duncan shifted in his seat, leaning in as if to block Johnson's questions. "I don't see what any of this has to do with what happened," he said.

"Just getting a broad overview of your wife's life," Johnson said, turning his attention back to Ethan. "Anything you can tell us might be helpful, even if it seems unrelated."

"I worked with my dad sometimes," Ethan said, not offering any more details.

Johnson took another tack. "I know this can't be easy for you, Ethan," he said. "I hear you lost your mom not long ago. Is that when you came to live with your dad and your stepmother full time?"

"Yeah," Ethan said.

"Did they live here, then, or in Portland?" he asked.

"They were in Portland, at the townhouse, then we moved here," Ethan said.

"Is that when you started attending The New School?"

Ethan nodded. His body relaxed a little and he became more animated as he talked about his classes.

"The food's pretty good, too," he added.

"So, you like your new school. That's good. Hard to switch in the middle of high school, though. How do you like living here in Middleton?"

"It's okay," Ethan said. "Not much to do here, but Dad said we could get a dog."

Johnson told him about Peaches, the Corgi he had as a child, then asked, "What was your daily routine here? Did the family eat together? Who cooked? Did you have chores?"

The openness on Ethan's face closed as quickly as it had opened. Glancing first at his father, Ethan said, "Monica said she was too busy to clean such a big house, so we had a maid service. They came on Fridays. The back deck is covered, so Dad could grill stuff even when it rained. When Dad worked late, I made my own dinner. Monica didn't cook like mom did. She mostly did takeout."

"We have a meal delivery service," Duncan clarified. "Very convenient. They bring the meals right to our door. All we have to do is zap them in the microwave."

"How was your relationship with your stepmother?" Johnson asked. "Did you guys get along well?"

"I didn't see her that much," Ethan said. "I'm pretty busy with school."

"What can you tell me about your stepmother's friends? Any of them ever come to the house? Did she get along with the neighbors?" he asked.

Wright watched Duncan's body language. Tensed and ready

to spring.

"Was there anyone you can think of who'd want to harm your stepmother?" he pressed on, studiously ignoring the dad. "Did she have any enemies you know of?"

Ethan shook his head.

Duncan got to his feet, "Okay, guys, I think we've about covered everything here. Ethan has been through a lot. Maybe you can give him some time. We need to deal with the funeral and everything. We can talk again in a few days, all right?"

He walked the detectives to the door, with Ethan trailing behind.

Wright let him think he won that battle, but it was only the first round. Both detectives knew Duncan could refuse to have Ethan interviewed without legal representation, since he was a minor. They had no power to force it. They also knew Ethan wasn't going to say anything worthwhile with his father there. They'd have to come at this sideways.

When they got to the front door, Wright turned to Duncan and asked, "Did your wife happen to keep a paper calendar? A Day-timer or At-A-Glance or anything?"

"Not really. We have a flip calendar on the refrigerator where I had Ethan write in the nights he needed to stay at the school for events, things like that," he said.

"Do you mind if I take a look at that? I don't need to take it with us, I can just snap some pictures," Wright said.

"Sure," Duncan said, leading Wright down a hallway to the kitchen.

As Ethan turned to go up the stairs, Johnson caught his eye.

"I know how tough it is, Ethan. I lost my mom when I was around twelve," he said.

He was confident Ethan knew which mom he was talking about. The only one Ethan probably thought of as his mother.

"What was your mom's name?" Johnson asked, maintaining eye contact.

"Virginia," he said. "She was named after her grandmother."

Johnson nodded, then said, "My dad remarried, too. I didn't like her much, but luckily, she wasn't around long. They split when I was about your age. How did your folks get along?"

Before Ethan could answer, his father returned, Wright in tow.

20

With the detectives gone and Ethan back in his bedroom, Duncan went back to the kitchen to finish the dishes. He'd have to make a grocery run later. All he could find for the breakfast sandwiches Ethan had requested was some stale bread and slices of cheddar almost too hard to use. No sausage. In fact, nothing to make anything, just a stack of those pre-packaged delivery meals in the fridge. There were only three left. Two salmon and the one with quinoa nobody ever ate. At least there was butter. Monica had taken to putting a thick slice of it in her coffee every morning. Heard it was good for the brain or something.

He took a look around the kitchen. Things were going to change around here. He just had to get through the next few days. He'd have the funeral tomorrow if he could, but they told him he had to wait until the Medical Examiner released the body after the autopsy. He still didn't understand the need for one. It's not like they had to figure out the cause of death. She'd been shot, not poisoned like in some Agatha Christie novel.

Duncan wiped down the counters well enough to last until Maria came tomorrow, then got a yellow-lined pad and a pen.

He poured himself more coffee from the now-cold pot and zapped it in the microwave before pulling out a bar stool and sitting down. Not bothering with creamer, he took as long a drink of the lava-hot brew as his mouth could tolerate and started making notes.

When he was done with the grocery list, he flipped the page over and jotted down some instructions for his office manager, Adrienne. A funeral would be expected. She'd organize something simple and tasteful. And short. Just enough time for business associates and clients to stop by and pay their respects. He certainly wasn't going to invite Monica's 'friends.'

Monica. Poor Monica.

When did things change? Or, more accurately, when had he finally begun to see the woman he was married to for what she really was? His mind drifted to a Friday afternoon last September, less than four short months ago, before he knew everything, back when he thought the situation was still salvageable.

How naïve he had been.

***

SEPTEMBER 2020

4:00 P.M. FRIDAY

He walked down the hall to get coffee. Seeing the remnants from the day had turned to sludge, he made a fresh pot. Four heaping spoonfuls. Fully leaded. He was one of the lucky ones who could drink caffeine all day and still sleep like a baby at night.

Ever since the divorce, he'd started a new policy at the office. Early-Out Fridays. Everyone had to be gone no later than 2:00 p.m. Surprisingly enough, it didn't hurt the business at all—in fact, productivity had gone up. Everyone deserved to get a head start on the weekend, spend some time with their families.

If he'd established policies like this earlier, Virginia may not have left him. She'd been patient, but eventually, she'd gotten tired of raising Ethan alone.

When he got back to his office, he pulled out the bottom drawer of his desk and lifted out a five by seven photo in a thin, silver frame. It was one he had taken of her when they went to Italy, just before she left, in a vain attempt to save their marriage. While they were gone, Ethan got to go stay with his favorite cousins with his Aunt Lynn, Virginia's older sister. She happened to have a swimming pool. Ethan was very happy with this arrangement.

For two weeks all the stress had melted away. It was everything a second honeymoon should be. They'd dined late, slept in, and explored every back road and castle they could find. He'd snapped this picture of her one afternoon in that pretty, blue sundress that showed off her figure. They had stopped for a picnic. Refreshed and relaxed, she was perched on a low stone wall, cooling her feet in a river, swinging her tan legs, beaming a radiant smile at him.

But within a week of returning home, they'd slid back into their usual routines, him putting in too many hours at work, her frowning in the kitchen in stony silence. This was the only photo of her he had left. When she'd died, her sister set aside a box of scrapbooks and other mementos for Ethan, but besides the one in Adrienne's office, this was the only picture Duncan had left. All photos of his first wife had been banned by his second.

At first, he thought Monica's wanting him all to herself was kind of cute. He hadn't minded or really even noticed when she got rid of things. Monica pretty much had free reign of decorating the St. Clair townhouse, so he barely noticed when she rearranged a photo wall or reorganized a closet.

It wasn't until later that he'd realized the picture of the trip to the Grand Canyon when Ethan was twelve was missing. Gradually, over the next few months, anything from his old life, his family life, Monica managed to quietly replace.

And now they were here. Him working late nights to avoid going home. Her spending more and more time at her charity events, dinners, and injecting fresh pieces into her extravagant wardrobe. She said they were all tax write-offs, but from what he could tell, even though he had made her Director of Client Relations in Quantum Engineering, she wasn't bringing much, if any, new business in and didn't seem concerned about it.

And poor Ethan. He seemed to have finally accepted Monica, or at least tolerated her, but he'd also adopted his father's coping mechanisms: staying late at school several nights a week, volunteering for projects, and the like. The only bad thing about staying away was that in avoiding Monica, Ethan wound up avoiding him, too. He was becoming a stranger to his own son. He'd have to do something about that—bring him into the office more often. Get him involved in one of his projects. There were some low-level things Ethan could do now that he was old enough.

He knew marriage was a compromise. He also knew when he met Monica, he wasn't marrying Betty Crocker—or he should have. Like many men on the rebound, he'd let the lower half of his body make decisions for the upper half.

But, he reminded himself, he needed to look on the bright side, at the positives. Monica was sharp and bubbly, always put together, and wasn't so much younger than him that people dismissed her as his mid-life crisis. Not like Roger, who kept bringing twenty-somethings to the office Christmas parties—a new one every year.

When they went out, Monica made him look good. She knew enough engineering lingo to string a few coherent sentences together and nod and smile at the right places when his clients talked business. And even though she wasn't in the mood as often as she used to be, when she was, she was a passionate she-wolf in bed.

He'd made that bed, now he had to lie in it.

WHISPER CREEK

Duncan took one last look at Virginia's photo, sighed, and put it in the back of the bottom drawer, under some folders. As long as he was here, he might as well get some work done. He glanced at the clock. The McGregor project had a change order. With the office quiet, he could make good headway on that. At least Monica didn't complain when he worked late.

***

The microwave ding brought Duncan back to the present. He retrieved his mug and downed the last swallow of the bitter coffee. Grimacing, he rinsed it out and put it in the sink. Yep, he thought, hard to believe I was ever that stupid.

<h1 style="text-align:center">21</h1>

Cyndi Birdwell, the Chief Medical Examiner in Portland, worked six days a week, arriving promptly at five thirty each morning and often staying later than anyone else. She did, however, believe in taking a civilized lunch break. Hers was 11:00 a.m. to 1:00 p.m. No exceptions.

Unlike her fictional counterparts on TV, you would never catch her munching on a ham sandwich over a dead body or shoveling in ramen noodles at her desk. Cyndi always went out. And always enjoyed exactly one glass of wine with her meal, preferably a sturdy red.

You could always count on her results to be accurate and timely. Even with the two-hour break, there was rarely any backlog of bodies to work through in Cyndi's lab.

Although he'd been a detective for five years, Wright's hometown of Newberg, fortunately, didn't have a high murder rate, so this was only his third autopsy. The first was a middle-aged trucker—traffic fatality during a rare winter ice storm. The other driver was drunk. The second was an overdose—unfortunately, like every zip code in the U.S., Newberg did have higher drug-related crime than it used to.

Vick's VapoRub in his pocket, Wright was prepared. Johnson was an old pro. He'd been with Portland Homicide Division before transferring to Newberg-Dundee a few years ago. Corpses didn't seem to bother him.

A morgue assistant walked them back to where Birdwell was waiting, standing at the head of the table on which Monica LeGrange's body lay. The diminutive woman greeted them and indicated where they could stand to observe. Not for the first time, Wright noted how attractive Cyndi Birdwell was. Smooth, olive skin. Short and slim. If it weren't for the laugh lines at the corner of her warm, brown eyes, you'd swear she was a coed at OSU. He wondered what she looked like with her hair down. Today, it was pulled back into a bun and covered. Masked and gloved, she got right down to business, exuding a calm, unhurried competence as she worked.

Over the next two hours, Wright and Johnson observed as organs were removed and weighed, and tissue, blood, and urine samples taken and preserved. All standard procedure. As was recording the contents of her stomach. He doubted it would be helpful to know that only four ounces of partially digested soup was in there. Not much in her intestines, either.

"Pretty thin," Birdwell commented, "not a big eater . . ."

"No sign of sexual assault . . . no semen," she said, "So, no recent sex, consensual or otherwise."

If she hadn't told them, they would have asked. She knew this was a murder investigation. Who she was having sex with could be important.

When the bullets were removed, they paid closer attention. Wright jotted down the specifics.

She held the first one up to the light.

"Close range . . . .22 hollow point magnum . . . probably a handgun . . ."

Wright watched as she finished describing the location and trajectory of each of the bullets and placed them in evidence bags to be sent to the state lab for ballistics analysis. The state lab had some new 3D imaging technology that could analyze both surface pattern and depth. It was good they had the bullets, but it'd be even better if they had the gun to match them to.

Cyndi wrapped it up and left her assistant to close. Wright didn't need to stay to watch this part. It made him queasier than the autopsy itself.

Peeling off her gloves, hat, and mask, depositing them in the hazardous materials receptacle on the way out, she briskly walked the detectives back down the hall. She stopped just outside her office.

"I'll send the full report as soon as I can, hopefully by tomorrow, but for now all I can say is from the trajectory, the shooter was either taller or stood on higher ground than your victim."

She paused before going in. "If you decide you need further testing for anything, I've got the samples . . . let me know."

Wright noticed her hesitation. She'd been about to say something more, but he also knew her well enough to know she wouldn't make any subjective guesses without proof first.

"Thanks, Cyndi," Wright said. "Appreciate you getting right on this one."

"No problem. Anything at the scene?" she asked. "Anyone you're looking at?"

"Not yet," he said. "No one stands out. Everyone has an alibi, but they all stink. We're working on it."

"When we get it narrowed down to fewer than a dozen suspects, we'll let you know," said Johnson.

Cyndi laughed.

"Good luck. Wish I could have told you more, but that's all she's saying now," Cyndi said.

Wright thanked her again, and said they'd be in touch.

Maybe he should just come out and ask her what was niggling at her. But it was too late now, she'd already disappeared into her office.

They stopped at the desk, signed out, and pushed open the heavy doors to the parking lot. The clouds had cleared while they were inside, and bright sunlight almost blinded them temporarily.

Next stop, Quantum Engineering. They wanted to see where their murder victim had worked and talk with Adrienne, the office manager. Hopefully, she'd be able to give them a list of Monica's friends and coworkers. They'd also pick up Monica's computer. Even if it had crashed, they may be able to get something off it. Hopefully they hadn't thrown it out yet.

This part of any investigation was always a grind. Too much information and none of it specific enough.

22

Located two blocks east of Pioneer Courthouse Square, Quantum Engineering wasn't a large firm, but boasted a prime location in a beautiful, old, stone building right downtown. Wright lucked out and found a parking spot just around the corner.

A pony-tailed receptionist welcomed them with a helpful smile. Wright wondered if she knew about Mrs. LeGrange's death. If so, she was taking it well. So did the rest of the firm, it appeared. He saw several people in the background, presumably engineers, at their desks or working on some project in the glass-walled conference room in the back, conducting business as usual.

Wright showed her his badge and asked to speak with the office manager. She looked slightly alarmed, but smoothly got on the phone right away.

"Ms. Thorley? You have some visitors to see you—a Detective Wright?" she said. "Okay."

She then smiled at them again and said the office manager would be right out.

A few seconds later, a short, squat woman in a muted

pinky-peach plaid suit, tan nylons, and low-heeled pumps came up to get them. He didn't know they even made nylons anymore. He vaguely remembered his mother wearing panty hose for church, cinnamon-colored, but he was fairly certain his wife didn't own a pair.

After brief introductions, Ms. Thorley hustled them back to her office, which, like the woman, was plain. Taking a seat behind her desk, she indicated two chairs opposite, folded her hands in front of her.

"Terrible business," she said, "Mr. LeGrange is so upset. Please let me know what I can do to help."

They thanked her for being willing to see them so promptly, then Wright pulled out his notebook. He felt this looked less formal than an FI card. He wanted to put her at ease. If there was something to be learned about Monica LeGrange, this woman probably knew it. Office managers knew everything.

"We're trying to get a picture of who Monica LeGrange was. Anything you can tell us will be helpful. Who her friends and coworkers were, what her daily routine was, what she did here at the firm. But first, can you tell us a little about yourself and what you do here. How long have you worked here?"

"Of course," Adrienne said. "I've worked with Mr. LeGrange since he opened the firm twenty-two years ago, in 1999. It was just a two-person operation back then. I managed the reception duties and all administrative work, but the company grew quickly. Mr. LeGrange was soon well known—he does excellent work—and we were able to hire more help almost right away. We currently have a staff of fifteen full-time employees, including engineers, and an ebb and flow of interns and temporary administrative help, depending on the project load we have at any given time."

She pointed proudly to a picture on the wall to her left of a much younger Duncan LeGrange, standing in front of the same building, under an older Quantum Engineering sign. On his right was a younger Adrienne Thorley. In this photo, Duncan had all his hair and Adrienne's was a thicker, shoulder-length brown, tucked behind one ear. It was gray now, chopped off in one of those efficient, shapeless bobs some older women preferred.

"That's us, way back when," she said.

"Who is the woman on the right?"

Adrienne's voice took on a sad tone. "That's Virginia, Mr. LeGrange's wife," she said. "Sadly, she passed away not long ago."

"His first wife?"

"Yes."

"Why did they divorce?" Wright asked.

"Oh, that's not for me to say," Adrienne replied, sitting back. "Mr. LeGrange worked long hours back then. Most first marriages don't survive those early years of doing what it takes to get a business up and running."

"When did the current Mrs. LeGrange come into the picture?" Wright asked.

Adrienne sat up straighter and her lips pulled together a little tighter. She didn't answer the question directly.

"Monica was one of our office supplies vendors—copy ink and the like," she said.

Then, as if she was casting around to think of something positive to say and still be truthful, she added, "They married soon after they met."

"We understand she worked here at the firm," Wright said, "What exactly did she do here?"

"Her title was Director of Client Relations and Marketing," Adrienne said.

"And what does that entail?" Wright asked.

"Well, I'm not exactly sure," Adrienne said, keeping a neutral demeanor. "I handled her expense account and I know she took clients to lunch, attended events, was involved in charity balls, things like that."

"Was she involved in the day-to-day running of the office?" Wright prompted.

"No," Adrienne said. "Definitely not. Monica didn't keep an eight-to-five schedule. In fact, she wasn't in the office much at all. Mr. LeGrange and I continued the work of the firm as before."

After asking a few more questions, Wright asked, "Mr. LeGrange said we could pick up his wife's computer."

"You are welcome to it, it's up at the receptionist's station. We were going to ship it out today for a credit. Apple does that if you ship them your old one. She hadn't had this one very long. Monica liked new things. Normally, I could give you her back up drive—we have everything on backup, that's something we've been doing recently due to all the cyber ransom incidents people are experiencing, but I couldn't find her hard drive in her office."

Wright asked for a list of friends, but Adrienne just shrugged. "None here. Monica kept her own calendar. I know she had a membership at the Power Pilates—it's over on 10th street. You might want to check there."

"Or Nordstrom's," she added with a sour face.

Out on the sidewalk, computer tucked under his arm, Johnson said, "Wow. It looks like we should be asking for a list of Monica's enemies instead of her friends."

"Yeah," Wright said. "No one in that office is exactly grieving her loss. And I didn't see any group photos with the second Mrs. LeGrange in Adrienne's office, did you?"

"Nope," Johnson said.

"No love lost there," said Wright. "I don't think Monica was as essential to the business as Mr. LeGrange indicated earlier. At any rate, the husband and the office manager have very different views of what and how much she contributed to the company."

23

Logan hadn't noticed it while she and Huey worked in the computer lab, but when they broke for lunch and walked across the quad, the campus felt eerily quiet without the students there. At least the salad bar would be intact. Nick and Brittany always put out a full salad bar, even if it was just staff.

The aroma of something meaty and wonderful greeted them as they walked in, hung their coats on the back of their chairs and went to load up their trays. Nick was scooping big spoonfuls from a steaming tray of something with mashed potatoes on top.

"Shepherd's pie!" he said, "Thought we could use some comfort food today."

Logan agreed. Nick loaded her up, but she'd be coming back for seconds, she was pretty sure. It smelled delicious. She glanced at the dessert tray on her way back to the table. Nick caught her looking.

"Apple Betty," he called out, ". . . with your choice of vanilla bean ice cream or whipped cream."

Logan almost swooned.

After lunch, she and Huey returned to the lab and got

another couple of hours in before they decided to call it a day. Huey had some repair work he wanted to get to, and Logan had promised Carla she'd join her for a short, afternoon hike. Well, more of a talk-and-walk probably, but at least she'd be outside and moving. She wanted to work off that second scoop of ice cream she'd had with the Apple Betty, and she missed her beach runs when she was away from home. Carla said she usually took Freya out around four.

The sun was still high when they met at the bridge. Dark green pines looked cut out of the cerulean blue sky. Only a breath of wind drifted through, delivering sharp smells of pine and cedar, stirring the cool, crisp air. Even the crows were still. Nature, taking an afternoon nap. They decided to take the forest loop behind the cabins and then walk back along Whisper Creek to the bridge, about a forty-minute stroll.

Carla checked her pockets for poop bags and treats.

"Every walk is a training walk," she said. "Freya's pretty good about ignoring squirrels, but she's *very* interested in raccoons. If any of those are around, or if, God forbid, Gabby's cat is out, she'll bolt. I'm working on getting her to sit/stay imme-diately, no matter what. Dogs can't generalize and apply their training from one location to another. So I practice all of her commands in lots of different places. It's for her safety as much as for whatever she may go after. So far, she hasn't chased cars, but if she ever did, that instant obedience could save her life."

Logan didn't know much about dogs, but Carla's logic made sense. Freya was lucky to have an owner who was taking the time and effort to train her. Carla said she brought her to work with her most days, now. She doubted Rita would tolerate a poorly behaved dog in the office.

As they entered the forest, Logan was really glad she came. Sunlight streamed through the lofty, nodding branches of conifers high above their heads. G.I. Joe kept the simple trail clear of rocks and fallen branches, but other than that, the path remained in its soft, natural state.

The two women settled into a comfortable pace and neither felt the need to fill the silence. A woodpecker's distant tapping and a brief burst of a western tanager's song were the only sounds punctuating the quiet. Freya did her business and then trotted ahead, stopping to sniff an interesting fern or rock here and there, taking in myriad scents undetectable to the humans.

They followed the path around behind the cabins, then went down to the banks of the creek to enjoy watching the clear water flow past mossy logs and burble over and around its bed of boulders and rounded river rocks. Gnarled tree roots rose above the muddy banks, reminding Logan of giant's toes grimly maintaining their grip on the earth.

"If we get much more rain this winter, that one's coming down, I'll bet," Carla said, pointing to a large pine leaning over the creek. "It's just a matter of time."

Carla let out the leash so Freya could have a little more room to explore—nose leading the way, darting excitedly, zig-zagging back and forth across the stream. Logan watched as the young dog, golden coat glistening in the afternoon sun, splashed and twisted in the water, pouncing on sparkling drops of light skipping across the surface with joyful abandon.

"Definitely a water dog!" Logan said.

"Yep, she's in her element," Carla agreed.

Suddenly, Freya stood stock still in the middle of the stream, water dripping off her coat, looking intently at a spot on the opposite bank. Before Carla could reel her back in, she lurched forward, pulling the leash out of her master's hand.

"Freya! Come!"

Instead of returning to Carla, Freya came to an abrupt stop

a few yards away, barked once and remained stock still, staring into a shady area in the mud a few feet above the water.

Carla went in after her, grabbed the leash and dragged her up the opposite bank.

"Freya," she said, "What has gotten into you? Sit!"

Freya did, but her whole body remained laser focused on the muddy edge of the water just below her feet. The creek bank was undercut on this side by the flowing water, so from this angle, Carla couldn't see what had her dog's attention.

Before Logan could climb out of the creek and join them, Carla asked, "You see anything?"

"Not really. Nothing on the edge or in the water, but underneath here," Logan pointed, "there's a little burrow or hole. Could be something in there."

"Maybe," Carla said. "Don't stick your hand in there. You don't want to get bit."

She straightened up and tried to shake the water out of her shoes. "Freya's only trained to find human scent. This is her alert pose, but she could be confused. If there's a glove or hat or something that got swept in there by the current, I want to reward her, but if she's off—keying on a squirrel or something, I'd like to know."

Logan had no intention of blindly reaching her hand inside a dark hole, but she was curious, too. Freya was completely focused on whatever was in there and refusing to budge.

"No worries, let me see if I can find something to poke around in there," Logan said. "I'll be careful."

There weren't any loose sticks on the ground, so she broke a thin but sturdy branch off a fallen log nearby. Her Timberlands were waterproof, but she was in too far. They were filled with ice cold water and her toes were already numb. She'd have to stop by the cabin before dinner and change.

Standing to the side of the hole in case some frightened creature launched itself into her arms, she carefully reached in with the stick, keeping it along the bottom, so as not to poke any little critters in the eye. Freya remained stock still, and Logan held her breath. After a minute or two of gingerly exploring, she hit the back of the burrow.

"Nope, nada—looks like nobody's home today," Logan announced, relieved at not finding any rabid raccoons in residence.

She pulled out the stick. About halfway, it hooked on something. Something with some weight. Careful not to lose whatever it was she had snagged, Logan carefully pulled it out the rest of the way. Just as it was emerging, the object slid the last few inches and plopped into the stream.

For a moment, all Logan could do was stare. The stark, solid black body and straight lines were in complete contrast with the sun dappled, natural surroundings. This man-made object did not belong here, but here it was.

Resting peacefully on the stream bed, the swift current washing away its sins, was an instrument designed and manufactured by humans with only one purpose—to kill other humans.

Freya whined.

Carla belatedly petted her on the head and gave her a treat.

"Good find, Freya," she whispered. "Good find."

24

For the second time in the last twenty-four hours, Logan reached for her phone and dialed 911. After establishing that it wasn't going to get carried away with the current, dispatch told her to leave the gun where it was, not touch it, and stay there until someone arrived.

After rewarding Freya with multiple treats and lots of praise, Carla went to find dry clothes for both of them and a warm blanket or coat to wrap around Logan until she could change. The sun was setting and along with it, the temperature was dropping.

Logan sat on the bank so she could keep an eye on the gun. Wet to the skin from her thighs down, she was already starting to shiver.

Just then, her phone rang.

"Hello?" she said.

"Logan McKenna?" a man asked.

"Yes," she said, forcing her teeth to stop chattering.

"This is Detective Wright. Dispatch says you've got a gun there. Has anyone touched it?"

"No, it's still in the stream, but I'm keeping an eye on it. Do you want me to take it out?"

"No, not unless you have to. We're on Highway 99—be there in twenty minutes," he said. "Do you have someone with you or are you alone?"

It hadn't occurred to her to worry that whoever hid the gun might come back for it, but it did, now. Now, she really hoped Carla got back quickly. Better yet, that the police would roll up soon to take charge of the evidence, if that's what this was.

"Yes, Carla Morgan is/was with me. It was her dog that alerted to the gun in the first place," she said. "We'd never have found it otherwise. It wasn't lying there in plain sight. Carla just went to get some dry clothes for us, she'll be right back."

"Good. Stay put," he said.

***

Popping the Kojak light on the roof, Wright hit the siren and floored it. They'd be there in fifteen if the stars aligned and commuters got out of their way. The longer the gun was in the water, the greater the chance any fingerprints the killer might have left would get washed away, but if she removed it from the stream, they'd risk prints being smudged or obliterated completely.

He pressed the gas pedal down just an inch more—as far as he dared without getting them in a wreck. It would be getting dark soon, and he didn't like the thought of the two women being out there by themselves.

***

Logan kept her eye on the gun, ready to hook it with the stick or block it with her foot if it looked like it was going to get washed downstream. It gave her the creeps to think she might be looking at the weapon used to kill Monica, but what were the chances of finding a gun stuck in a mud hole not more than forty yards away from where she was shot *not* being the murder weapon?

Wright and Johnson arrived about the same time Carla and Freya returned. While Logan changed out of her wet shoes and gratefully pulled on the warm coat Carla brought her, Wright pulled on gloves, carefully retrieved the gun, and placed it in an evidence bag. Johnson began taping off everything from Whisper Creek to the chicken coop, with a few yards on either side for good measure.

Once he had the gun secured, Wright took Logan and Carla's statements. Freya didn't have much to say but looked quite proud of herself. By the time they were done, the sun was dropping down behind the hills.

For the second evening in a row, spotlights lit up the garden area and crime scene techs started combing the ground. Nothing much was to be gleaned except the murder weapon. If it turned out to be that. Wright couldn't wait to send this one to the state lab to see if they could get a match on the bullets or any useable prints.

If bullets and gun matched, they'd have someplace to start. No one had bothered to file off the serial number on this one, a .22-caliber handgun. Hopefully, it was registered to one of the fifty people they had FI cards on. This case might be solved before the weekend, after all.

***

Brittany wiped down the last of the stainless-steel counters at the service window that opened into the dining room and called over her shoulder to Nick, "You about done back there, hon?"

"Yep," he answered, "just need to take the greens out. Back in ten."

Nick shouldered open the back door and breathed in the cold, clean air. He loved working here. As a cook, of course, but at The New School, specifically. Looking back, it was a miracle he'd made it this far. Raised by an aunt after his parents left—one by way of the grave, the other by way of the bottle—he'd been lost for a while. Floated around, got into some trouble as a teenager. When his aunt kicked him out, his grandfather took him in and gave him another chance.

Grandpa Kelly kept him on the straight and narrow, taught him to cook. He had a little diner down on third street. Made sure that when Nick wasn't at school he came straight to Kelly's Kitchen. He set him up with his homework every afternoon in a corner table and let the waitresses fuss over him while he cleaned up from the lunch crowd and started prepping for dinner. It was a second chance at a future Nick was grateful for every day. Grandpa had been gone now for many years, but Nick still missed his scratchy whiskers and the t-shirt stretched over his lean frame that always smelled faintly of good grease, garlic, and onions.

Nick dumped the vegetable and fruit scraps into the wheelbarrow, lifted up the handles, and steered it toward the compost pile, which was just around the corner. Brittany was a genius when it came to designing the layout of the garden. His herbs were nearby, the raised beds were just beyond, the chicken coop on the far side, and the compost pile behind the dining hall. She had created a perfectly coordinated kitchen and garden workspace. He was a lucky man. How many men had the perfect wife, two beautiful kids, and the perfect job?

He couldn't help but reflect on how close he'd come to losing it all. All because of one woman. Monica. Well, she wasn't a problem, now.

WHISPER CREEK

After spreading out the compost and turning it under, Nick rolled the empty wheelbarrow back to the kitchen. Leaning it up against the outside wall, he practically skipped up the back steps. They planned on putting the twins to bed early tonight, so he and Brittany could have some grown-up time. He didn't like having to schedule time alone with his wife, but since the kids came along, that's about the only way he got any.

But first, he went to make sure everything was ready. The two women who worked in the kitchen wouldn't be returning until Monday, so G.I. Joe said he and Carson would finish the dishes and lock up.

Nick entered the tiny space he euphemistically called his office. A scarred, oak desk shared the ten-by-ten room with racks of industrial size cans of tomato sauce and corn. Various cleaning and paper products filled another shelf. A clipboard with the sign-in sheets and schedules hung on the side.

Something on the narrow shelf above his desk was slightly out of place, protruding slightly over the edge. A small, metal lockbox. Nick reached up and lifted it down. It felt much too light. Hands shaking, he placed it on the desk in front of him and sat down in his chair.

It was unlocked, but then, it wouldn't take a genius to find the key, it was hanging on the hook by the door along with the rest of the keys. Angry at himself for being so careless, he sat there for a moment, staring at the box. Then, half knowing what he would find, he forced himself to push the latch with his thumb and lift the lid.

All thoughts of a romantic evening with Brittany disintegrated. If he hadn't been sitting down, he would have passed out.

The gun was gone.

25

After giving their statements to the detectives and taking Freya a few yards off the path to do her business after all the excitement, Carla and Logan trudged back to the dining hall. Logan's pants were still wet from the knees down, but at least now she had dry boots. She almost went home first, but decided she was hungrier than she was cold. If they hurried, they'd make it before the kitchen closed.

When they got as far as the chicken coop, Brittany was arguing with Detective Wright.

"I just got them to start laying again. I am *not* moving them!" she said, hands on her hips.

Wright explained they needed to tape off an extended area to keep people away from the stream. No one was going to bother her chickens. The crime scene techs would work mainly down at the stream. They were almost done. He was on his way to the office to update their director, Ms. Wolfe. If she had any questions, that's where he'd be.

Brittany huffed, but didn't argue any further. She spotted Logan and Carla.

"Wait up, guys!" she said. "I'm almost done here."

"What'd they find down there anyway? All the police would say was that it was an 'object of interest' that may or may not have any bearing on this case," she intoned, mimicking Wright's cop voice.

She finished checking the nesting area and spread some fresh straw on the floor inside, securing the door on her way out. A pile of dirty straw lay just outside. She said Carson or G.I. Joe would be taking that to the compost pile later. They were going to clean and lock up for them tonight. She and Nick were leaving early.

"*I*," Brittany informed them with a Groucho Marx wiggle of her eyebrows, "have a date with my husband!"

The wind shifted and the acrid smell from the pile of dirty straw outside the coop almost made Logan's eyes water.

"Wow," Logan said. "That packs quite a punch!"

Brittany laughed, "Yep, chicken poop has a unique stink. High ammonia content. Great for the garden, though. Makes good soil after composting."

The strong smell reminded Logan of something, but she couldn't place it.

Luckily, the aroma of fried chicken washed away the scent as soon as they walked into the dining hall.

Carla put Freya at a down/stay command at her feet while they ate. It was amazing to watch. The dog just lay there, her chin on her paws, perfectly content. It was either the breed or the training. It couldn't be the breed, because her neighbor's Golden Retriever back in Jasper—about the same age—would have been barking, play bowing, begging for scraps, or running around the room, or all of the above, probably simultaneously. If she ever got a dog, Logan was going to bring it up here for Carla to train.

Rita came in just as Carson started closing the roller window in the serving area, but he filled up a plate for her and handed it through.

"Thanks, Carson," she said. "Glad you're feeling better."

The young man nodded.

"Thanks," he said. "And thanks for bringing me breakfast the other day. That helped."

"How are you two doing?" Rita said as she sat down with her dinner.

Logan worried Rita would object to Freya being in the dining room, but apparently she either didn't mind or was making an exception tonight.

"Is that our wonder dog under there?" Rita said, smiling.

Freya thumped her tail in acknowledgment of the compliment.

Getting the nod from Carla first, Rita tore off a piece of chicken and gave it to Freya.

"It's just meat—no breading. Good deeds should be rewarded," she said.

Next, Rita wanted to hear all the details, from Freya keying on the muddy hole on the side of the creek bank to the retrieval of the gun.

"Well, at least they should be able to find the guy," Carla said. "I mean, unless the serial number was filed off the gun, they'll be able to trace it, right?"

"I thought so, too," Rita said. "But Detective Wright quickly disabused me of that notion."

"Really?" Carla said. "Don't they have all that on record somewhere? I mean, they have to do background checks on you when you buy a gun where you give them your name and address and whatever, right?"

Logan knew a little about this issue from hearing her brother Rick and his fellow officers complain, but she didn't interrupt.

"It turns out that the police can't just type in a number, have their computer search a national database, and spit out the name of the gunowner," she said.

"Why not?" Carla asked.

"There *is* no national database," Rita said, adding honey to her buttered roll.

"What?" said Carla.

"Yep," Rita said, "It's all manual. Even if the gun's serial number is intact, the best they can do is call the manufacturer to get the name of the dealer or wholesaler they sold the gun to. Then, they send that store or wholesaler a request to get the name of the person who bought that specific gun."

"How long does that take?" Carla asked.

"He said it can take up to a week, but with a homicide, they might get the answer in twenty-four hours," she said.

"Well, that's good, right?" Carla said.

"Yeah," Rita said, "As long as the gun hasn't been resold. If that's the case and the state doesn't require background checks for resales, it's a dead end."

"That's ridiculous!" Carla said.

"I agree," Rita said.

Logan jumped in. "Me, too. Cops hate it. The gun lobby is pretty powerful. And there's a reason some people don't want the government tracking who has what guns," Logan said.

"Why?" Carla asked.

"They're worried a national database gives the government power to come take their guns whenever they want to," said Logan.

"Jeez," Carla said.

Rita popped the last piece of buttered roll into her mouth and washed it down with the last of her mineral water.

"Let's just hope the gun you found was only sold once," Rita said. "He said it has a serial number. Hopefully, they'll get a match. They're also going to try to pull up fingerprints, but he's not hopeful."

"Did he say how the investigation is going?" Logan asked. "Do they have any suspects? He wouldn't tell us anything."

"If they do, he's not saying. Just said it's an 'ongoing investigation,' etc."

Carla looked frustrated.

Logan understood why. Carla was the one who had to field the phone calls from parents. Logan assumed the concerned calls would only turn increasingly more frantic as the week progressed unless the killer was found. Today was Wednesday, so hopefully they'd find the guy before students came back on Monday.

26

After depositing their dishes in the designated tub, the women said their goodnights. Rita went back to her and Nicole's rooms above the office. Logan and Carla started walking toward home.

Hunger satisfied, all Logan wanted now was a long, hot shower and a gazillion hours of sleep. The spike of adrenaline from finding the gun had faded, and with it, so had the last reserves of her energy. Huey wanted to finish up his backlog of repairs first, so she didn't have to be at the lab until around nine. She planned on sleeping in. Unless Nick's cinnamon rolls called, of course . . .

When they got over the bridge, Logan waved goodnight to Carla and Freya and used her mini flashlight to pick out a path to Glenda's cabin. An early diner, Glenda was already home and curled up with a good book in front of the fire.

A few security lights illuminated the main buildings back on campus, but here in the forest, the night lay soft and deep. Spotting a fallen log on the edge of the path, Logan decided to sit down for a minute and allow her swirling thoughts to settle before she got to the cabin and had to relay the events of the day all over again to Glenda.

She turned off her flashlight and let her eyes adjust to the dark. Letting the silence settle around her, she tuned in to the nocturnal stirrings in the forest—the whoosh and sway of the forest's breath moving through the trees. The distant call of an owl. Something skittered through the shrubs to her right. Behind her, she heard the soothing susurration of Whisper Creek.

A few minutes later—or maybe more, she wasn't sure—Logan was startled out of her meditative state by the sound of two people crossing the bridge and hurrying up the path she'd just left. She recognized the voices.

"Are you sure?" Brittany asked.

"Yes," Nick said, spitting out the word.

"What are we going to do?" she asked, anxiety mounting in her voice. "Are you going to report it?"

Logan strained to hear Nick's response, but if he gave one, she couldn't hear it. Whatever he said was swallowed by the night.

***

THURSDAY, MID-MORNING

Logan hadn't slept well. She kept going over and over the snippet of conversation she overheard, wondering what Brittany and Nick were talking about. She left that part out when recounting the day's events to Glenda.

She'd planned on taking Brittany aside after breakfast, but when she started to, she changed her mind. What would she say? 'Hi Brittany, I was eavesdropping on your conversation last night and wonder what it is you think Nick should report . . . to the police?'

No. She needed to give this some more thought. Everything seemed normal at breakfast, both Nick and Brittany were working, running around in the kitchen, joking with everyone, just like every other day. Maybe she'd imagined Brittany's anxious tone of voice. Maybe she wasn't referring to reporting something to the police—she hadn't actually used the word police—maybe it had to do with something completely unrelated, like food deliveries being late or something.

Student meals were included in their tuition, so there wasn't any money to speak of that could have been stolen, but maybe they kept some petty cash and that was missing. Logan couldn't imagine Teresa or any of her crew stealing anything, though.

It was late when she heard Nick and Brittany last night. She was tired. It'd been a hell of a couple of days. Her exhausted mind must have draped innocent words with ominous overtones. It was probably nothing. Time to get her head back in the game where it belonged—on her work.

***

Huey was waiting for her in the lab. He'd already had breakfast.

"Morning, Logan," he said. "Did you and Carla really find a gun yesterday?"

"Well, technically, Freya found it," Logan said. "I was just along for the ride."

She filled him in and gave him the large mocha coffee she brought for him, with two extra squirts of hazelnut syrup, and pulled up a chair.

"Thanks," he said, taking a drink. "Just finishing up here."

"Okay, whatcha working on?" she said.

"There," he said, winding a small piece of electrical tape around a cord tightly. "That should hold it for a while."

"Before we get started on MuMu," he said. "I want to show you something."

Huey pushed his current project aside and pulled a small, flat, black device out from behind the monitor. Rummaging through a box of loose cords, he found one that fit and plugged it into the side, attaching the other end to the USB port on his computer.

"I forgot I had this," Huey said.

"What is it?" Logan asked. "Is this what you wanted me to see?"

Huey leaned back in his chair and folded his arms. He waited a beat, then said.

"Monica LeGrange's backup drive."

"Wow," said Logan. "But why do you have it?"

"She gave it to me a few weeks ago, told me to repair it. Said it got dropped," he said.

"*Told* you? That seems pretty nervy. Is that part of your job? Do a lot of parents ask you to fix things for them?" Logan asked.

"No, Monica had no problem with nervy," he said. "I only agreed to take a look at it so she'd leave my lab. I planned on keeping it a few days, then giving it to Ethan to take back to her and say I didn't have any luck. I forgot I had it until today."

Logan knew this shouldn't be the first question out of her mouth, but she was curious, "Does it work?"

"Don't know. Haven't tried it yet," he said, double clicking on the icon that had appeared on the desktop.

Nothing happened. Huey tried several different ports and cords, but the icon just sat there on the desktop, mocking them.

"Well, we should turn it over to the police, anyway," Logan said, secretly disappointed they hadn't gotten in. Do you want me to call that Detective Wright? I've got his card."

"No," said Huey, "I've got his card, too, but they won't need this. They'll have Stacey going through her computer. This is just the backup drive. That will have more current files anyway."

Stacey was the forensic cybercrimes tech with the Newberg-Dundee Police Department. Huey often helped her out when she had a case that required more expertise than she possessed. Huey could also hunt for things unofficially, using methods that she, being law enforcement, was not permitted to use.

"That's the first thing the police will do," Huey said, "you said she was texting someone that night when you saw her, right? They'll have Stacey go through all her technology—phone, computer, whatever else she had. They won't need an old backup drive. It's been at least a month since she gave it to me to fix. There'd be no current data, anyway."

27

WEDNESDAY NIGHT

Carson came in, shut the door behind him, and threw himself on the bed, raking his hands through his hair, squeezing his eyes shut, then staring at the ceiling. He'd managed to hold it together all day without anyone becoming suspicious, but the strain had been unbearable. He couldn't keep this up.

There was no *way* they weren't going to find out! He'd used his phone! What an idiot. The police could always track your phone—know where you were, when you were there, who you called or texted. Probably what you had for breakfast. He thought about destroying it, pulling out the sim card and stomping on it, but he needed it to call Matt. He needed a ride and money. He had a little, but he'd need more than the few bucks he'd squirreled away to get far enough away from the cops.

He'd met Matt in rehab. He didn't know if he was still clean or not, but his was the only number he had. The others he'd deleted. That was one of the first things they told you to do. To cut all ties with your past. He was supposed to get a new number so they couldn't call him either, but he hadn't gotten around to it yet. He'd deleted all of his old drug contacts, so he couldn't call them, but they still had *his* number. Once they knew he was serious about staying clean, the invitations to party or to 'try some good stuff'—always newer and better, of course—gradually tapered off, then finally stopped. Except Monica. He thought he was free and clear until she called.

Damn her! Why couldn't she have just left him alone?

Suddenly, a craving hit him so strong he could taste the high. That hadn't happened in months. For a split second, he thought of reaching for his phone, of planning a few days relief from all this. See if Matt was still using. He could just take a little, then get clean before the next drug test. They trusted him now. They only did them once every couple weeks.

No! He was *not* going to go through that hell again. He'd worked too hard! He was *not* going to give in! He reached for the six-month sobriety chip he kept by the bed on his night-stand. No, no matter what, he was not going back.

This made him think of Blanchett House and Rita and G.I. Joe. What would they think of him if they knew?

Shutting his mind to everything else, Carson focused on his immediate problem. Escape.

He just had to get to Portland, lay low with Matt, pick up some work in a kitchen or car wash and then as soon as he could scrape together enough money for a bus ticket, get the hell out of Dodge. He knew a couple of places that didn't ask for ID and paid under the table. He'd have Matt do the shopping, pay cash for everything. Except for walking to work, he'd stay in Matt's apartment. He could disappear for a couple of weeks.

He dialed the number.

Hallelujah! Matt picked up right away—sober as a preacher.

He told him his job here was up and there was more work to be had in the city. Luckily, Matt didn't ask questions. As long as Carson was clean and sober, yes, he could come stay with him for a while. He'd appreciate the company. It was so hard sometimes. Boring. Everything was boring compared to getting high. They could keep each other on the straight and narrow.

Carson decided the best plan was for him to wait until Mrs. Wolfe and Nicole were asleep before leaving. No one else lived in the house. G.I. Joe used to have this room, but he had his own cabin now with the rest of the staff members on the other side of Whisper Creek. No one would hear or see him walk right down the road, which was sure to be deserted by the time he got out. If a car did drive by, he'd just hide in the brush until they passed.

Matt said he was working late, but to give him a call when he was ready and he'd come out and give him a ride, if he didn't mind it being after his shift got over at midnight. Carson said he didn't mind. He really didn't, because this way he didn't have to explain to Matt why he needed a ride in the middle of the night. If Matt thought he was in any trouble, he probably wouldn't take him in.

Decision made, Carson looked around his room. He'd have to leave behind the nice clothes G.I. Joe bought him, and the Bible Carla had given him. The Bible was too heavy and he wouldn't need nice clothes for a while. He felt bad leaving like this, so taking their gifts seemed wrong. He did take the money though. $189.67. He needed that.

If he just hadn't taken Monica's call . . .

Slamming the door shut on useless regrets, he finished stuffing his bag, making sure his sobriety chip was safely tucked into one of the interior compartments, zipped tight. The one thing he was proud of. No one could take that away from him, no matter how things turned out. He laced up his work boots, threw his warm jacket over his backpack, which he'd hung on the bedpost, and then lay back down to wait, fingers laced behind his head. He wanted to leave a note, but what was there to say?

As he waited for the sound of footsteps, running water, and other getting-ready-for-bed muffled noises from the rooms above to settle, Carson's mind had nothing to do but wander down memory lane to where he took his first wrong turn.

28

DECEMBER, 2020

"Hello?"

"Well, hello handsome," Monica purred.

"What do you want?" Carson said, keeping his voice low. He'd deleted her number, but she had obviously kept his.

He'd finished working for the day and was back in his room, but still, he didn't know how soundproof it was and he didn't want anyone to hear him talking with someone from his past. Carla's desk was just across the reception area. If there was a lull between parents coming to pick up their kids, she might hear him.

He hadn't heard Monica's voice for over a year, and it was jarring. It felt weird to be talking to her now.

"That's no way to greet an old friend," Monica said. "I was just calling to congratulate you."

"Oh," he said. "For what?"

"For landing on your feet, Silly," she said. "Hadn't seen you around. One of the girls said you were doing the rehab thing.

You could have told me. You didn't have to drop off the face of the earth like that."

"I didn't tell anyone," he said.

"And by the way, you didn't need to go to rehab," she said. "You were fine."

If you call losing most of your teeth and giving blow jobs for your next fix, 'fine,' sure, he had been hunky dory.

When Carson didn't respond, she continued, "Well, I'm sure it was tough going through rehab, but at least you got yourself a nice, new job out of the deal—out there at The New School."

At the words New School, Carson felt the bottom of his newfound sense of security drop out from under him. How did Monica know where he was?

"What?" was all he could manage to say.

Monica just barreled along, as if she weren't carrying on a one-sided conversation.

"Oh," she said, "I saw you the other day. My stepson goes there. Yeah, that's a news flash, right? It was great when it was just me and Duncan, only had to put up with a stinky kid on weekends, but the kid's mother kicked the bucket and I inherited a surly teenager. I had to move to the godawful suburbs so he could have fresh air and a yard for a dog . . . yada, yada, yada. Can you imagine me living in the suburbs, Carson?"

Her laugh was harsh and hollow. How had he ever been attracted to this woman?

"Why are you calling, Monica?" he said.

As soon as he'd saved enough money, he was definitely going to have to buy a new phone. But would that help? She knew where he worked now.

"Well, now that you've got rehab out of your system, I thought you might be ready to have a little fun . . ."

Fun . . . He used to share Monica's idea of fun. One of his best customers, they met every Friday morning. Nine-thirty on the dot. Outside. Pioneer Square. On the concrete steps just outside Starbucks. He in his raggy jeans and backpack. She in her Manolo Blahnics and Hermes bag. Their delivery system was simple. He would tuck her drugs into the Starbucks bag with whatever giant, gooey pastry was on offer that day.

Monica didn't need to worry about calories. Her regular order took care of that.

She was perfect. They all were. All the Portland second wives. Perfect as their plastic surgeons and hair stylists could make them. Carson remembered how she looked. He wasn't a big fan of fake boobs, but hers were nice—not huge, like hooker boobs. Tasteful. He may have been a drug addict, but he was a guy. He noticed.

Then one glorious summer morning, with a wicked grin, she'd crooked her finger and invited him back to her river-view, loft townhome to share some of the good stuff he'd just sold her. He wondered briefly if there was a husband to worry about, but she said he was a boring workaholic, always at the office. She worked there, too, but didn't have to go in early. No one expected her until noon.

They took very good advantage of the next couple of hours. She used him to a frazzle. This went on for a few weeks, every Friday after his delivery. Then, one Friday, no invite. No explanation. The party was over. It was back to business as usual.

How had he ever thought that was fun?

". . . I pick up the pimple monster on Thursdays around 4:30 p.m. That's when I saw you last time I was there, going into your room on the other side of the office. So next time I come to pick him up, you can slip a little something into my purse. It shouldn't be too hard. You were always good at thinking up something clever, Carson. It'll be like old times."

"I'm clean, Monica," he said. "I don't have anything. What part of rehab don't you get? I'm sure you can find another connection downtown. Or go to whoever you've been getting stuff from. I've been clean and sober for three months. You must have another supplier by now. Either way, I can't help you."

***

He was surprised, but she hadn't called back right away. She must have found another source, because it wasn't like her to give up so easily. He hadn't heard from her for weeks. Then, last Friday, she called again, her voice tinged with anxiety. He recognized the signs. She needed a hit. Whoever she had been using must have either gotten arrested, overdosed, or gotten clean. That's when he got to see her desperate, dirty side.

"Well, Mr. Three-Months-Clean-and-Sober," she growled into the phone when he turned her down again, "I know you're lying. I know you've got some. There's no way you kicked it. You're no better than me. You just want to keep the good stuff for yourself. I *know* you, remember?"

Carson wanted to hang up, but he couldn't. Some part of him remembered a sliver of the young woman Monica had been at one time or might have become. The light, laughing Monica that swirled and twirled across the hardwood floors in her loft apartment those few Fridays long ago.

But that Monica wasn't this Monica. Who knew what this Monica was capable of? After many group therapy sessions at Blanchett House and long talks with G.I. Joe since he came here, he had gained some insights into himself and what addiction did to you. Addicts were self-centered, which fit Monica to a T. She didn't have to come to him for drugs. She could have found someone else to buy from, but she was angry.

Angry at him, yes, but angrier at herself. Filled with self-loathing that she had somehow fallen farther down the ladder than someone she'd always thought of as many rungs below her.

In a weird way, it made perfect sense. She wasn't willing to do what it took to overcome her own addiction, so she couldn't stand seeing anyone else make it. Now all she wanted to do was drag him back down to her level. Any way she could.

"Tuesday, Carson," she said. "I have to be out there for one of Ethan's nighttime things. The geek helps with lighting or something. Duncan, Ethan, and I—the happy family of three—oh, make that four—the sainted dead mother is always with us!"

Monica's voice hinged on the verge of hysteria now, "I'll be there for several hours, sitting through a stupid talent show, so you'll have plenty of opportunity to figure out how to get me what I want.

"And you know what, Carson? I don't care if you're really clean or not. I know you still have connections. If you don't want your new boss to find out what you've been up to, not only will you make sure this happens, but this delivery will be *free*. Make one wrong move and I'll be happy to fill her in."

"I haven't been up to *anything*," he said. "I keep telling you, I'm clean!"

"I'm sure those places have strict rules, right? Curfew, random drug tests. I'll take you down and you know I can do it. If you make me go somewhere else, I'll save a little back and plant it in your room or put a few drops in your water bottle. I know my way around the dining hall out there. You'll never see it coming. Who are they going to believe? A former drug addict or the co-owner of an engineering company; a good wife whose husband adores her, and the dutiful mother of one of their students?"

She knew she had him.

"So, that's settled, then" she gloated, "See you Tuesday!"

***

Carson listened intently but didn't hear a thing. He'd laid awake for hours already, but waited another thirty minutes to be sure. Finally, he felt confident Mrs. Wolfe and Nicole were sound asleep. Making sure nothing in his pockets or backpack jingled, he slowly opened first his bedroom door and slipped out.

The parking lot was all gravel, so he kept to the smooth, dirt edges, stepping softly until he reached the road. No streetlights in the boonies. He fumbled with his phone in the dark.

When Matt picked up, Carson let out a huge sigh of relief. Matt was home and wanted to come get him now, since he'd picked up an early morning shift. When a yellow hatchback slowed to do a U-turn, Carson quickly tossed his phone into the woods. He would have smashed it first but didn't have time. But he wasn't too worried. Getting rid of the phone met his main objective—not being tracked by the police.

29

Back in his room, Ethan felt sick. The police had just left. He'd listened at the top of the stairs to the questions they asked his dad. He'd watched a lot of cop shows and he knew anytime the police said their questions were 'just routine,' they were anything but. And then, when they asked if his dad had a gun, he'd about shit his pants. That had to mean his dad was a suspect!

Then later, at the door when the older detective asked him how his dad and Monica got along. They were digging.

But it wasn't the cop's questions that had him feeling nauseous. It was his dad's answers. Dad seemed to go overboard acting like everything was fine—more than fine—like the three of them were one big, happy family. Like Monica wasn't . . . well . . . *Monica!* That was *so* not true!

His head hurt. He wanted to tell them the truth, but he'd followed his dad's lead. In the end, he'd tried to say as little as possible.

Ethan threw himself back on his bed. Maybe his dad just didn't want anyone to know what their family was really like because he was embarrassed. Dad was kind of a private person.

When he was eleven, they went to his grandparents' house for Thanksgiving and one of his uncles had gotten really drunk and thrown a bottle of beer at the TV while the men were all in the family room, watching the game. On the way home, his dad had made a point of telling him not to share that story with anyone—something about not airing dirty laundry in public.

Maybe Dad still loved Monica, in spite of everything, and didn't want anyone to think bad about her? Maybe that's what happened when someone died. You wanted to erase their bad points. Well, if that was the case, it was going to take a gimongous eraser! Monica had too many bad points to count.

Now that he thought about it, his dad had always glossed over Monica's faults and acted all nice around other people, particularly lately. But he remembered all too clearly how they talked to each other at home, or more like avoided talking to each other. They didn't yell much. His dad pretty much just gave in most of the time to avoid arguing. It made Ethan furious. He hated to see his dad get pushed around like that. He spent a lot of time in his room.

They did get into it one time, though, although it was Monica who did most of the yelling. At the time, he wondered why no one called the cops, but either the neighbors decided to mind their own business—no one ever mentioned it—or the yelling couldn't be heard outside the house. Maybe they thought that any admission of domestic problems in someone else's home meant they were susceptible, too.

It had been tense around the house for several days, everyone sticking to their own schedules. Things came to a head two weeks before Christmas. He and Dad had finished dinner and cleaned up, then he'd gone upstairs to finish his homework. He wanted to get all of the reading done for his U.S. History class that night, so he could stay late at school the next day to help Huey with the lighting for the little kids' Christmas program at The New School.

Dad took his computer to his chair, which wasn't unusual. He often worked while watching TV, but when Ethan came down a couple of hours later for a quick snack before turning in, his dad was just sitting there in the dark, TV off, computer on his lap, nursing a tumbler of amber liquid. A bottle of Maker's Mark was within reach.

Dad had been sort of grimly quiet all night. He didn't ask.

Monica got home around eleven. He heard her kick off her shoes, throw her car keys on the table in the entryway, then start up the stairs. His dad's voice cut through the quiet.

"Monica," he said, "In here."

She stopped, then Ethan heard her walk back to the kitchen.

"Oh, hi, Hon," she said, opening the fridge. "Sorry I'm late, Jessica can talk forever! You're so lucky you don't have to go!"

"Shut up," he said, in a quiet voice full of fury that Ethan had never heard before. "Just shut up."

"Excuse me?" she replied, shutting the refrigerator door. "You can't talk to me like that!"

"I'll talk to you any way I like," he said. "You don't deserve better."

What has gotten into you?" she said. "Are you drunk?"

"No," he said, "Not that it's any of your business. I certainly have a right to be. Where were you tonight? And don't say with Jessica at the planning meeting . . . I know you weren't there."

Ethan strained to hear them, but Monica had moved into the family room, farther away. For several seconds, Monica didn't answer. Ethan could all but hear her brain spinning, trying to come up with a good answer.

"Of course, I was at the planning meeting . . . ," she said.

"Stop lying, Monica!" his dad boomed.

Ethan had no trouble hearing that one.

When Monica spoke again, she'd lost the innocent tone.

"I don't need to listen to this," she said flatly, clicking her heels back into the kitchen.

"The hell you don't!" he said. "I've given you so much, and you . . . you've given nothing . . . you just take and take! I opened everything to you—my heart, my home, my business, I even let you into the life of my son!"

"Into *his* life? Ha! You dumped him into mine! I didn't ask to be a full-time mother, but here I am! I've tried to make something of that teenage lump, but nothing I do is appreciated! By him or by you!"

"Yes, that was a mistake. You aren't cut out to be a mother, that's for sure," he said. "Or a wife, it turns out . . ."

"What?" she yelled.

"Don't bother, Monica," he said, jumping out of his chair. "I put up with you taking over my life and giving nothing back. I put up with your spending every goddamn dime I make, without you working at all . . ."

"I work! I work my butt off! I take clients to lunch and decorate the office and your house so it doesn't look like a 1950s reject . . . ! I bring lots of money in—maybe not directly, but . . ."

"Try not at all, Monica," he sneered. "But that's not what this is about. This is about your crossing the line that finally opened my eyes. This is about you screwing around, Monica."

"How dare you!" she said.

"How many have there been? Huh?" he shouted, slamming his hand down on the kitchen counter.

"I want you out," he said. "I may have made a mistake in marrying you, but I don't have to keep making it."

30

Legs splayed out in front of him, slouched in his chair, Wright sat staring at the driver's license photo of their victim, taped front and center on the mostly empty whiteboard. The conference room was windowless and the air was stale. It could have been high noon or coming up on dinnertime. He had no idea, but the chatter from the bullpen had died down, so he was guessing it was closer to five. Suzie knew not to count on him to keep regular hours when he was working a homicide, but he'd told her he'd be home to eat with the family tonight.

Forty-four hours. It had been approximately forty-four hours since someone shot Monica LeGrange and even though the link chart was fuller, they were still no closer to arresting anyone.

Who were you, Monica and why did someone want to shoot you?

"See anything?" Johnson asked as he came in and poured himself a cup of coffee from the pot someone had set up in the back of their temporary command center/conference room. If they didn't solve this case by Monday, the Major Crimes Response Team would be disbanded and it'd be just him and

Johnson working it along with a dozen other cases they had waiting for them.

"Nope," Wright said, swiveling around to face him. "Stacie have any luck with the computer?"

"Negative," Johnson said. "She'll keep trying, but she doesn't think there's much hope there. If she can't get into it, she'll send it to the staties. Maybe they'll be able to."

Johnson sat down and both detectives turned their attention back to the whiteboard. It was almost four-thirty and they had the room to themselves. Everyone else had either gone home for the night or were following up on leads. Power Pilates had given them a couple of names of instructors she'd taken classes from. They got the places she got her hair and nails done from the calendar at her home. Hopefully they'd get something there.

Wright liked building a physical link chart. Not that he wasn't computer savvy. He kept Excel spreadsheets with data and made sure all the FI cards were digitized, but for putting it all together—going over the 'what ifs' with Johnson, he liked the physical, visual power of having a picture of his murder victim in the center, surrounded by people and locations they were connected to in some way. The killer was in there somewhere. He just had to find him.

The detective he'd replaced used to use a bulletin board with different colors of strings for different types of connections, but he found it simpler to just use a whiteboard and one black marker. He wasn't *that* anal.

Right now, the only photos they had on the board were Monica's in the middle, her husband, Duncan, her stepson, Ethan, and for locations, her forested, suburban home in Middleton, Quantum Engineering, Power Pilates, Jansen's (her hair and nail salon), and Cheryl, her massage therapist. According to Duncan, Monica had been an only child and her parents lived in Florida, somewhere. He didn't have any contact information for them. He said they hadn't been close. In fact, he'd never met them.

Other than clients she'd taken to lunch or social galas she and Duncan had attended, there seemed to be no one of any significance in Monica's life. Even the neighbors only knew her well enough to say hello, and they said they rarely saw her. According to them, she used her remote and drove straight into the garage—entered the house from there. She wasn't the type to spend much time watering the roses in the front yard or going to neighborhood BBQs.

How lonely that must have been, Wright thought. His street had a block party every year and he and his wife knew every family on the street. He couldn't imagine not having those connections to keep him grounded in the real world when this job could so easily corrode his faith in his fellow human beings.

Johnson got up and reached for the marker, uncapping it. Across the top of the whiteboard he scribbled the words LOVE, LUST, LOATHING, and LOOT.

Wright nodded, "That about covers it."

"According to someone much smarter than me, those are your main motives for murder," Johnson said. "FBI Workshop," he added, by way of explanation.

Wright considered the list.

Johnson drew a line through one of the words, "We can take out lust, I think. They reserved that one for serial killers who get a sexual thrill out of killing their victims, usually after humiliating, torturing, and raping them—or some combination of the above."

Wright agreed they could eliminate a serial killer in this scenario. That didn't fit this homicide, and unless it was his first, no similar crimes had been committed in the area.

"So that leaves Love, Loathing, and Loot," Johnson said, taking a professor's stance at the whiteboard.

"What about jealousy? Anger?" Wright asked, playing the part of a diligent student.

"Ahh . . . but what *causes* the jealousy? What *causes* the anger?" he asked. "What's the underlying motive, Grasshopper?"

"Love, Loathing, or Loot . . . ?" Wright asked, the innocent, wide-eyed pupil learning at his master's knee.

"Ahh, yes, Grasshopper!" Johnson said, "You are beginning to understand . . ."

They both smiled at the Kung Fu reference. Johnson had been in diapers and Wright hadn't been born yet when the show first aired, but they'd both been streaming it lately. Johnson always gave Wright David Carradine's part while he played the role of the Kung Fu master.

Just then, Wright's phone dinged. He dragged it toward him across the conference table. It was from one of the sheriff's deputies on the team. He'd been contacting gun dealers in the area all day. It was a long shot, but if the gun had been purchased nearby, they might get a match on the serial number in the store's background check files.

He smiled at Johnson.

"Got him!" said Wright, reading the text he'd just received. "On October 23, 2020, the Walmart Supercenter in Sherwood, Oregon sold a twenty-two handgun, same serial number, to a Nick Zimmer residing at The New School on Whisper Creek Road."

"Up for a ride?"

Johnson grinned.

While Wright called Suzie to let her know he'd miss dinner

after all, Johnson called to get Judge Lorens on the phone for a search warrant for Nick's office and home. There was another text from the lab saying they had print results, but since they knew the gun was Nick's, it wasn't urgent. He'd call them back first thing in the morning.

31

The energy in the car was palpable. Finally, they had a lead to follow. If the ballistics report matched bullets to gun, they'd have enough to arrest him, but for now, they were just going to ask Nick some questions.

This being his third trip up there in as many days, Wright didn't need to GPS it.

On the way, Johnson read Nick's FI card out loud to refresh their memories. He'd grabbed the wife's, too. All they had were the initial statements, no follow up interviews had yet been conducted.

"Nick Zimmer, 47, cook, runs the kitchen with his wife, Brittany, 36. One-year-old twin girls . . . both worked for the school since it opened. They live in one of the staff cabins across the creek in the back."

"They were the magic act," Wright said, remembering the outfits. Hard to miss a six-foot-three man in drag. "What's the timeline? Where was he when the McKenna woman saw Monica walking into the garden area?"

"They performed first, then were in and out of the kitchen, cleaning up and setting up the coffee and dessert station for intermission. Said they watched the rest of the show from back there, behind the audience. He could have slipped out anytime without being noticed."

"Except by the wife," Wright noted. "She'd know."

"Priors?"

"No outstanding warrants," Johnson said.

He could check for warrants on his phone but would have to wait until he was back at the station to do a thorough criminal background search.

A few minutes later, they drove under the wrought iron arch. Wright parked on the side of the lot, out of view of the windows that faced the road. Bypassing the office, they walked around the main building and headed directly to the dining hall. No sense announcing their arrival. The faint clatter of dishes reached them through the closed doors, which were unlocked, so they let themselves in.

Unlike the night of the murder, the place looked pretty empty. On the far left was the stage. The velvet curtains were closed. The room felt somewhat cavernous with all the folding chairs put away. Only a few round tables were set up with condiments and napkin holders on the right, between them and the kitchen. Through the pass way, they saw Nick at the stove, stirring something. Brittany was loading up a salad bar.

Nick lowered the flame on what he was cooking and pushed open the swinging saloon doors to come out and meet them. On the way, he asked Brittany to keep an eye on the pot so it didn't burn.

"Detectives," Nick said, wiping his hands on a towel he had tucked into his pants. "What can I do for you?"

"Just following up on a few things, Mr. Zimmer," Wright said. "Is there someplace we can talk?"

Nick gestured toward the nearest table and pulled out a

chair. "We can talk here," he said. "The staff will be coming in for dinner in about twenty minutes, so I can't talk long."

Wright ignored the time limit. He'd talk with him as long as he needed to and not a minute less. Right now, he wanted to see if Nick was a liar or not.

Both detectives watched his body language closely. After a few softball questions, Wright jumped right in.

"Mr. Zimmer," he said, "As I'm sure you know by now, a gun was found not far from here in Whisper Creek yesterday. Do you know anything about that?"

"No," Nick said, shaking his head.

He came from another direction, trying to catch Nick off guard. It was an interview technique that had worked well for him in the past.

"How well did you know the deceased, Monica LeGrange?" he asked.

"Not very well, we all knew she was Ethan's stepmom, of course," Nick said, "but just to say hello to when she'd come to pick him up."

Brittany had come up to sit beside him. He reached for his wife's hand, "We didn't know her better than any of the other parents."

Wright returned to the issue of the gun.

"Do you own a handgun or does anyone else you know on campus own a firearm?" he asked.

Nick hesitated for a split second, then said, "I don't know if anyone else has one, but I picked up a .22 last year to keep critters away from the chickens. The raccoons kept raiding the nesting area for eggs. Coyotes were after the chickens, mostly, not the eggs. They couldn't always get in, but they'd spook the chickens anyway and they'd stop laying."

Brittany put a hand on her husband's arm. Wright wondered

why they didn't ask if the gun that was found in Whisper Creek was Nick's.

"We'd like to take a look at it," Wright said.

"Why?" Nick's jaw twitched.

"Just part of the investigation," said Wright. "Process of elimination."

Nick clenched his jaw, looking reluctant to answer.

"I don't have it," he said, finally.

"Oh? It's not here?" Wright said. "Is it at your home?"

Brittany answered for them.

"No, someone stole it," she said.

Wright looked at Nick.

"When?"

Again, Brittany answered. "We don't know."

"When did you discover it was missing?" Johnson asked.

"Yesterday," Nick sighed. "I noticed the lock box I keep it in was crooked on the shelf. When I opened it, it was empty."

"Did you report the theft?" Johnson said.

"Not yet," Nick said, avoiding direct eye contact.

"Why not?" he asked.

"I will," he said. "I was going to, just haven't had time with everything that's been going on. I'll do it today."

"Well, as long as we're here, we can take a stolen property report and take a look around while we're at it. The department's spread pretty thin right now. No sense calling property crimes when we're already here. We'll need any sales receipt you have."

Nick took them back to his office. His earlier reluctance seemed to give way to resignation. Johnson went through the motions of taking the stolen property report, while Wright poked around and checked the office and door for signs of a break-in.

"No signs of forced entry," Wright said. "You're sure the gun was here the whole time? You never took it home?"

"No, like I said. I bought it to scare off the local wildlife. I've only had it a few months," Nick said.

"Nick would never have a gun in the house around the girls," Brittany said. "He never brings it home. It's always here in the office."

Johnson's phone dinged and he glanced at it. Wright looked at him hopefully, but he shook his head and put the phone back in his pocket. The judge still hadn't come through with the search warrant.

They didn't want to tip their hand and let Nick know he was a probable suspect until they had the lab report. If they got a match on the bullets, or better yet, any prints, they'd have enough to come back with an arrest warrant.

On the way out, Wright asked, "Oh, when was the last time you fired your gun, Nick? Maybe that will help us narrow down a time frame for when it was stolen."

"Not sure," Nick said. "Sometimes I take it out for target practice if there's time between lunch and dinner. There's a hill behind the art barn. I set bottles and cans and stuff up on a board out there. That's the safest place to shoot. Nobody's ever out there."

"You a good shot?" Wright asked, smiling now, bonding, shooter to shooter.

"Not really," Nick said. "I've never hit anything; the noise is usually enough to scare them off."

"Do you remember if you took it out Tuesday?" Johnson asked.

Nick shook his head. "I don't know," he said. "I could have."

"Okay," Wright said. "Can you think of anyone else on campus who might have a firearm? A delivery person, even."

"Wow," Nick said. "I hadn't even thought of that. I've never seen one, but anyone could have one, I suppose."

Johnson finished scribbling, then slipped his notebook and pen into his inside, jacket pocket.

More relaxed now, Nick pressed his hands on his thighs and stood up, "Well, thanks for taking the report. If you've got all the information you need, I need to get back to work. You guys want to stay for lunch? We've got plenty. Made a big pot of chili—one *con carne* and one veggie—take your pick. Cornbread and all the fixings."

Brittany popped her head around the corner, suddenly becoming the bubbly hostess. "Hot fudge sundaes for dessert!" she tempted, smiling widely.

Wright thanked them for their offer, but said they needed to get back to the station. When they got in the car, Johnson huffed.

"Lesson number one, Grasshopper . . ." he said, "*never* turn down free food. Especially when it smells that good."

Wright acknowledged his error profusely and pointed the car in the direction of McDonald's, which was only a few minutes from the station, hoping to redeem himself. Offering to pick up the tab mollified the Kung Fu Master somewhat.

32

Logan worked with Huey for another hour before he had to leave and go help Glenda set up her new computer. The health office had just gotten a new upgrade. Since she had a little time to kill, Logan decided to go up to the office and talk Carla out of one of her giant oatmeal and raisin cookies to tide her over until lunch.

When she got there, Carla wasn't at her desk, but she heard rhythmic vacuuming noises around the corner in Carson's room. After grabbing her cookie, she went to investigate. Carla saw her at the door, made a few more passes across the floor, then unplugged the vacuum and wrapped the cord in an efficient figure eight around the hooks on the handle. Pushing it back out into the hallway, she parked it in the corner.

"Hey, Logan," she said. "How can one man make such a big mess? I just cleaned in here two days ago . . . it actually stinks in here! How is that possible?"

Logan smiled. She knew Carla didn't have to take care of the rehab interns from Blanchett House, but like most moms, she couldn't help jumping in and cleaning up after kids, no matter what their age, then complaining about it. Logan knew the feeling. She'd wanted to do the boy's laundry the other day.

She glanced down at the dirty clothes that lay right where she'd seen them last time, in a pile by the door.

Shoving the last bite of cookie into her mouth, brushing the crumbs off on her jeans, Logan swallowed, then said. "Want some help?"

What the heck. Couldn't hurt to spoil Carson a bit. Life was hard enough.

Carla put her hands on her hips.

"We can throw those in with the sheets," she said, nodding at the clothes as she stripped the bed.

"You got it," Logan said, bending to pick them up.

When she lifted the shirt and pants off the shoes, the source of the smell became apparent. Carson's nice, new shoes were caked in mud and bits of straw . . . and a smell that Brittany had recently identified for them as . . . chicken shit.

A dozen thoughts fired through Logan's brain simultaneously, all of them culminating in the following, now glaring, facts. She grabbed Carla's arm and sat her down on the bed.

"Tell me if this makes sense," she said.

Carla had a good head on her shoulders. She'd set her straight if her brain was making connections that weren't there. She ticked off her thoughts one by one on her fingers.

"Fact One—Carson was wearing those clothes and shoes the night of the Talent Show. He was wearing that outfit when he came in with G.I. Joe just as the show was starting. I noticed he'd cleaned up. They were nicer than his work clothes.

"Fact Two—It started raining *after* he and Joe came in, so his nice shoes didn't get muddy on the way over."

"Fact Three—We know G.I. Joe said Carson left at intermission because he wasn't feeling well.

"And Fact Four, the most damning of all, that's not just mud, but muddy chicken poop on those shoes. Carson could only have gotten it on his shoes sometime between intermission and when I saw Monica's body."

With each new fact, Carla's eyes grew more worried. She paused to digest the information before answering.

"There could still be a logical explanation," she said. "We need to give Carson a chance to explain."

Logan agreed and they went in search of G.I. Joe. He and Carson usually worked together, or he'd know where the young man was. They found Joe pruning some evergreen shrubs behind the Art Barn. Alone.

When Carla asked where they could find Carson, Joe said he'd sent the boy into town to deliver some *Joe's Black Gold* to Blanchett House and pick up some things at Ace Hardware, including WD-40. Not something he normally ran out of, but he must have forgotten to put it in his order last time.

"What time do you expect him back?" Logan asked. "We really need to talk with him."

G.I. Joe didn't ask what about, just shrugged his shoulders. "Probably sometime after dinner," he said. "You know how he loves spicy Chinese food—kung pao—too hot for me, but I told him he could stop by Yang's if he wanted."

"He's been working hard, thought he deserved a treat." he added, as if to defend giving his protégé some time off.

"Well, tell him to give me a call if he gets back in the office after I've left for the day," said Carla. "I'll leave the front door unlocked for him. I'll ask Rita to keep an eye out so she can lockup after he gets back."

"Oh, no need to bother Mrs. Wolfe," G.I. Joe said, "I'll stop by and lock up. I've been making extra rounds at night anyway, since . . . you know . . . that woman was found."

"Okay," Carla said. "Thanks, Joe. We'll let you get back to work."

Once they were back in the office, Carla pointed out the window at a green truck parked out front. "I just have one question. If Carson drove into town, whose car did he take? Carson doesn't have one and that's G.I. Joe's truck."

Something was obviously not right, but they weren't sure what. Logan decided to trust her instincts. G.I. Joe was covering for Carson, that much seemed clear. But maybe it had nothing to do with Monica's murder. Maybe Carson had fallen off the wagon and G.I. Joe was keeping him out of sight for the day until he could pass a drug test again.

The 'why' could wait until after dinner, but if Carson didn't return tonight, they'd have to go to Rita in the morning. From there, it'd be out of their hands. Rita would probably call the police. At the very least, Carson would lose his placement here. She just hoped G.I. Joe didn't lose his own job. Rita's rules were strict.

Speaking of dinner . . .

A girl always thinks better on a full stomach.

Logan and Carla decided to leave the room as it was for now, locking the door, just in case. Logan hoped that wasn't necessary, but being the sister of a cop, she knew it was better safe than sorry.

It was one of those cold, windless, winter days when the sun shone bright, but didn't raise the temperature much above freezing. Even though they were only going across the quad, Logan pulled a beanie on, securing her thick hair against her ears, and stuffed her hands in her pockets.

When they got inside, they each loaded up steaming bowls of thick chili con carne topped with big squares of cornbread with honey butter. Glenda waved them over to her table where Gaby, the art teacher, was regaling everyone with the horror story of how she'd managed to blow up a large, sculptural piece she'd worked on all week in the new kiln. Hadn't got the settings right, or there was an air bubble in there somehow. She had time to try one more time before students came back on Monday. Glenda was thrilled with her new computer and for the rest of the meal, no one mentioned murder or mysterious, missing former, or maybe not so former, drug addicts.

Logan had just returned to the table, balancing a large, hot fudge sundae on a plate with another of Carla's huge cookies, when Huey came in and pulled up a chair next to her. He had no food.

"What's up?" Logan asked. "Aren't you hungry?"

33

Logan looked up at the kitchen window, which Nick was about to close.

"I'll get something in a minute," Huey promised.

"You'd better hurry," Logan nodded again toward the kitchen.

Huey nodded hello to Carla and Glenda, seemingly undecided.

"Go ahead," she said, "I'll wait here. I'm sure they have some left."

"Okay, but wait here," he said. "I'll be right back."

"It'll take me a while to work my way through this anyway," she grinned, slicing down with her spoon to load it up with just the right balance of vanilla bean ice cream, brownie, and hot fudge sauce.

By the time Huey returned, Logan was sitting by herself. Glenda and Carla had already gone back to work, to escape— as Glenda said—'all that computer gibberish.' The two women found technology useful, but only as a tool. They did not enjoy the technical underpinnings that so fascinated Huey when he talked shop.

Logan waited for him to take a few bites of chili before asking him what he wanted to talk with her about. Something was obviously on his mind. Huey glanced around the dining hall before answering, and even then, he spoke in a low voice. Nick and Brittany were the only ones still here and they were back in the kitchen.

"Remember that backup drive I showed you this morning?" Huey asked.

"Sure," she said, unconsciously lowering her own voice. "Monica's, right? Did you get into it?"

"I probably shouldn't have, but, yes, I did," he said.

Logan leaned over, "Why, what was on it?"

"First," Huey said, wiping his mouth and taking a sip of water, glancing up at the kitchen, where Brittany was wiping down the exterior counters.

"You almost done?" he said to Logan, not answering her question. He stood up to bus his tray, having taken only a few bites of his chili.

More than intrigued, Logan quickly scooped out the last of her sundae, licked the spoon, and hurried to follow.

When they got back to the lab, Huey sat them both down in front of his computer and placed his hand on top of the hard drive sitting to his right.

"After you left this morning, Stacie called to update me on a project I'd been helping her on. I asked how the investigation was going—if she got anything off Monica's technology. She said the detectives still hadn't found the phone; they were waiting on the phone records. They did bring her the victim's computer, but it was a lost cause, too damaged to get anything off it."

Logan looked at the black box under Huey's hand, the remaining source of information about Monica's life. He must have found a way to fix it.

"So, this is it, then. Any luck?" she asked.

"Unfortunately, yes" he said. "Turns out it wasn't broken, just needed an updated device driver."

Logan waited for him to explain. Whatever had been on Monica LeGrange's computer was the woman's own business. But something was upsetting Huey. She hoped it wasn't what she thought it might be.

"First, I checked her emails," he said. "Looking for any she may have sent or received the day of the murder. Nothing unusual there. She had two different Gmail addresses she used all the time, easily accessed, one for business, the other personal— things she'd signed up for, hair appointments, and a couple of female friends she met for lunch, things like that."

"That doesn't sound bad," Logan said.

"There was another account," he said. "With only one contact."

"Who?" Logan asked, not really wanting to know the answer.

"Nick's," Huey said.

Logan's heart sank.

"And there were attachments," he said.

"Attachments?" she said, feeling like a fool for repeating everything Huey said. "What kind of attachments?"

"Not the kind you'd send home to mother," he explained. "And nothing he'd want Brittany to ever see."

He angled the monitor toward her, jiggled the mouse until the inbox came up, then rolled his chair back to give her room. She appreciated the gesture. She didn't want to see these images with Huey.

Logan reached for the mouse and double clicked on the first email. Several images of Nick and Monica that left nothing to the imagination assaulted her vision. She quickly closed the window.

This was information she did not want to know. These pictures verified Glenda's suspicions that Nick and Monica had been involved. There was no way of knowing when those pictures had been taken, so no way of knowing if the affair had been ongoing or a one-time fling. Not only would these now be made public, but worse still, they would implicate Nick in her murder.

Logan sat back.

Up until two minutes ago, all her images of Nick were positive. Nick and Brittany, laughing and joking in the kitchen, working together in the garden. Last summer, Nick swinging his daughters around and around in dizzying circles to their shrieks of delight; Nick down by the creek while Brittany spread a blanket and unpacked an impromptu picnic. Such a beautiful family. This would crush them.

No wonder Huey was upset. He knew he'd have to turn this backup drive over to the police . . . the only question was whether or not they should warn Nick first. It was inconceivable that their friend could have had anything to do with Monica's death, wasn't it?

Once Nick saw those pictures, they weren't sure how he would react. He might decide to get rid of his computer or worse, run. Even if he was innocent, which Logan and Huey assumed he must be, any of those actions would just make him look more guilty. No, better to have the police confront him and have him explain. That was Nick's best chance.

They went back and forth on the options, but finally decided to give the police the backup drive but include it with a couple of other pieces of equipment Huey had been meaning to return to Stacie. And not take it over until tomorrow afternoon. He wouldn't lie, exactly, just use some delay tactics, not make a big deal of it. Stacie would get into the backup drive eventually, of course, find the files and turn them over to the detectives, but the delay might give them time to find the real killer, making Nick's involvement with Monica a moot point. At least, that was their plan.

What a mess.

Huey reluctantly began packing the drive into a medium-sized box, along with some adapters Stacie needed, stuffing bubble wrap around it to keep it from shifting inside. Even though it was only a twenty-minute trip down into town, he wasn't taking any chances.

***

When Huey left, Logan felt at loose ends. It was all she could do not to march over to the dining hall and talk to Nick, but she knew that wasn't in his or Brittany's best interests. The photos would set a bomb off in their marriage. She just hoped that was the worst of it.

She tried to work, but couldn't concentrate, so she locked up the lab and walked out into the quad.

Usually, the sight of the familiar campus was comfortable and warming: the buildings, the gardens, the dining hall with the broad, welcoming porch from which emanated warm, nourishing aromas throughout the day. It was a good school. She believed in it—and the people who worked here—many of whom had become good friends. They weren't just here for a paycheck, but because they were drawn to Rita's vision of what education could be; just like she was.

But not today. Today everything looked gray, neglected, and cold. Monica LeGrange's murder seemed to have ripped a wide gash right through the middle of campus and destroyed the peace she usually felt here. She fervently wished she could unsee those pictures.

VALERIE DAVISSON

34

The sun had gone down, and it was so cold outside the windows near the kitchen were fogged. Warm, humid air laced with a mix of cleaning solution and fries hit their faces as Wright followed Johnson inside. Both men knew what they wanted and no one else was in line, so they ordered. Their food came in record time, even for McDonald's. Only two other tables were occupied. One by a family with a small boy and a baby asleep in a carrier. The other by two men in hard hats and orange vests, their faces grimed from their white foreheads down.

Wright dipped a hot fry into the miniscule ketchup container and got it into his mouth without dripping any on his shirt. Johnson had already polished off his Big Mac and was working on a small cheeseburger. His fries were history, so he stole some of Wright's.

They'd been discussing their visit with the Zimmers.

"He's hiding something," Wright said. "So's the wife."

"You think *she* could have done it?" Johnson asked. "He

owned the gun, but she had access to it. She claims she never shot it, but who's to say? Jealous?"

Wright buzzed an 'Mmmmmm' on his straw, taking a long drink of his soda. He made his own concoction of black tea, lemonade, and Coke.

"Could be," he said. "But so did everyone else. We've got nothing that puts any of them together and the worst the office manager had to say about Monica was she was a lazy shopaholic. Never said she was a cheat, and probably would have. She didn't have much else good to say about her. Besides, if Mrs. LeGrange was as into status and money as the office manager thinks, why would she go after a lowly cook when she'd already landed an engineer? Why risk losing a whale for a minnow?"

"Depends," Johnson said, "Could be she liked living dangerously . . ."

Wright considered this.

"Brad done with their financials yet?" he asked. "Maybe Duncan wasn't as well off as he appears. A lot of small businesses folded last year. Maybe he was on the ropes and the wife was the rich one. Kill her, get the money."

"We'll check, but most of the companies that went under last year did commercial," Johnson said. "Duncan's firm does a mix, residential for some wealthy clients and just a few jobs for the city. Unless he lost some contracts, he's good. Brad said he and Monica had joint checking accounts, no financial drama there, no huge debt as far as he could tell. We can have Brad keep digging."

Wright didn't question his partner's instincts when it came to finances. Johnson invested on the side and was pretty knowledgeable when it came to the stock market and Portland real estate. He even had money in Bitcoin. Swore cryptocurrency was the future of commerce and banking. Johnson claimed that within five years, they were all going to be using crypto instead of dollars. Which he said were going away. China was buying gold, and soon, the American dollar would no longer be the reserve currency of the world.

Wright didn't know about that, but he had bought 2 percent of one Bitcoin, just in case. That was all he could afford. Even then, it set him back $1,000.

Johnson wiped his mouth, wadded up his napkin and tossed it into the now-empty bag along with the burger wrappers piled on his tray.

Wright said he'd call the state lab in the morning and Johnson would see if they had any luck with the phone records. Nothing more they could do tonight.

They were losing the momentum they'd gained this afternoon, but both knew progress in any investigation came in fits and starts—you just had to keep pushing.

***

FRIDAY MORNING

Johnson was on the phone when Wright came in. He'd made up for missing dinner by making his daughters panda pancakes with chocolate chip eyes and driving them to school. He'd smoothed things over with Suzie over a glass of red wine and a slow dance in front of the fire. He'd have preferred to skip directly to the roll-around-on-the-sheepskin-rug portion of the evening, but he'd learned to be a patient man. The former usually led to the latter.

While he waited for Johnson, he hung up his coat and flipped open his computer. He began scrolling through the spreadsheet he'd created from the FI cards, updating Nick's information from their interview yesterday.

They'd initially taken a closer look at the handyman, one Joseph Maynard, the one they called G.I. Joe, but he didn't seem to have any connection to their victim and his worst crime was loitering. A former alcoholic, a Vietnam vet, he'd been clean and sober for several years. Ms. Wolfe vouched for him unconditionally.

Wright didn't like admitting it, but he knew that probably the only reason Maynard's card got flagged by the officer who took his initial FI statement that night was not because of any connection he had to the victim or for any reason, really . . . other than that he was black man and looked nervous when being questioned by a cop. Racial bias was an invisible, deep vein of trouble that ran through society at large, not just among cops. Until that changed, he didn't see much hope for his own or any other police department suddenly becoming color blind.

An email notification popped up on the top of his screen. The lab results were in. They emphasized these were preliminary. The final reports would follow in a few days.

There were two attachments. He clicked on the prints report first.

Only a few salvageable prints could be obtained from the gun. A lengthy, technical explanation listed the reasons why. First, some of the prints had been smudged. The rest were difficult to retrieve. Ninhydrin and DFO were not productive, but they had finally been successful using cyanoacrylate fuming.

From the rest of the paragraph, Wright understood that although sweat prints were easily washed away from glass or metal surfaces submerged in water, lipid or oily fingerprints sometimes remained and could be clear enough for matching.

As expected, the prints found were Nick's. He didn't have a criminal record, but the school's director, Rita Wolfe, kept all staff and student fingerprints on file even though they were not required to as a private institution. Student fingerprints were collected as part of a national child ID program. One of the wealthier parents recommended it. Each student had a photo ID and fingerprints on file in the National Crime Information database in case of kidnapping or getting lost in the woods. Staff fingerprinting was similar to that required for employment in public schools.

It was Nick's gun.

There was a partial print they hadn't been able to identify yet, from the end of the barrel. Slightly smudged, it was inconclusive, but because of the direction of the whorls they could see, they were certain it wasn't Nick's. One of the women probably touched it when they retrieved it from the stream. As soon as they could pull up a really clear image, they'd check the women's prints first, then locally, and VICAP.

Satisfied, Wright eagerly opened up Door Number Two, the ballistics report. This is the one he'd been waiting for. And it was worth the wait. The .22 hollow-point bullets he'd watched Cyndi Birdwell pluck from Monica's chest were a solid match for Nick's gun.

Walking over to the whiteboard, he picked up the marker and drew a thick, black circle around Nick's photo, which they'd added to the board yesterday, then a dotted line to Monica.

Johnson ended his call and Wright filled him in, forwarding him the lab's email so he'd have the details himself. They were itching to go pick him up, but they knew if they waited until late enough in the day, they could take their time putting him in a room and stretch it out until Monday. By then, hopefully, they would have enough evidence to arrest him. If not, they'd have to let him go.

In the meantime, they'd keep digging for any connections they could find between Monica LeGrange and Nick Zimmer.

They still knew next to nothing about their victim's life.

Johnson took the phone company and Wright went to talk with Stacie. She'd called a minute ago, but he'd let it go to voice mail while he was going over the ballistics report with Johnson. Maybe she'd been able to get into Monica's computer after all.

This is how homicides were solved. More grunt work than glamour. They'd keep at it, adding connections, building their case.

35

Wright decided to time their arrival just after dinner, when the staff had left the dining room and just Nick, Brittany, and maybe G.I. Joe and his helper would be there. When they arrived, Brittany had already left to go relieve the babysitter, so it was just Nick and Maynard, the man they called G.I. Joe. His helper must have left early, too.

The two detectives worked well together. The whole process went surprisingly well. They emphasized to Nick that he was not under arrest. They just wanted to ask him some more questions, have him take a look at the gun to identify it for certain as his, clear up a few inconsistencies in their report. Although upset, Nick had been cooperative. Promising this wouldn't take long at all, they had their suspect in the car and tucked into an interrogation room in less than an hour.

Nick hadn't asked for a lawyer—yet. Hopefully, after cooling his heels in there for another hour or two—they'd offer to order in some pizza, try and drag out the clock—he'd be in a chatty mood. Because they hadn't formally arrested him, they didn't have to read him his rights. Still, anything he said could and would be used against him.

***

As Wright and Johnson went over how best to approach Nick before he lawyered up, Huey was at the front desk, signing in. Huey was a familiar face, often there to work with Stacie, so the officer on duty waved him on back.

Stacie thanked him for bringing back the items she'd given him for repair and said she'd get to them as soon as she could. Once she got into the backup drive and saw the videos, Huey knew she'd have to show it to the detectives and Nick's name would zoom to the top of the suspect list. He didn't have much time.

Picking up his pace, he walked quickly to his car. He needed to do some more digging and not in any approved areas. He didn't often use his less-than-legal hacking skills, but this situation called for him to break a few rules.

When he got back to the lab, he fired up his computer and made a pot of coffee. It wasn't as good as Nick's, but it would do. This was going to be a long night.

***

After Huey left for the police station, with nothing left to do and a few hours to kill before dinner, Logan decided to burn off some energy and turn her mood around with an afternoon hike. Needing something more strenuous than the gentle walk she'd taken with Carla and Freya the other day, she decided to drive up the road a few miles to a trail she'd been meaning to try. G.I. Joe had recommended it. He and his quasi-adopted daughter, Teresa, often hiked there when she visited from Portland.

Going to the cabin first to change and fill up her water bottle, Logan stopped at the office to let Carla know where she'd be since she was going alone. She wasn't anticipating getting lost or injured, but her father had drilled safety procedures into her and Rick from the time they were toddlers. They always had to let someone know where they were going and when they'd be back.

As she'd hoped she would, Carla gave her a cookie for energy and said she wished she could go, too, but had a ton of work to catch up on.

***

When she got to the trailhead, which was not much more than a wide turnout, Logan parked near the wooden sign at the entrance. There were no paper trail maps left in the plexiglass holder, but according to the map painted on the board it didn't look like there were too many ways to get lost. It was pretty much a single, four-mile loop. It was rated at medium difficulty and carried the usual directives about not feeding wildlife and watching out for mountain lions. A photo of a mountain lion was helpfully posted in case hikers had forgotten what they looked like, with a note scribbled on it that the last sighting was in 2017. Logan patted the pocket with the pepper spray her brother, Rick, the cop, insisted she always carry—more to deter two-legged varmints than four, but still.

Adjusting her water bottle on her belt, she patted her other pocket to make sure Carla's cookie was in there along with her phone. She'd made sure it was charged before she left. Another dad rule.

The trail was steep, with loose rock in places, but easily identifiable and dry. She'd checked the hourly weather report before leaving and rain wasn't due in again until later that night. G.I. Joe said this trail wasn't as well maintained as the ones in Forest Park, the urban park in Portland he enjoyed, but had great views and about halfway up, there was an eagles' nest. If the eagles had moved on, there were always hawks to be seen, riding the thermals in the valley below.

An hour in, Logan stopped for a rest. Her thighs were burning and she felt much better. This was just what she needed. She wasn't thirsty, but knew she needed to stay hydrated, so unhooked her water bottle and took a long drink. She left a little to wash down that cookie. She pulled out her phone. Carla told her she'd let her know if Carson returned. She checked her messages while she munched and sipped.

Nothing from Carla, but there was a voicemail from Brandon's dad, Mark, forwarding the contract his attorney had drawn up to nail down the specifics of how they could share the money coming in from the videos. Apparently, Brandon was already working on a second one. He asked her to take a look at the contract and get back to him with any changes.

He included the dollar amount they'd earned so far. When she saw the total, she about fainted. Wow. It was enough to pay off their house in Depoe Bay and have a good start on Ian's college fund. She'd have to have that money talk with Ben sooner rather than later.

She sure hoped it wouldn't change their relationship. She hadn't told anyone besides Bonnie about their engagement—yet—so no harm, no foul, if money screwed everything up. She wasn't sure why she was so worried. Having more money was supposed to be good, right? Would it affect the comfortable, yet delicate balance of love and trust they'd only recently achieved? Until now, they each contributed equally to the relationship.

She'd just started to relax and allow Ben fully in. She didn't want to mess that up.

It put her in mind of a poem she'd once read called Reluctance.[1]

WHISPER CREEK

Reluctance

I'll pick and choose for show and tell
Until you think you know me well,
But dark and wounded parts of me
I'll never, ever let you see.

I think that if you saw inside,
If heart and soul were open wide
Such pain and heartache you'd discover
You would go and love another.

But if someday you'll cherish me
And understand the world I see
Perhaps I'll let my fences down
And you can wander all around.

She'd knocked down her fences and let Ben in. Hopefully, he'd want to stay.

36

By the time Logan made it back to campus, ragged clouds scudded across the darkening sky, threatening rain. She grabbed her coat off the seat next to her and hustled out of her car, hoping she'd make it inside before the sky opened up. She didn't.

Semi-drenched, she trotted up the stairs, shook herself off and wiped her hiking boots on the entrance mat before walking into the office. She didn't see Carla at her desk. Figuring she must be in the dining hall already, Logan started to head out into the quad when she heard voices coming out of Rita's office.

"Yes," Rita said. "Thanks, Arlyn. I'll have my cell on me. He can call anytime . . . and Arlyn, I owe you one."

"Well, that's good, at least," Carla said, following her out into the hallway. "I just can't believe it . . ."

"Nothing else we can do tonight," Rita said, locking the door behind her.

Rita never locked her door—no one did around here. Guess nobody's feeling very trusting these days, thought Logan. Having a murder on the premises will do that to you.

Carla spotted Logan and filled her in. A lot had happened while she was out communing with nature.

***

The police just left. They'd taken Nick into custody—not a formal arrest, she clarified. But, to be on the safe side, Rita was finding him an attorney—that's what the phone call was about. In the meantime, they were heading over to the dining hall to help Brittany and finish the dinner preparations for the staff. Everyone was in shock—operating on autopilot.

Logan wondered what had prompted this new, aggressive move on the part of the police. Huey had said Stacie wouldn't get into the backup drive until Monday, at the earliest, so they couldn't have the pictures yet. She wasn't sure if Huey had gone into Portland this weekend to visit with his sister. If so, he wouldn't have heard about Nick. If he wasn't at dinner, she'd have to give him a call.

Dinner was a quick and somber affair. Sour Cream Chicken Enchiladas and Cherry Dump Cake—the meal Nick and Brittany had prepared before he was picked up—was one of Logan's favorites, but she barely tasted it. No one talked much. Until the attorney called back, or Nick returned, there wasn't much to discuss.

Most of the staff had taken the weekend off, so there wasn't a heavy load of dishes, but everyone pitched in bussing tables, and Logan and Carla stayed to help Brittany close up the kitchen. Rita told Brittany she could take some personal leave. She promised she would but wanted to make sure things were set for next week. Once that was done, she could concentrate on getting Nick back home and taking care of the girls. The babysitter was with them now. Teresa and her kitchen crew were coming in tomorrow. Brittany's plan was to get things organized tonight and hand things over to them first thing in the morning.

Rita thanked her and gave her a firm hug.

"We'll get through this," she told her. "Don't you worry."

Brittany was on the verge of tears, but she kept it together and reassured Rita she'd be fine. After Rita left, and making sure Logan and Carla knew what to do, she melted into the back office to start working on a temporary schedule for next week.

When they were almost done and getting ready to leave, G.I. Joe emerged from the dishwashing area, striding quickly over to where they were pulling on their coats. It wasn't until then that Logan realized Carson wasn't with him. And she hadn't seen him at dinner, either.

"Logan," he said, "Carla," he nodded, acknowledging both women. "I know it's getting late, but if it's possible, I really need to talk with you."

He was a handsome man. Logan wondered briefly why he hadn't remarried. He'd been clean and sober for years. Joe was a kind, hard-working man. He may have had his troubles, but he was good now. His original family—a wife and daughter— had rejected his overtures at reconciliation, but there must be someone for him out there.

Stuffing his hands in his pockets, he looked nervously back at the kitchen.

Logan quickly cycled through and rejected the various options for a private place to talk here in the dining hall or back in the main building. Brittany was in the kitchen; Rita was either in her office or upstairs with Nicole if she was done working for the night.

Carla must have done the same, because she suddenly turned to Logan and said, "Glenda's out in Sherwood, right?"

Glenda had recently developed something of a romance with a retired Air Force colonel she met online and often stayed with him on the weekends, leaving after lunch on Fridays, returning Sunday for dinner.

An intelligent man with a finely tuned sense of humor, the Colonel, as they all called him, had become something of an amateur ornithologist in retirement and had introduced Glenda to bird watching. They spent many happy hours, binoculars in hand, exploring the Tualatin River National Wildlife Refuge.

"Yes!" Logan said, "That works. We'll have the cabin to ourselves. Does that work for you, Joe?"

G.I. Joe looked relieved. "Thank you, yes. I'll meet you out there in a few minutes. I just need to lock up the front. Brittany will get the back door when she leaves."

He didn't volunteer and they didn't ask, but they knew it must be about Carson. So much else had been going on, Carson's disappearance—which they now assumed it was—had dropped way down the list of urgent problems to be solved. What day had they first noticed he wasn't in his room? The day after the Talent Show—Wednesday. G.I. Joe said he'd gone into town to do an errand for him, but he'd lied about him using his truck; it had been right out in front of the office in the parking lot. Just another knot to unravel in this whole mess.

37

Carla lit a fire while Logan put on the teapot and dug around for some cookies. She almost forgot and was going to offer Joe wine. Hearing his soft knock on the door, she placed the tray on a low table they could all reach and went to let him in. Although Carla reassured her that Freya was trustworthy, Logan made sure her canine guest had her own supply of treats so she wouldn't be tempted to steal theirs. And to make double sure, she sat near enough to where the beautiful golden lay stretched out by the fire that she could snatch them out of harm's way if necessary.

Over the next twenty minutes, G.I. Joe came clean. He admitted to covering for Carson when he didn't show up for work Wednesday morning. He was hoping there was some logical explanation. He assumed he'd return by nightfall, but he hadn't seen or heard from him the past two days. And now he was frantic.

"Why don't you just talk with Rita?" Logan asked. "I'm sure she'd know what to do."

"Yes, but she'd have to report it to Blanchett House, and . . . I'm still hoping it won't come to that. I trust you, Ms. McKenna," he said.

"Call me Logan, please," she said.

"Logan," he paused. "I know how you helped Huey and his sister with all that trouble up in Portland. And you, Carla. You've been like a mama bear to the new kids, including the Blanchett House program interns. You're both good people. And you know the police are more likely to answer your questions than mine. Maybe you can find out where he is before Blanchett House or Mrs. Wolfe discover he's missing. The conditions for his being here are very strict."

In case they didn't fully understand, he continued, "You don't know how hard it is to get into a program like Blanchett House offers. I don't want him to lose this chance," he said, slumping back into his chair.

"I know he's a good kid . . . there were no signs he was having trouble. We do a random drug test every few days, so there's no cheating. All his tests have come back clean. I just want to find him and get him back here safely. Once I find out what happened, I can try to make it right with Mrs. Wolfe."

"Can you help me?" he asked. "Will you help me find him?"

Logan stood up and warmed her hands by the fire. How many chances should one person get? Carson was a drug addict. Drug addicts lied. Carson appeared to have lied to the police about being in the vicinity of the chicken coop that night—the night Monica was killed. But that didn't make him guilty of murder. But if he wasn't guilty of something, why did he run?

The only way to answer those questions was to try to find the runaway—if that's what he was. Logan was torn—neither she nor Carla wanted to keep secrets from Rita, but it wasn't really keeping secrets if she didn't ask.

Sins of omission weren't as bad as sins of commission, right? Logan was fuzzy on that, not having attended much Sunday School growing up.

WHISPER CREEK

In the end, they both agreed to do what they could to help, but only for the weekend. Come Sunday night, they'd need to notify Rita. She rationalized in her mind that Rita had enough on her plate getting the school ready for students Monday morning. But if she asked, of course, they'd tell her the truth. They made sure G.I. Joe understood that.

G.I. Joe gave them all of the information he had about Carson's background and former life in Portland, which wasn't much. Logan said she could contact Rheanna, a musician friend of hers whose day job was as a police dispatcher in Portland, to see if she'd heard anything. Carla said she'd call the hospitals and the highway patrol to see if there'd been any accidents. They really didn't have much to go on. They didn't know if he was walking or had been picked up by someone, caught an Uber, or had been abducted by aliens.

Satisfied they had done all they could for now, they said goodnight. G.I. Joe thanked them again and left for his own cabin. Carla and Freya followed suit a few minutes later. Logan cleared the table and washed the mugs and plate, placing them on the dish drainer to dry before taking herself to bed.

What a day!

After she ran a brush through her hair and got into her pajamas, Logan went back to the living room to call Ben and enjoy the last of the fire. Tucking one leg under her, she grabbed her phone and checked her messages. One from Tilly, who was housesitting the Jasper house—how weird that she now called it the Jasper house versus just 'home'—one from Amy, and one from Ben. Tilly said the house was fine. She had a batch of mail saved for her. Did she want her to forward her mail up to Oregon, or would she be coming back soon? Logan had left her return date open. Tilly was going through a divorce and needed a place to stay while she was figuring out her next move. It had worked out for both of them.

Amy said Liam's parents were coming for a two-week visit from Scotland next month, and the center had taken in a severely injured southern sea otter last week who may or may not make it. The otter was being kept in a holding tank on the lower level. Sadie, the orphaned sea otter pup she and Logan had rescued a few years ago, was now a big girl and reigned as queen of the large tank on the main floor that was open to the public. She reveled in being the star of the show and playfully showed off for the children every time a field trip came through from the local elementary school. Amy ran the education component at the Sea Otter Center in Jasper and had helped raise Sadie from a pup.

Ben's text said 'Miss You . . .'

Logan answered Tilly and Amy, then decided at the last minute to do a video call with Ben instead of just a phone call. She missed the big guy's face. She wanted to look into his eyes when she told him how much she loved him. Even though they texted several times a day, it wasn't the same.

After wading through the murky slime of lies and murder the last few days, she needed an infusion of Ben's clear goodness. She needed to *feel* good conquered evil—not just believe it in an abstract way. Ben kept her universe in balance.

She tapped the video camera symbol to call, then suddenly jumped up from the couch and ran in to yank open the dresser drawer and retrieve the velvet box. She slipped her engagement ring back on her finger just as Ben picked up and settled back on the couch.

"Hello, Beautiful," he said, smiling.

***

Long after she and Ben said their goodnights and she'd banked the fire and gotten into bed, Logan lay awake. She wasn't guilty of murder, of course, but she was guilty of not being completely above board with Ben. She still couldn't bring herself to tell Ben about the money she had coming in from the music video and because she lied about that, she hadn't told anyone about their engagement. Then, when the murder happened, she didn't feel it was the right time.

Logan kicked the covers and punched her pillow.

Monday. She'd do what she could to help find Carson tomorrow for G.I. Joe. By Monday the attorney Rita found for Nick would hopefully go down and get him released from jail. Then she'd look over the contract Brandon's dad's attorney had sent—she still hadn't gotten around to that—and get the final numbers on what she had earned, as well as the projections.

Now that she had a plan, she felt marginally better. Once she knew Nick was safe and her other obligations fulfilled, she could relax. Or at least accept that she could not fix or control everything. Carson would either surface or he wouldn't. Rita would forgive him or she wouldn't. The police would find out who killed Monica, or they wouldn't. Either way, in a few days, she was flying back home to Ben. With her ring on.

38

Nick's arrest, or rather, his being picked up late Friday and held as a 'person of interest' by the police, threw everyone into a tizzy. First the murder, then finding the gun, now this. No one knew quite what to do. But in spite of the shock and worry they were all experiencing, and the very personal anguish Brittany must be going through, ready or not, students were coming back on Monday and The New School needed to be ready. Life was like that. Crises didn't wait for a convenient time to occur.

Brittany got the kitchen crew to come in early and go over the modified schedule. She assured Rita that she and Nick had already planned the menus for the week and were ready to go. Teresa would take over most of the cooking—she was in training with Nick anyway—and everyone else could spread the remaining work out between them. Brittany was taking the twins to her mother's, then going down to the jail to see if she could get in to see Nick.

Carla looked relieved she wouldn't have to do a Call Out to

all the parents. Even though they had an automated system for just such emergencies, parents always called for more information and the system got jammed.

One of Rita's donors and long-time friends, Judge Simpson—the man Logan overheard her talking with on the phone last night when she got back from her hike—gave her the name of a good defense attorney, a buddy of his from law school. Even though they worked opposite sides of the courtroom when he was with the DA's office, the two men had remained friends. He assured Rita this guy was the best.

Logan found Rita's loyalty to Nick admirable. She hadn't hesitated. Didn't ask why the police pulled Nick into the station and locked him up in a holding cell. Didn't ask how Nick's gun wound up in a muddy hole on the banks of Whisper Creek. Didn't question Nick's claim of innocence—even when the judge called her later to tell her in confidence that the detectives had pretty solid evidence that Nick's gun was the murder weapon.

What Logan and Huey knew, but the police and Rita didn't, yet, was Nick's history with Monica.

Logan was torn, but in the end, both she and Huey decided to let the police discover that themselves, once Stacie got into the backup drive. Hopefully, by then, Nick would have an attorney to advise him.

In the meantime, Huey continued to dig for more information. Even if they couldn't hand anything he discovered without a search warrant over to the police, they'd at least be able to share it with his defense attorney. If the lawyer thought it was valid and could be used to clear Nick's name, he would know the legal way to go about obtaining it officially.

Given the circumstances, Logan decided to stay for a few more days at least and do what she could to help. She'd talked with Ben until late last night, catching him up on everything that had happened. It was so good to hear his voice. The only thing better would have been to have him here and feel his warm arms around her and lean into his solid chest. In spite of her trying to redirect her thoughts, other warm parts of him came to mind, too.

Before she called, she'd taken her engagement ring out of the box and slipped it back on her finger. Even though Ben would have no way of knowing if she was wearing it or not, it just didn't feel right to have it off. It felt right to have it on . . . where it belonged. For the first time since he'd given it to her, Logan felt a girly excitement. She wanted to wear it and share the wonderful news, but it didn't feel like now was the time for the big announcement.

How could she celebrate when Nick was in jail? Hopefully, there'd be time for that soon. All they had to do was find the real killer.

She slept with it on, but in the morning, she pressed her ring back into its slot in the velvet box and placed it carefully back into the drawer. Then she walked over to the dining hall to join Glenda for breakfast.

This morning's fare was simpler than usual, just an oatmeal bar, cold cereal, and fruit, but after a little of everything, Logan checked in with Brittany to offer her help for next week in the kitchen. After the two women hugged, Brittany introduced her to Teresa and showed her where everything was. They decided that since Logan's culinary skills were limited, she would provide the most benefit by filling condiment containers, wiping tables, and running the dishwasher. Relieved she wouldn't be trusted with anything people actually had to consume, she happily complied. Schedule in hand—she was to report back at 4:30 p.m.—Logan wandered over to the lab to see if Huey was around.

"Hey, Huey," Logan said, looking around the lab.

"Over here," Huey's disembodied voice came from under one of the student workstations, where he was doing something with wires.

He made one last push, then scooted out and brushed off his pants before accepting the large mocha coffee Logan was holding out to him.

"Thanks," he said, taking a long drink. "Pull up a chair and we can get started. I think it's working now."

They worked companionably the rest of the day, breaking only for lunch and when Logan took a short walk with Carla when she took Freya out to go potty. She'd just gotten back when Huey's phone rang.

"Hello?" he said.

"It's Stacie," he mouthed silently, pointing at the phone.

Logan waited, unconsciously holding her breath, wondering if Stacie had gotten into the backup drive yet and seen the pictures of Nick and Monica.

Huey listened for a few minutes.

"Really?" he said.

Another few unbearable minutes went by.

"Okay," Huey said. "Thanks, Stacie . . . yeah, don't worry. I appreciate your letting me know."

Logan looked at him expectantly.

"Well . . . ? What did she say?"

"Well, she said two things," he said. "One, she got into the drive and saw the pictures, but she's going to keep a lid on that until Monday. That's the best she can do and she's sticking her neck out by doing that much. She'll put it in a written report and leave it for the Detectives. They'll see it when they come in Monday morning. That should save her bacon."

"That's great!" Logan said. "What's Two?"

"Two is the fingerprint report," he said.

"Is that why they hauled him in?" she asked. "That's stupid. Of course, the prints on the gun would be Nick's, it was Nick's gun."

"No. There was one partial print on the barrel from someone else. The state lab finally was able to identify it," he said.

Logan looked confused.

Huey's pursed his lips, then blurted out, "It's Ethan's."

"You mean Monica's stepson, the one who helped out at the talent show?" Logan asked. "How did his print get on Nick's gun? The gun that killed his stepmother?"

"I have no idea."

39

Wright stared at the board. This was getting ridiculous. They'd only been in the office for a couple of hours, and already their case had splintered into at least three different directions, each of which they would have to track down to see which were legitimate leads.

Here it was Monday, and when they'd started their day, they had one suspect but nothing connecting him to the victim. Now they had three suspects with a plethora of motives and evidence . . . *all* connected to the victim. He glared at all the black lines.

It looked like a goddamn spiderweb.

Wright and Johnson had decided to come in early, wanting to take one more pass at Nick before they were forced to release him. They'd tried periodically on Friday to catch him in a lie before tucking him into a jail cell for the weekend, but he'd stuck to his story.

Yes, the gun was his. Yes, he was upset that it had been stolen, and even more upset that it had been used to shoot someone, but no, he didn't know who took it or exactly when it had gone missing. He only knew Monica LeGrange in passing, just one of many parents he saw on campus now and then.

They'd done some digging, but it looked like Nick was who he said he was. Gainfully employed as head cook at The New School since it opened, married—happily as far as they could tell—with two young daughters, twins, cute as cupcakes. No criminal background. Clean as a whistle. Got along with his coworkers. A trusted employee. Even his kitchen crew liked him.

No one was that perfect. There must be something.

Anxious to get that something out of their suspect, Wright pulled into the parking lot around 6:30 a.m. Johnson right behind him. When he got to the conference room, Stacie's report was waiting for him on his desk. Johnson went down the hall to get coffee. Their goal was to have Nick brought up from the jail and stuffed into an interrogation room by seven.

They would apologize for keeping him over the weekend, and thank him for his cooperation. As soon as the office staff got here at 8:00 a.m., they would get him processed and out of here. He'd be home in time for lunch. In the meantime, did he want some coffee and a breakfast burrito or a donut while he waited?

Impatient to get down to the interrogation room, Wright skimmed Stacie's report, going right to the conclusion. Stacie had already tried to get into Monica's damaged computer and failed. He assumed this was simply a formal summary of that attempt.

As he reached for the three-hole punch so he could add the report to the murder book, he stopped and reread the last paragraph, then flipped open his computer and logged in to view the videos Stacie had sent.

The elusive back-up drive had been located. Apparently, Monica had dropped it off for repair with the computer guy at The New School, who had dutifully turned it in once he remembered he had it. Wright didn't know if he's seen the videos. It was working now. Stacie must have fixed it.

He double clicked on the first icon. It blossomed to fill the screen. Taken from an angle high up and to the left, it was Monica, laughing, riding Nick for all she was worth. He'd seen the victim's naked body, of course, at the autopsy, but seeing her live like this was something else. There were three videos, each more damning than the last. Adventurous to say the least. If they were all taken in the same night, Nick had stamina, he'd have to give him that.

Wow. He'd have to ask Stacie if she had dates and times, but no matter when these were taken, Nick knew Monica a *whole* lot better than he'd let on. This definitely gave them probable cause.

"Got him!" he said, signaling Johnson over as he dialed downstairs to see if Nick had been brought over yet.

At about the same time Wright was viewing more of Nick than he ever wanted to see, Johnson was going through his own inbox. The phone company had finally come through. He had just sent the multiple-page document to the printer.

"McCallen," Wright said, "Is Zimmer here yet? What room did they put him in? Oh, and is the ptomaine trolley out front? We want to make sure our special guest doesn't go hungry."

Finding the videos had put them a few minutes behind schedule, but with the new evidence they now had, hopefully they'd have time to get in touch with a judge so they could enter the room with a formal arrest warrant in hand, along with the breakfast burrito.

"He was," McCallen said. "Just left."

"What do you mean, left?" Wright said. "They take him back to the jail? Why?"

"Nope," McCallen said. "His attorney picked him up. Had

all his paperwork in order. Sorry, I thought you knew."

Wright's brain scrambled to catch up. *Damn.* Nick hadn't asked for an attorney, so someone must have sent one.

"Okay," he said. "Thanks . . . yeah, don't worry about it, not your fault."

It was a setback, but not devastating. They wouldn't be getting a confession out of Nick this morning or be able to arrest him, but they knew where he was, and once they had the warrant, they'd go bring him in. It was just a delay. Wright put a call in to a judge.

While they were waiting, they decided to go through the phone records Johnson just received. Given the personal, or at least very intimate, relationship they now knew Nick had with the victim, there was probably a lot of incriminating evidence in those phone records. They'd add them to the warrant request. More nails in Nick's coffin.

40

Retrieving the printouts, they sat down at the conference table and divvied up the list. The records contained a list of all outgoing and incoming calls, Facebook messages, and texts from Monica's phone. The content of the calls was unobtainable, just the dates and times were listed, along with the numbers of the people with whom she communicated. But the transcripts of the recent texts were all there. They got to work.

Things got complicated from there. It should have been simple. There was a smattering of phone calls and texts between Nick and Monica, but those were over two years ago. Nothing until the night of the murder. A short call from Monica to Nick, then one call back, followed by a text at 5:45 p.m. Nick made himself perfectly clear.

This has to stop. If I have to, you know what I will do.

Next came several phone calls from Monica to him, all hang-ups. Apparently, Nick had nothing more to say to her.

If that was all they found, they'd be done. Case closed. Tie it up in a bow. Everybody go home. But things weren't that neat.

With the images Stacie sent, combined with a footnote she included in her email about the partial fingerprint they'd ID'd, the phone records, and additional information they dug up, Nick wasn't their only suspect.

Not wanting to give the defense team any excuse to claim they hadn't followed the evidence where it led and considered every suspect before rushing to arrest Nick, they were glad now his lawyer came and got him out. They needed time to put all of this together and track down these other leads. Let him think they had nothing . . . for now. They were confident they'd still come back to Nick.

Which brought them to the board. All those new, black lines radiated out from Monica's pretty face.

Nick's driver's license photo was already up there, as were Monica's family members: her husband and stepson, Ethan.

Johnson tacked up the driver's license photo of the newest addition to their rogues' gallery, twenty-six-year-old Carson York, drug addict fresh out of rehab, employed at The New School as part of a halfway house deal with Blanchett House in Portland.

His number showed short messages back and forth between his phone and Monica's, arranging meetings downtown, but with no personal content of a romantic or sexual nature. The frequency dropped off the last few months, but a few days before she was killed, she'd called Carson twice. Short. One return call, then nothing.

Johnson pulled up his FI card.

"This was the kid we interviewed in his room up at the main house. Said he was sick, left during the show," Johnson said.

"Anyone verify that?" Wright asked.

"His supervisor, G.I. Joe," he said. "He's the one who told us where to find him when we asked if anyone had left before we got there. Said they worked together all day, cleaned up, then came back to the dining hall for the show."

"What time did he leave?"

"Says here, intermission," he said. "I'll call him."

"Anything besides drugs?" Wright asked. "Any assaults?"

"Nope," Johnson said. "Not in Portland, anyway. Could have a record somewhere else."

"What do you think?" Wright said. "What's his connection to Monica? I don't think he was one of Quantum Engineer's clients she was schmoozing."

"Drugs are equal opportunity slayers," Johnson said. "Maybe he was her dealer."

Wright considered her phone calls to Carson.

"Maybe she wanted to score, saw him at the school, thought she'd tap him for another hit," Johnson added.

"Maybe," Wright said. "But his boss says he was clean—out of the life."

"Yeah, but it doesn't take much to fall off the wagon. He'd only been off the stuff a few months. Maybe Monica made him an offer he couldn't refuse. Or maybe he was on the straight and narrow and didn't want what she was offering. Maybe she wouldn't take no for an answer and bam, he popped her."

"But where would he get the gun?" Wright said.

"Maybe he saw Nick put it away sometime. He worked in the kitchen sometimes. Sometimes in the garden."

They sat and stared at the board some more. The four words Johnson had printed across the top were still there:

LOVE, LUST, LOATHING, LOOT

"Okay. Nick's more lust than love," Wright said.

"And lust can turn to loathing pretty quick," Johnson said. "That's two strikes against Nick."

"Carson," Wright said, going on to the next suspect.

"Well, loot for sure, if he was her dealer," Johnson said. "But if he was selling her drugs, she'd be paying him. What would be the motive to kill her?"

"Which brings us to our least likely suspect, Ethan," Wright said. "Ethan was close to his mom, his real mom. From what he said at the house, and what we've learned about his step-mother, there was no love lost there. Lust? I suppose that's a possibility. Seventeen, raging hormones and all, but I didn't get that from him. Did you?"

"No," Johnson said. "I got that he avoided being around her whenever possible, not that he had a crush on her. If he found out about Nick, maybe . . . would that be enough to make him kill her?"

"We need to find out what the hell his fingerprint was doing on Nick's gun," Johnson said.

41

Logan wasn't sure what she'd been expecting, but when students arrived and started filling the dining hall Monday morning, other than Nick not being there, things felt almost normal. She offered to help prep and serve breakfast, but Teresa and her kitchen crew had everything covered. They did accept her offer to help G.I. Joe bus tables since Carson was still not there.

She and Carla broke the news to him last night that they had been unsuccessful in tracking him down. Logan had tried to emphasize the positive.

"No news is good news, right?" she told him.

When this didn't cheer him up, she added, "At least we know he's not in the morgue, the hospital, or jail. If he fell off the wagon, he can get back on. When he resurfaces, I'm sure he'll get in touch with you."

G.I. Joe nodded, but didn't seem convinced.

"Maybe Rita will give him his job back," she said lamely, knowing this was probably not going to happen. Rita couldn't risk having anyone around the school who wasn't solidly committed to staying clean and sober.

Rita must have forgiven Joe for trying to cover for him, though, because he was still there.

Later, she would tell her that Joe's character was never in doubt. He had earned the right to be trusted. Joe's only flaw had been a soft heart and wanting the young man to succeed.

Everyone's mood lightened considerably when Nick walked in just as breakfast cleanup was complete. Rita's judge friend had come through and the attorney had gotten him released. He said they would have had to do that or arrest him, anyway. Students were already in class.

Logan had never seen Nick look so rough. Three days growth of beard and wearing the same clothes he left in on Friday. He thanked Rita profusely for finding him an attorney and getting him out. The lawyer said they had nothing to arrest him for and no reason to hold him any longer. Hopefully, this nightmare was over.

Once he'd accepted hugs and 'welcome backs' from everyone, he checked on the kitchen, then said he was going home to clean up and get some much-needed sleep. He promised to be back in time to help with dinner.

Freed from kitchen duty until after lunch, Logan decided to work with a couple of music students she'd missed, then join Huey in the lab. The hour before lunch was his prep time.

When she arrived, Huey and Ethan were sitting at the back table, talking. Ethan looked like a rabbit about to bolt. Huey placed his hand on his arm.

"It's okay," he said to the boy, "Logan's a friend, she already knows. She's okay."

"Hi, Ethan," Logan said, wondering what she'd just walked into.

Then she remembered—the fingerprint. She'd been so busy trying to track down Carson and then, so happy about Nick being released, she'd forgotten all about Ethan's print being found on the murder weapon. Of course, this would be good news for Nick, but not such good news for Ethan.

Logan came in and sat down on the other side of Ethan, but not close enough to crowd him.

"Hi," he said, still looking skittish.

"Hi, Ethan," Logan said. "I'm sorry about your stepmother. This must be a really tough time for you and your dad."

Ethan nodded, but didn't say anything.

"We were just talking about how Ethan's fingerprint got on Nick's gun," Huey said, "and where to go from here."

Turning to Ethan, he said, "Why don't you start from the beginning and tell Ms. McKenna what you told me. She's got a pretty good head on her shoulders. Logan helped me and my sister a few years ago. And her brother is with the police in Southern California. She knows how cops think and how things work. I'm sure you have nothing to worry about, but she may have some good ideas about what to do next."

"Okay," Ethan said, pressing his hands on his thighs, sitting up a little straighter. Huey got him a coke from the mini-fridge near his desk and handed it to him.

Logan watched as Ethan's Adam's apple bobbed up and down as he drank half the can in a few gulps. He was so young. He put the can down and glanced over at her before starting. She tried to relax and keep her face impassive and open, non-judgmental, no matter what he had to say.

"I don't want to get Nick in trouble," he began. "If my dad finds out, he'd probably get Nick fired."

He paused to take another drink of coke.

"It was no big deal, really. Just . . . A few weeks ago, I was out walking, killing time after my last class before I was due at the lab. I was helping Mr. Le build one of the sets we're going to use for the spring show—it's gonna be really cool. I remembered I needed to pick up some wooden tulips from the Art teacher, so I did. I was walking back from the Art Barn when I heard some sharp popping sounds, loud, maybe like a car backfiring, but there aren't any roads back there—nothing but open fields—so I went to see what it was."

Logan waited for him to finish off the last of his coke before he continued.

"When I came around the bend, I saw Nick. He was shooting at a bunch of empty cans he'd set up along a log, at the other end, against the hill."

Ethan turned his attention back to Logan, "He was practicing. Said he got the gun to scare off the coyotes and racoons from Brittany's chicken coop. When I asked, he let me try it a couple of times. He said he'd talk with my dad before we had any more lessons, just to make sure it was okay with him.

"He really emphasized gun safety," Ethan added eagerly, racking up points in Nick's favor. "Said you should never leave a gun loaded and definitely never just laying around. You should always keep it in a safe place, away from kids."

"Did Nick ever show you where he kept his gun, Ethan?" Logan asked.

"Yeah," Ethan said. "In a metal box, a gun safe, he called it. In his office. Students don't go in there."

Logan and Huey exchanged glances over Ethan's head.

42

Logan took a minute to think about how she would ask her next question. One wrong word could make Ethan clam up, but she needed to get him to answer the questions she knew the police would ask—if they did their jobs and followed up on leads other than focusing on Nick.

It would be uncomfortable for Ethan to talk with her, but a lot less intimidating—or incriminating—than talking with two homicide detectives, who were surely on their way. She was surprised they weren't here already. They should have read Stacie's report by now. They would have to follow through to see why Ethan's print was found on the murder weapon.

Of course, Stacie's report contained incriminating evidence against Nick, too. But he had a lawyer. This kid didn't.

"That doesn't sound so bad, Ethan," she began. "Nick probably should have gotten your father's permission—and the school's—before letting you handle his gun, but as you said, he was planning on doing that. Nick has a very good track record here. He's a big part of this school and has worked here ever since it's been open. I'm sure Mrs. Wolfe would take that into account. And you seem to have a very good relationship with your father. Your dad may be upset, but I'm sure if you explain the circumstances, and that Nick was going to clear it with him before you had any more lessons, he won't be too angry."

Ethan considered this.

Now, Logan took a step into the sensitive area she'd been skirting.

"Your family seemed really close," Logan said, aiming for a light tone. "Your dad and stepmom sat at our table that night, before the talent show started. He was very sweet to her. I'm sure it must be very hard for you both. You must miss her."

Ethan looked over at Huey before answering.

"No," he whispered fiercely. "I don't."

Then, in a flood of adolescent emotion, Ethan spilled his guts, telling them what life with Monica was really like. He said she even used drugs, although he didn't know the extent of it or what she took. He overheard her on the phone once, talking and laughing with one of her friends about it. He started paying attention after that. Sometimes her pupils were little dots and she had tons of energy, but she always managed to look and act normal by the time his dad got home.

Wrung out after his outburst, Ethan wiped his eyes, then blew his nose on the tissue Huey handed him. Huey patted him on the shoulder. Logan felt sorry for the kid, but this changed things somewhat. It gave Ethan motive—at least, that's how the detectives would see it. Ethan wouldn't be the first stepson to hate his dad's new wife. But did he hate her enough to kill her?

***

"Ethan," Logan said, "I'm sure you had nothing to do with your stepmother's death, but you need to know the police are going to ask you how your fingerprint got on Nick's gun. Everything you've told us makes perfect sense. All you need to do when they talk with you is tell the truth, just like you did to us. Don't add anything and don't leave anything out.

"But," she added, "I would strongly suggest that you talk with your father first. Tell him what you told us. He'll probably want to have an attorney present when you talk with the police, just to make sure you feel comfortable and everything is recorded properly. Okay?"

She didn't add that having an attorney present would almost certainly be a necessity if the police were at all inclined to suspect him of murdering his stepmother.

Which begged the question—Who really killed Monica LeGrange? Who agreed to meet her in the chicken coop on a rainy, winter night, walked right up to her and shot her twice at point blank range? Who would do that? Was it a crime of passion or premeditated?

Ethan wanted to call his dad right then, but he was already late to relieve Carla up at the office. He was covering the phones again and there wouldn't be any privacy there. Since Ethan had computer class right after lunch, Huey told him he could call from the lab before he let students in or step outside if necessary. An hour more wouldn't matter. His dad would decide what to do from there. Ethan looked very relieved to have the burden of his fears and worry shifted onto someone else's shoulders.

Logan and Huey walked over to the dining hall and joined Carla and Glenda at their table. Glenda was telling them all about the night heron she'd spotted that weekend.

"He was standing very still along the opposite bank of the estuary in some reeds, all hunched up, like a little old man. Kind of short and fat compared to the great blue herons, with strong black and white strips along the side of his head, with a long crest swooping back off the top of his head," she enthused. "Spectacular bird. So unusual to see him this time of year. I wonder what happened to his mate? They're monogamous, you know . . ."

Logan's brain was running in the background, but she let herself relax into the good company and good food of lunch hour at The New School. More than anything, she just wanted to feel normal, like things were as they had always been. But she knew it wasn't so.

43

"**D**ad?" Ethan said.

"Yes, Ethan," Duncan said. "What do you need? Everything okay?"

Stumbling in places, Ethan blurted everything out, then drew a shaky breath.

"I should never have touched that gun," he said.

Duncan immediately took charge.

"Where are you, Ethan?" he said.

"I'm in the back of the computer lab—outside. Mr. Le said I could call from out here," Ethan said. "I know you're working and it's your first day back . . . I'm so sorry, Dad, I know you don't need this right now, but . . . ," His voice broke as he confessed everything.

His voice wavered and he started to sniffle, wiping his nose on the back of his jacket sleeve.

"I'm so sorry, Dad," Ethan said. "I just want to come home. Can you come pick me up?"

"Of course, Ethan, now listen to me," Duncan said. "Who else knows what you've told me? You spoke to Mr. Le, did you talk with anyone else?"

"Just Mr. Le's friend, Ms. McKenna," Ethan said. "She said to tell you everything and that you'd probably want to get a lawyer for me. How much do lawyers cost, Dad? Do I really need one? This is so . . . so . . . fucked up!"

"Watch your language, Ethan," Duncan said. "Listen. I want you to go back to the office. Get your things and wait for me there, preferably in Mrs. Wolfe's office. I'll give her a call right now. Under *no circumstances* are you to talk with the police without my being there—understand? *No circumstances.*"

"Okay," Ethan said. "I'll go right now. And I'm sorry again to bother you at work, Dad."

"That's not important, right now, Ethan. I'll be there as soon as I can," he said. "And don't worry, it's going to be fine—everything's going to be all right, son."

Shaking with fury, Duncan threw the files he had in his hand across the room. Having no heft, they didn't even make it to the wall, but simply flew open, their contents fluttering haphazardly to the ground, giving him no satisfaction at all. Clenching his fists, he stood very still, breathing slowly, pulling his emotions back in, getting himself under control.

"Mr. LeGrange?" Adrienne poked her head around the corner into his office, a slightly alarmed expression on her face. "Is everything okay?"

"Yes, Adrienne," he said. "I got distracted and tripped. I'm afraid I've made quite a mess," he said, bending to pick up the papers strewn across the floor.

"Here, let me help," Adrienne said, coming in. "It's no wonder. You probably shouldn't have come in today. It was too soon."

"Thanks," he said, "As always, you come to my rescue."

After getting everything back in order, Adrienne placed the file folder neatly back on his desk.

"Why don't you go home?" she said. "We can handle everything here for a few days."

"I think I'll take you up on that, Adrienne," he said. "There's more to do with funeral arrangements and all that than I thought. I just got another phone call about some things that still need to be done, but hopefully I'll be back tomorrow or the next day. I'll let you know. I can catch up on most of this paperwork from home, but call me if anything comes up that I need to handle directly."

He gave her shoulder an absentminded squeeze, grabbed his coat, computer, and keys, and walked out to his car.

She thought it odd that he didn't take the project files home with him.

***

The faces of the two men walking up the front porch steps were all too familiar. Carla stayed where she was, manning her workstation behind the reception desk. Logan acted like she was filing some papers, helping out in the office.

Ethan was tucked safely into Rita's office, awaiting his dad's arrival. Rita was up in Portland, but when Carla got her on the phone and explained the situation, she gave her permission. She felt strongly that Ethan's parent should be present before the police talked with him.

Logan inwardly smiled. These wolves weren't getting past them.

Putting a bright if puzzled expression on her face, Carla greeted them cheerfully as they entered, "Good afternoon, Detectives, what can I do for you?"

"We need to speak with one of your students, Ethan LeGrange. Is there an office we can use for a private conversation?" Wright said.

Carla pretended to look up Ethan's schedule on her computer. "He has computer class right now. That's his last class today. He has independent study after that. Can this wait until then?"

"No," Wright said.

"Okay," she said, reaching for the phone, "I'll call him up to the office."

Punching in an extension, she waited until someone picked up.

"Mr. Le?" she said. "There are two detectives here, they'd like to speak with Ethan. Could you send him up to the office?"

Wright couldn't hear the other end of the conversation.

"Oh, okay," Carla said. "Do you know where he is? Okay, I'll let them know."

Turning to Wright, she said, "Mr. Le said Ethan isn't in class. He doesn't know where he is, but it's possible his father came to pick him up early since he didn't have any other classes this afternoon. This is his first day back since his stepmother . . . since the incident."

Logan had to admire the way the woman lied through her teeth.

"Did he sign out?" Wright asked.

Logan winced internally. They hadn't thought of that. But Carla had a quick response.

"Not that I know of, but I was at lunch. Ethan was manning the desk for me as part of his service hours. All the kids here log a certain number of hours as part of their curriculum here. It's part of what makes the New School such a great place for the development of the whole child. He could have left then. He was gone when I got back, but I assumed he went to class."

She smiled innocently up at them. Wright scowled.

He didn't look convinced, but handed her his card and said, "Please give me a call as soon as you locate him. We'll be in touch."

Logan and Carla watched the two detectives get into their car and drive down the access road. Logan prayed Ethan's dad didn't pull in until after they were gone. When the detective's car turned onto the main road, Logan went to retrieve Ethan from Rita's office.

His father arrived a few minutes later. The only indication that Duncan knew they'd assisted in helping Ethan hide was a curt nod in Carla's direction before he signed him out. His son meekly followed him to the car. Logan knew that eventually the police would talk with him, but by then, his dad would make sure he had an attorney present.

44

Wright turned north on Highway 99 while Johnson punched in the Portland address, then settled back for the ride.

"Well, that was a nothing burger," Johnson said, "I'll bet anything that kid was there."

"Yeah," Wright said, "Probably. We'll catch him later, at home. The sooner we follow up on these two leads, the sooner we can go pick up Nick."

"You sure Nick's our guy?" Johnson asked.

"Aren't you?" Wright asked.

"I don't know," Johnson said. "Nick wasn't the only one Monica talked to that night. Carson was obviously her dealer, or at least a fellow user. And there's always the husband. He could have been pissed off about her fooling around with Nick."

"Then why weren't *their* prints on the murder weapon?" Wright pointed out.

"Could have worn gloves," Johnson said.

"And as for Mr. LeGrange, she wasn't texting him that night," Wright said.

They batted the options back and forth until a cultured, British woman's voice told them they had 'arrived at their destination.'

A former luxury hotel, the Majesty Arms had fallen well past 'worn' all the way down to 'derelict.' Although still graced with carved embellishments over the main entrance and each window, the granite facade no longer sparkled, but was coated in layers of dark, streaky grime. Converted sometime in the seventies to rented rooms euphemistically called studio apartments, the Majesty Arms *de*pressed rather than *im*pressed visitors.

Wright found a parking spot right outside. The majority of the residents didn't own cars and there were no businesses to speak of on this block.

If the door had a lock, it wasn't working. They opened the door and stepped inside the miniscule entryway. A woman was retrieving her mail from a row of rickety, metal boxes on their left. The stairs were straight ahead.

"Elevator's broken," the woman said.

Taking her at her word, Wright and Johnson started up the stairs. The man they wanted to see was on the fourth floor. They hadn't called ahead. When they got there, Johnson knocked.

A pudgy young man with dark hair, neatly trimmed, answered the door. He wore shapeless sweatpants, flip-flops and a faded OSU sweatshirt, and held a wooden spoon in his hand, half-coated in something red. An enticing aroma of garlic and onions wafted toward them. Wright's stomach growled.

"Mr. Wells, Matt Wells?" Wright said.

A faint spark of fear surfaced in Matt's eyes, but he didn't physically flinch or run away. "Yeah, I'm Matt. Who are you?"

"I'm Detective Wright and this is my partner, Detective Johnson," he said. "May we come in?"

"Uh . . . sure, I guess," Matt said, stepping aside to let them in.

The room was neat but sparsely furnished. Wright doubted anyone had actually purchased the mismatched furniture in the apartment. The faded, corduroy couch Matt pointed to must have come with the place or he'd picked it up off a curb somewhere.

"I'll be right back, I just need to turn down the stove," he said.

It didn't take long to survey the entire contents of the room. A small green end table with a 1970s orange lamp, a plywood laminate coffee table, and a small TV in the corner. Two sleeping bags were rolled up behind the couch and several pairs of shoes were by the door.

Matt came back in, sans spoon, wiping his hands on a thin dish towel. He sat in the chair and lay the towel on the arm.

"What can I do for you?"

"We're hoping you can help us locate someone, a friend of yours, a Carson York," Wright said. "Have you seen him lately?"

"Why?" Matt said, looking alarmed. "Is he in trouble?"

"We just want to ask him a few questions," Johnson said. "Do you know where we can find him?"

Matt swore under his breath. "Look, I don't want to get into any trouble," he said. "I'm on probation. I've got a good job, things are going good. I don't want to mess that up."

Wright leaned forward, "And you won't be in any trouble, Matt, if you cooperate with us. We just want to talk with your friend, but it's important. Do you know where he is?"

"Is this about drugs? He *told* me he was clean! He looked clean and he didn't say anything about running from anything," he said. "He just needed a place to stay while he got a job and saved up some money. It's really hard to get started after rehab or if you've got a record. We help each other out. It's all been good. No problems."

He looked up at them. "Are you *sure* he's mixed up in whatever you want him for?"

"Like I said, Matt, we just want to talk to him," he said, taking out his notebook, glancing at the sleeping bags behind the couch, "Now, when was the last time you saw Carson?"

Matt sat back, folding in on himself. "This morning when I left for work," he said. "He works afternoons and nights, filling in at a couple different places, dishwashing."

"Do you know which restaurant he's at tonight?" Wright asked.

"Fontana's," Matt said, "Little Italy. Dinner shift." He glanced at the clock. "Starts in about an hour. You're not going to tell him I told you, are you?"

"Not if we don't need to," Wright said.

Matt did not look reassured.

They confirmed the basic facts of how Carson got in touch with Matt after Monica was killed and got a ride into Portland, then headed out to Fontana's, leaving a forlorn young man to go stir his marinara sauce.

Little Italy smelled almost as good as Matt's apartment. They would definitely need to take a dinner break, but it might not be for a while. It would depend on how their conversation with Carson went. They might be driving back to Newberg with a suspect in custody.

Fontana's was a small, family trattoria squeezed in between two larger, more modern establishments. The back alley, where Johnson positioned himself next to a dumpster and the kitchen door, did not smell as good as the front.

Sure enough, within minutes, a white-aproned young man exploded out of the exit door, along with a cloud of steam, sprinting for all he was worth down the alley toward the street.

"Police! Stop!"

Damn.

Johnson took after him, wishing he were younger and had worn different shoes. He wasn't planning on a foot pursuit when he got dressed this morning.

45

"Logan," Huey said, "Got a minute?"

For Huey, Logan had nothing but minutes right now. Even if she'd been in the middle of something, she'd have dropped it to find out was going on. As it was, she'd just finished breakfast and her schedule was wide open.

She should probably just go home, but she hadn't heard anything about Ethan since his dad came and took him home yesterday. Nick wasn't under arrest, but his situation was still precarious, and no one knew where Carson was.

She hadn't seen much of Huey the last couple of days, but knew he'd been busy doing what Huey did best, digging around in cyberspace, looking for evidence to give to Nick's attorney to help clear him. Of course, both of them hoped he didn't find anything that would implicate Nick further. They'd face those facts if they had to.

And then there was Ethan. That poor kid was now pulled into the middle of all this.

Grabbing a few extra muffins and a cinnamon roll along with a refill on her coffee, Logan followed Huey back to the lab.

Normally, Logan didn't pay attention to how the lab looked, but this morning, it seemed drabber than usual, like every other computer lab in every other school she'd ever been in. Off-white, beige, and gray. Just computers, chairs, and wires. Bland, bland, bland. There must be a way to spruce this up, thought Logan. Add some color or plants or something.

They sat at the round worktable. Logan pushed a coffee at Huey and took one of the muffins for herself. She would have preferred the cinnamon roll but didn't want to be greedy. Still . . . if Huey didn't want it . . .

Huey took a bite out of a muffin before wiping his hands on a napkin and pulling over his laptop. The cinnamon roll beckoned.

"What have you got?" Logan asked.

"Several things. First, I got her phone records," Huey said, angling the laptop screen so she could see.

Logan scanned the record of calls and texts, scrolling down until she'd seen all the relevant pages.

"Wow," she said, sitting back.

"Yeah, I know," Huey said.

"That text . . . I mean, not only did he text her, but what he said makes it sound pretty threatening." She took a minute to absorb this information.

"We need to talk to him," she said. "There must be an explanation. . . . And if the cops have this, which they must—it's the first thing they would have requested—why haven't they already arrested him? Catching him sending a text to her right before she was killed . . ."

This has to stop. If I have to, you know what I will do.

"That's pretty damning," Logan said.

"Well, I can't say for sure why they haven't arrested him, not knowing what other information they have," Huey said. "But see this number here?"

"Yeah," Logan said. "Whose is it?"

"Carson's," Huey said.

"Carson York?" Logan said. "Well, that might explain why he ran. Do we know what their connection was?"

"I'm not positive," Huey said, "and there's no way to know what they talked about, other than the phone call was short, but while I was looking for background on Monica, I found an ER record that might be relevant."

Logan waited for Huey to explain.

"The ER doctor wasn't specific, but his notes sound like code for a drug overdose—amphetamines," Huey said. "She was released, probably with a warning if it was her first time. And knowing Monica, she probably flirted her way out of it once she was out of immediate danger."

"I get that Carson did drugs and now we know Monica probably did, too, but how would she have known him? Didn't he work the streets in Portland?" Logan said. "They didn't exactly travel in the same circles."

"Yeah, but she'd have to buy her drugs from someone. My sister says she used to see deals going down all the time downtown when she had the food truck, and not all of them were kids. She told me a lot of their customers wore suits. Up and comers who wanted an edge or something for a party on the weekend. Women like Monica would probably use cocaine to stay thin," he said.

"Okay, that makes sense," Logan said. "Monica and Duncan lived downtown before they moved out to the suburbs and their office is right downtown. Was there any other contact between Carson and Monica besides that night?"

"Yeah, not for a while. Back in the fall there are a few short Facebook messages and calls," Huey said. "Those sound like they're arranging meeting places or times. They don't mention drugs, but I can't think what else they'd have in common."

"The timing is right," Logan said. "Carson was on the street then. And we can check with G.I. Joe, but it looks like the messages and calls stop when he entered rehab and started the Blanchett House program."

Huey continued the thought, "Yeah, they could have reconnected here—Monica was on campus occasionally—and started up their business relationship again."

"But Joe says he was clean," Logan said, playing devil's advocate. "That's why it doesn't make any sense for him to have anything to do with Monica."

"If he wasn't back into selling drugs and if he didn't kill Monica, why did he run away?" Huey asked.

Logan tapped her fingers on the table, looking vaguely in the direction of the pastries. Huey grinned and slid the cinnamon roll over to her, then took the last muffin for himself. Shamelessly, she took two big bites and swallowed them down with almost the last of her coffee.

"What about Ethan's dad?" Logan asked. "It's always the husband, but no one's even looked at Duncan. Does he have any calls on there?"

"Well, yeah," Huey said. "There's one call that night, earlier, but it's probably reminding her about the show or when to be ready or something. No threatening texts like Nick's on there. In fact, none after the show started."

"Did they come in one car?" Logan asked.

"They walked in together," Huey said. "I assume so."

"You're sure they didn't call or text that night, during the show?"

"Yes," Huey said. "Just Nick and Carson. They are the last two people who had contact with Monica LeGrange."

Grateful to Huey for going to all this extra work for Nick, Logan was still frustrated that he'd found nothing to definitively help clear him. In fact, the text he'd sent to Monica was just one more bit of evidence for the prosecution. Their side of the scale was looking pretty heavy right now.

He had found the information about Carson, and they would pass that along to Nick's attorney—unofficially, of course—but she didn't think that would really take Nick out of the police's crosshairs, although it might help muddy the waters, spreading suspicion to include at least one other person.

An idea began to surface in Logan's mind. She turned to Huey.

"Can you get into someone's bank records? Finances? Taxes, whatever? A person or a business?" Logan asked. "I mean, will this get you in any more trouble than hacking phone records?"

Huey rolled his eyes and grinned. "Give me something hard to do, Logan, not this easy stuff. Whose financial records would you like me to exhume?"

Logan scribbled three names down on a piece of paper and pulled on her jacket.

"Here," she said, "Check these out. It's probably a long shot, but I'm going to run into Portland and do some digging of my own."

"Where are you going?" Huey asked as she hustled out the door.

"Better you don't know," Logan said, "that way you can claim innocence if I make a fool of myself."

46

Logan put the Rav in gear and slowly crunched away from the school, trying not to spray gravel up onto Rita's car. She had no intention of cracking the windshield or returning it with little rock pits in the paint. When she got to the arch, she did a California stop and pulled directly onto Whisper Creek Road. Ten minutes of meandering later, she turned north onto Highway 99.

Feeling like a cat let out of its cage, Logan popped open the moon roof and pressed down on the gas—keeping her eye on all three mirrors so she didn't get a ticket. The roads were dry and the highway smooth. Why not have a little fun?

The Rav wasn't Lola—nothing beats a top-down ride in a '58 Corvette convertible—but today, all the windows down, cold, fresh air whipping in—it felt pretty damn close.

She relaxed and enjoyed the ride, but sooner than she wanted she was in Portland, looking for Quantum Engineering and a place to park. She found a spot half a block away. She had no particular plan, just a hunch. They needed to know more about Duncan and Monica's marriage than phone records could reveal. Mentally riffling through several cover stories, Logan picked one and went inside.

A twenty-something receptionist looked up and smiled brightly at what she deemed to be a new client, possibly someone important.

Logan strode in, unaware of the striking impression she made. Dressed in her usual uniform of jeans, boots, turtleneck sweater and a leather jacket she'd had since Amy was born, sunglasses pushed up onto the top of her head, her hair pinned back to frame her high-cheek-boned, lightly freckled face. She looked like a Hollywood movie star.

Logan didn't dress to impress, but impress she usually did, even though her clothes sported no designer labels, and she often trimmed her unruly locks herself.

"Hi," Logan said, smiling back. "I'm here to see Duncan LeGrange, if he's available."

"I'm sorry," she said, "but Mr. LeGrange is out of the office today. Did you have an appointment? What was your name, again?" Looking at her calendar, she looked concerned, worried she had made a mistake.

Extending her hand, Logan said, "Logan, Logan McKenna. Sorry, I should have called first. I'm from The New School. just stopped by to drop off some materials and go over the assignment portal for Mr. LeGrange's son. I was going to sit down with his dad for a few minutes to explain how we can accommodate Ethan with some online sessions until he feels up to returning to school."

The receptionist looked unsure.

"We know this is a difficult time for the family. We want to make it as convenient as possible for Ethan to complete his work, without missing any academic instruction. We don't want him to fall behind in his studies," said Logan, with a perfectly straight face.

Just then a fifty-something, slightly frumpy woman came out of her office and walked up to the desk. She lay a soft hand on the receptionist's shoulder, releasing her from further obligation to this visitor. Her nails were short and painted a frosty, pale-pink color Logan identified with grandmothers. The young woman nodded and gratefully returned to her work.

Looking up at Logan, who had a good six inches on her, the woman extended her own hand and said, "Adrienne Thorley, Mr. LeGrange's Office Manager. What can I do for you, Ms. McKenna?"

Logan again explained her mission, then waited.

"As Lindsey has explained, Mr. LeGrange isn't in the office today, but if you follow me, I'll be happy to help. You can leave whatever work Ethan has to do with me. I'll see that he gets it."

Adrienne walked Logan back to her office.

"It was kind of you to drive all the way out here," she said, offering Logan a seat at a small conference table to the right of her desk. "You can show me what you have over here."

"Well, as I said, everything is online," Logan said, taking a seat and opening her laptop, hoping she could make this sound believable. "There are no books or worksheets to deliver. I just wanted to explain how Ethan can obtain assignments and submit his work through the school website until he returns."

Before leaving the school, Logan had stopped by Carla's desk to obtain the passcodes to get into his teachers' most recent lessons and assignments. She was familiar enough with the way students and faculty interacted online to deliver a relatively succinct explanation to Adrienne to pass along to her boss. At least, she hoped it was plausible enough not to raise any alarm bells. Despite her dowdy appearance, the office manager seemed to be pretty sharp.

When she'd covered everything she could think of, Logan decided to see how well Adrienne knew Duncan and Ethan and how much she knew about Duncan's personal as well as business finances. Maybe she'd be able to shed some light on their relationship. She didn't know exactly what she was looking for, she was just nibbling around the edges, trying to uncover secrets, if there were any to discover.

"Ethan sure is a good kid," Logan said. "He's a whiz in the computer lab and everyone sure likes him. I got to watch him work at the talent show that night. He did a great job on stage, helping Huey. Have you ever had a chance to see him in action?"

Adrienne smiled, softening a bit at the mention of her boss's son. "Yes, I've seen him rehearsing complicated lighting changes on the stage, working on sets. He's quite good. Mr. LeGrange would sometimes have me pick him up at school if he wasn't available. We're all very proud of Ethan. He's very talented."

After sending this week's assignments to the printer, Adrienne got up to retrieve them. Logan took the opportunity to look around the office for something to get the woman talking.

Finding some photos of what looked like the early days of the company, Logan asked, "When were these taken? Was this when the company first started? Is that you?"

Some of the photos hung on the wall, others were propped up on a shelf.

"Yes," Adrienne said, pointing with the papers in her hand, "that was our entire staff. Just me, Mr. LeGrange, and Virginia."

"Virginia?" Logan asked.

"Yes. Virginia LeGrange," she said. "Mrs. LeGrange."

"And what about this one?" Logan asked, pointing to a small, slightly out-of-focus black and white photo in a thin, wooden frame, tucked halfway behind the others.

In it, a skinny girl of about twelve, with rough cut, sun-bleached hair proudly held up a very large bird by its ankles. Behind her, a rifle leaned against an unpainted porch railing.

"Oh, that," Adrienne said. "That's my first turkey."

She quickly got up and retrieved the photo, putting it in a desk drawer. "I forgot that was up there. Just a silly family picture."

"Not at all, I think that's great. When I was that age, I wouldn't have been able to cook dinner, let alone provide the main course."

Adrienne acknowledged the compliment with a nod. "Dad taught all us kids to hunt. Said everyone should know how to feed themselves. If more parents taught their children correctly, we'd have fewer adults who . . . who don't know how to do anything but order their dinner at a fancy restaurant."

47

This detour was interesting, but Logan wanted to get the conversation back on track—on the topic of Quantum Engineering, the players who had formed it and how they were all connected.

"How wonderful to have worked here from the very beginning, to help build a company from scratch," Logan said. "That must be very satisfying."

"Yes," Adrienne said. "It really has been."

"My husband and I had a computer training business," Logan said. "Started with an old iMac and a prayer. A lot of long hours to get a business up and running, but fun. And rewarding."

They talked a few more minutes about the challenges small businesses face. After Logan alluded to corporate debt Jack had accumulated, Adrienne bragged about her boss's business acumen and that Quantum Engineering was very successful financially.

Logan filed that piece of information away.

"Of course, it was just the two of us managing our little computer business," Logan said. "For the first few years, we didn't have any other employees. Quantum Engineering must have gone through some upheaval when Virginia and Mr. LeGrange divorced and then when the new Mrs. LeGrange came on board. So much paperwork. Changing people at the top is a lot more complicated than people realize."

"Yes," Adrienne said grimly.

The impression Logan was getting from their conversation was that the exit of the first Mrs. LeGrange for the second had not been a smooth one.

"But sometimes change is a good thing," Logan rambled on, feeling like she'd stirred the right pot. "It sounds like Monica was really involved in the business, helped it grow. Probably good to have new blood from time to time, right? Shake things up, fresh ideas and all that."

A harsh laugh escaped Adrienne's lips. When she spoke, it was with unexpected venom.

Looking Logan square in the face, she said, "The *real* Mrs. LeGrange did more to help Quantum Engineering by staying home, being a good wife and mother, than Monica ever did, no matter how many fancy titles she put behind her name."

Tapping the papers crisply on the table in front of her to straighten the edges, Adrienne rose in one fluid motion. Putting her friendly, efficient, office manager face firmly back on, she placed Ethan's assignments on her desk and escorted Logan to the reception area. When they arrived, she held open the door, all formal and distant.

"Thank you for stopping by, Ms. McKenna. I'll see to it that Mr. LeGrange understands how to access and submit Ethan's assignments online. I'm sure he'll appreciate it. Drive safely, now."

Jeez! Don't let the door hit you on the way out.

Obviously, Adrienne regretted having let her guard down.

Logan doubted Duncan's office manager showed her true feelings very often.

Back in her car, Logan took a second to regroup and process what she'd learned so far. According to both Ethan and Adrienne, Monica wasn't the beloved wife and company asset her husband had claimed she was, so why had Duncan pretended otherwise?

He had been so loving to his wife during dinner before the talent show. No signs of animosity or resentment. And later, Duncan portrayed her as a loving mother to Ethan, too. From what Ethan told her and Huey, Monica was anything but. Why the lie?

Or could he really be that blind? Did Duncan know about her fling with Nick? Her drug use? How she really treated Ethan? Ethan hadn't said much about his dad's relationship with Monica, mostly he'd just talked about how awful she was to him.

It was possible Duncan really was clueless. Men—and women—saw what they wanted to see when sex was involved. It happened all the time. From the little she'd learned of spousal abusers from her neighbor's experience a few years ago, her husband had been charming and romantic when they first met, but quickly become controlling and violent after marriage. Abusers counted on the wife not wanting to admit to her friends and family she had made a mistake. And then there was the abject fear. But that came later.

She supposed it could be the same for a man—when the fresh, new sex-kitten he marries on the rebound from his divorce turns out be a wildcat with claws, more interested in his bank account than his bed. If so, that gave him a lot more reason to kill Monica than Nick or Ethan.

But Duncan's prints weren't on the gun . . .

Damn . . . she'd forgotten about that. She had to give the cops credit for following the evidence, but still. Logan knew there was something there. If she could just figure out what it was.

Making a decision, she called Huey for Ethan's home address.

In for a penny, in for a pound . . .

She could use the same schoolwork pretext for stopping by.

Duncan was lying. That seemed obvious. Did Ethan know more than he had shared with her and Huey so far? What had he told the police, if anything? Had they questioned him yet?

She'd keep looking for answers, but none of the answers were good. Unless it was a stranger off the street, no matter who killed Monica, someone Logan knew was going to get hurt. She didn't know if Oregon had the death penalty or not, but being in jail for life was worse than death, in her opinion.

She thought of the vulnerable, young boy who'd broken down and cried in Huey's classroom. If Ethan's father really murdered his stepmother, where did that leave him? He was almost eighteen, but still a minor. His mother dead, his father in jail . . . she couldn't imagine. And what if Ethan was the one who pulled the trigger? Was that why he was so torn up? Had Ethan acted in a moment of hormone-driven rage at the woman who was destroying his and his father's lives?

The thought made her sick, but Logan wanted to find the truth. Her very nature made that the only course of action, the only goal to strive for. She'd faced some truths in her own life and had survived. Others would too.

The truth was supposed to set you free, but as far as Logan could see, for Ethan, Nick, and Duncan . . . and Carson, she almost forgot about him—if any of the scenarios she'd come up with were true, no one would be truly free. The ugly aftermath of hate and violence would cling to anyone left standing.

48

Logan put her phone on silent and walked up to the door. She pressed the doorbell once and waited.

She heard footsteps, but whoever it was stopped on the other side. Seeing the security peephole, Logan put on her best non-threatening smile. The I'm-not-a salesman-or-a-Jehovah's-Witness-or-a-cop face. No ulterior motive for dropping by.

Just as she was about to give up, Ethan opened the door.

"Hi, Ethan," Logan said. "I just stopped by to see how you're doing. We weren't sure how long you'd be out of school and Carla wanted me to show you the portal we set up so you can stay current on your work. Do you have a minute?"

Ethan stood frozen in the doorway.

"I'm not supposed to talk to anyone," he said, "but I think Dad meant the police, not you."

"It'll just take a minute," Logan said.

Ethan shifted his weight onto the other foot, then opened the door to let her in.

"Is your dad home?" Logan asked.

"Dad just went to the office for a couple of hours," he said.

"He should be back, soon. We're supposed to meet with an attorney this afternoon."

Logan followed him into the kitchen, which was warm and reminded her she hadn't had lunch. Moisture condensed on the inside of the large, sunny windows and Ethan went to stir something spicy on the stove.

He filled up a good-sized bowl he had waiting next to the burner, then at the last minute remembered his guest. "You want some? It's just chili and hotdogs."

"Sure, I could eat," Logan said, "If you've got enough to share."

He reached up for another dish from the cupboard, filled it and brought both bowls, steaming hot, to the small table by the windows.

"Cheese?" he asked.

"Absolutely," Logan said.

He went back and got a bag of grated Tillamook cheddar from the fridge, then reached back in for a beer. He brought both to the table.

Logan's eyebrows rose a half inch of their own accord.

"You want one?" he asked.

"Uh, no, thanks," Logan said.

He popped the top and sat down.

She almost said something but reminded herself this was not her child. Maybe his dad let him drink at home. If not, hopefully Duncan wouldn't blame her since she was the only adult in the room.

An open bag of tortilla chips was already on the table. They doctored up their individual bowls, then dug in. The chips were a little stale but added the necessary crunch.

When they were done, Ethan cleared the table, putting the dishes in the sink without rinsing them, washing the pot, or wiping down the counters. Logan had to smile. Typical teenager. She was so glad Amy was raised and running her own home, now. She didn't miss those battles with her teen over laundry and housework. Somehow, when kids got their own place, they magically started taking care of things. It was one of those quirks of nature—just when kids were old enough to become good roommates, they left home.

Knowing she may have only a small window of time before Duncan came home, Logan got out her laptop and steered the conversation to where she wanted it to go. Ethan would talk or he wouldn't. But she had to try.

"How are you doing?" she said, "Have the police tried to contact you, yet?"

"Carla called Dad yesterday and told him they came by the school just after we left," he said. "He said if they showed up here, not to answer the door. That's who I thought was at the door."

"So you said your dad found you an attorney?" she said.

"I think so," he said. "He wants to talk with us first, but Dad says he's a really good one."

Suddenly, Ethan teared up, his Adam's apple began to bob up and down as if he were trying not to cry. Logan's heart went out to him. She knew how even small things loomed large for teenagers emotionally; she couldn't imagine how frightening this situation must feel to a seventeen-year-old. Any adult would be scared, let alone a kid.

She was torn between wanting to comfort him and wanting him to open up and tell her the whole truth. Every instinct told her he was holding something back.

But right now, she just felt sorry for him. He seemed to be unravelling before her eyes. The beer he just downed probably hadn't helped his emotional frame of mind.

"Look at me, Ethan," she said. "You're going to get through this."

She didn't say, 'It's all going to be okay,' because Logan never lied to kids. She had no idea whether everything was going to be okay. But she was confident that he could get through whatever he was facing. He was not alone. He had a lot of people in his corner.

Ethan's shoulders began to shake.

49

"Ethan," she said, "I can't help if I don't know what's bothering you. Are you worried about your fingerprint on the gun and talking to the police? Do you want me to call your dad and ask him to come home?"

"No!" he said, "I'm not worried about me! I'm worried about Dad!"

"Your dad?" Logan asked, "Why?"

"Because I think . . . it's possible . . . he might have. I think he might have done it—to protect me," he said miserably, slumping back into his chair.

"What makes you think that?" Logan said.

"She was destroying our lives! That's why," he said. "I can't talk to the police about this. I just can't!"

"They'll take him away," he added in a whisper. "I can't lose Dad, too."

Logan was sure he was referring to losing his real mom, not losing Monica.

"Okay, Ethan," Logan said. "Just spit it out. I'm listening. When you're done, we can figure something out. What to do."

Ethan took a deep breath.

"We were just fine. I was sad Mom and Dad split, but we were okay. They didn't fight. They both came to my games and school stuff. Then, Dad met Monica and all that stopped. Monica weaseled her way in, and it was all about her. He didn't do it on purpose. I don't think he even realized how different things were."

Logan kept her mouth shut.

"Things weren't great, but they were okay, I guess. I still lived with Mom then. But when she died, I had to move in with Dad and Monica full time. That's when it got bad. It started with little things, like forgetting to pick me up after school some afternoons when Dad was stuck at the office. Or, when I had braces, she was supposed to take me to the orthodontist and didn't show up. Ms. Thorley had to come out and find me a couple of times so I wouldn't miss my appointment. She's nice.

"Monica hid things pretty well, but gradually, Dad started realizing the way things really were. Finally, when Dad found out about her fooling around—that was after we moved here—they had a big blow-up fight. I was actually glad. I figured that was it, that he would divorce her."

Logan waited, but she had a feeling she knew what happened next.

"But things got worse instead of better," he said. "They didn't get divorced. I saw a letter on his desk once, here at home. Something from an attorney, but he finished his shower before I could read it all. I Googled him, though—the attorney—and the website said he handled divorces.

"The only part I did read was something about securing what was left of my college fund and cutting up his wife's credit cards or Dad would lose the house, too."

"I'm sorry, Ethan, that must have been horrible, but that doesn't make your dad a murderer. What makes you think he did it, besides having a good reason to?" she asked bluntly.

Ethan's voice lowered to almost a whisper.

"I told the police he was always in his seat when I looked out," he said. "During the show, but he wasn't. After intermission, his seat was empty. He was back by the last act. I saw him when I turned up the house lights when Carla's dog went out into the audience, but I'm not sure how long he was gone."

Logan sat with this information for a minute.

"Well, that still isn't proof he was outside," Logan said, "He could have just gone to the bathroom and his prints weren't on the gun. Besides, your dad would have no way of knowing where Nick's gun was kept, would he? He couldn't have taken it."

Ethan's face brightened and he shot up straight in his chair, "Right! I didn't think of that. There's no way he could have done it! He didn't know anything about that gun until I told him about it yesterday!"

Logan was relieved for Ethan's sake that Duncan seemed to be off the hook, but that left Ethan right back on it.

50

Feeling guilty for missing her lunch KP duties, Logan drove as fast as she could back to the school without getting a ticket. She went directly to the kitchen to apologize to Brittany and see if there was any dinner prep she could help with. When she got there, she found Carla sitting at one of the tables, one arm around Brittany's slumped shoulders. Students were back in class and the rest of the dining hall was empty.

"What happened?" Logan said.

"It's Nick," Carla said, "they arrested him right after lunch. At least they had the decency not to do it in front of the kids."

Logan remembered passing several cars on Whisper Creek Road. She hadn't paid attention to who was in them.

"Did you call the attorney?" Logan asked.

"Yes," Carla said. "Nick still had his card. He's on his way over to the police station, now."

Logan didn't ask about bail. With a murder case, she knew bail would either not be available, or be set so high they couldn't post it. It was highly unlikely the police would be letting Nick walk around free anytime soon. She wondered why they decided to arrest him now and not over the weekend. What had changed?

Anger rose within her. This was just wrong! So many lives were being torn apart. Ethan, Nick, Carson . . . until the real killer was caught, one of her good friends, a seventeen-year-old boy, and a young man trying to get his life back together would all be suspect. The cops were focusing on Nick, but no one was free and clear. Should she share what she knew about Duncan's true relationship with his wife? About there being holes in his alibi? If so, and the cops followed that lead and found evidence against him, that would just hurt Ethan in a different way.

She had to find some answers. Right now, all she had was a muddy mess of questions.

First things first. Always the pragmatist, Logan first asked Brittany if there was anything she could do to help in the kitchen. Brittany thanked her for her offer, but said Teresa had everything under control and there wasn't much else anyone could do until they heard from Nick's attorney. She was going back to her cabin, now, to wait for his call. Carla had to get back up to the office. They agreed to meet back here for dinner.

Huey had classes until four, so Logan would have to wait to update him until then. She wondered if he even knew about Nick's arrest. No sense upsetting him in class and this wasn't news she wanted to share in front of students anyway.

For now, she went back to Glenda's cabin for some thinking time. She wanted to put together everything she had learned today with what she already knew to see if any of the new information made anything clearer.

There was no better place for a good thinking session than a good soak in Glenda's enameled cast iron, clawfoot tub. If she kept the bathroom door open, she'd be able to see and feel the warmth of the woodburning stove. Walking back over the footbridge, she realized how low the temperature had dropped. She was definitely chilled. Even her bones were cold. She couldn't wait to immerse herself in the hottest water she could stand. She might even sprinkle in some of the lavender herbs Glenda kept nearby.

Thirty minutes later, tub filled as high as she dared with the hottest water she could get from the faucet, Logan stepped in carefully so as not to slosh water on the floor. Holding onto the sides, she lowered her body inch-by-inch into the scalding water. Lying back, she relished the feeling of the water washing over her skin, enveloping her. Immersed up to her chin, her muscles began to completely unspool as she breathed in the lavender-scented steam.

Suspended there like that, Logan allowed her thoughts to drift, meandering down whatever paths they encountered, stirring details she'd missed, nudging them to the surface of her consciousness, discarding others as useless. What was it Ethan said about the gun? His dad didn't know where Nick kept it, but who would, besides Ethan, Nick, and Brittany? And who was Monica texting with so intently when she saw her hurrying into the dark through the garden that night? Nick or Carson? And what about Duncan? How much did he know about his wife's extracurricular activities? Did he know about the drugs? Just how much had he hated Monica? Enough to kill her? Why didn't he just divorce her?

She wasn't sure how much time had passed, but the interior of the cabin was subdued and the bathwater cold when she woke. Disappointed she'd lost the lovely warmth she'd gained, Logan pulled the plug out by the chain, stepped out, and quickly toweled off. Grabbing her clothes, she hopped over to the fire to finish pulling on her jeans and boots and shimmy into her sweater. Rubbing her hands together, warming them in front of the flames, she grabbed her cell phone to call Ben, but seeing what time it was, decided to get over to the dining hall to meet Carla and Huey first. She sent a short text letting him know she'd call him later.

She didn't want to be rushed when they talked. Logan enjoyed not only their long, rambling, late-night conversations, but having Ben tuck her into bed—virtually if he couldn't be there in person. The sound of his warm, male voice had become a comforting bookend to her day. Just the thought of it made her feel grounded and safe.

Glancing quickly at the dresser that held the velvet box with her ring, she smiled. Just one more reason to solve this mystery. She couldn't properly share her upcoming nuptials until she knew her friends were safe.

Shrugging on her warm jacket, she hustled out the door to the dining hall. It was time to pull the troops together. After dinner, if it was okay with Glenda, she was going to invite Carla, Huey, and G.I. Joe back to the cabin to bring everyone up to speed and brainstorm ideas. Five heads were better than one.

51

Keeping her tone of voice nonchalant, Adrienne told the receptionist she could take her break now and to forward the phones back to her before she left. She'd cover whatever calls came in during lunch. Before her supervisor could change her mind, the girl began straightening her area and gathering her things.

"Do you want me to bring you back anything, Ms. Thorley?" she asked.

"No, thank you, Lindsey," Adrienne said, "I'll pick something up later."

They both knew Adrienne always ate at her desk, but for some reason, they went through this charade every day.

Adrienne walked to the break room at the end of the hall, retrieved a paper bag from the community fridge, and brought it back to her desk. She opened the bag and took out her lunch. Turkey on wheat, lettuce and tomato, no mayo. A large slice of dill pickle wrapped in waxed paper to avoid getting the sandwich soggy. Salt and vinegar potato chips and a Diet Pepsi. The deli down the street knew her order by heart.

The office was quiet. Duncan stopped by earlier to meet with one of the engineers about a troublesome job he was completing for the city, but he was home with Ethan now. He'd seemed upset but hadn't said why. She'd had the files he'd left behind yesterday ready for him. He'd barely nodded in her direction.

Adrienne tried not to take this personally, but it rankled. After all she'd done for him!

She chewed methodically, taking a swig of the Diet Pepsi now and then, enjoying the strong fizzing—almost burning— sensation at the back of her throat. She'd had allergies since she was a girl and only Pepsi could cut through the morning phlegm she always woke up with. While everyone else in the office walked around with a Starbucks glued to their hand, Adrienne traveled with her diet soda. A cold can was always within reach. The mini-fridge in her office was fully stocked in case the deli ever ran out.

Anyone walking by her door would see only a dowdy, middle-aged office worker sitting there. Minding her own business. Placidly eating her lunch before going back to work.

What they couldn't see was what was running through her mind. Today's film was a memory of how this all started, all that had led to this moment, this problem she was faced with. She shouldn't have lost her composure with that Logan woman, shouldn't have opened her big mouth. Worry began to swirl in her gut, but she pushed it down. How much had she understood? Nothing she could do about that now.

A natural problem solver, Adrienne didn't waste time on regret. By reviewing the events carefully, zooming out for the big picture, then focusing closely on each detail, she'd find a way—a clear path to cleaning up this mess.

***

It started last Christmas. The office was decorated, employee bonuses arranged, and she'd just sat down to plan the holiday office party. They usually closed from Christmas Eve until the day after New Year's. The annual gathering was always lunch at Yang's on Christmas Eve Day. Yang put on a huge spread. Everyone looked forward to it. But that was before. Before Monica.

This year, Duncan's new wife, without consulting anyone, had booked herself and Duncan on a fourteen-day cruise that left on December 16th. What nerve!

But Adrienne knew better than to bring it up directly with Duncan. When she'd tried to talk with him about the high balance on the Mastercard Monica kept running up and she kept paying off, he'd defended his wife and had given Adrienne the cold shoulder for a week. No, she couldn't go to Duncan. She'd have to deal directly with Monica herself.

She waited until Duncan was out for the morning, on site with a client, and Monica made one of her rare appearances at the office. She'd have to catch her before she took off again for lunch with her girlfriends. The stars aligned and Adrienne took her shot, flagging Monica down as she hurried past her office, digging in her Louis Vuitton bag for her car keys.

"Monica?" Adrienne said, in the friendliest voice she could muster. "Have you got a minute? I need to talk to you about the office party."

"I'm on my way out, right now, Adrienne," Monica said, barely slowing down.

"It's important, Monica," Adrienne said. She added a bit of flattery to sweeten the pot. "Since you're in charge of client relations and marketing now, I knew you'd want to handle this yourself."

Monica acted put out but was obviously pleased that Adrienne was consulting her instead of studiously ignoring her as she usually did. Usually, Adrienne treated her like she was a piece of gum on her shoe. Adrienne was aware of this and kept her conciliatory tone as she invited her to sit down at the small conference table in her office. She had the calendar already pulled up on her computer. This shouldn't take long, surely the woman would see reason.

She began by briefly summarizing the problem, then added, "Mr. LeGrange always invites a few important clients to join the office party at Yang's, so since you're in charge of client relations now, I knew you'd want to know. It's also good for company morale. I'm sure you can see why it's important we reschedule your cruise.

"I checked with the cruise line, and they say there's no problem in moving your dates forward a couple of weeks. They have an even better cabin available on January fifteenth . . . or even . . ."

"No, not changing it," Monica said flatly. Adrienne expected her to pop up and leave, but something made her change her mind. She flipped her blonde hair back over her shoulder and settled back into her chair. "And who told you to try to rebook my trip?"

"Well, I just thought . . ." Adrienne said.

"No, I don't think you did," Monica said. "I can't wait another minute to get out of this dreary, dripping, eternally gray city, let alone another whole month, just so you guys can have your little annual Christmas party. Besides, Duncan's looking forward to this trip." A small smile played on Monica's lips. "And I know you care about what Duncan wants."

Adrienne's face reddened, but she kept her voice even, "I doubt it. Mr. LeGrange gets seasick if he even looks at a boat."

"Oh, he can get one of those little seasick patches or whatever. He'll be fine," she said. "Don't you worry about my husband, Adrienne."

Lines clearly drawn in the sand, things may have ended there, but Monica stood, smoothed invisible wrinkles out of her skirt, and made things even clearer.

"You need to get some things straight, Adrienne," she said, in a low voice. "Up until now, you've run the show around here.

You've had 'Mr. LeGrange' and Quantum Engineering, all to yourself. I've put up with your condescending, dismissive attitude for months. Frankly, I had to," she admitted.

"But this,*" she said, indicating her perfect body, "is worth more than* that.*" She swirled her hand dismissively in Adrienne's direction.*

"You don't need to know the details, but I hold your Mr. LeGrange's rather puny balls—oh, but you don't know that firsthand, do you Adrienne? I'll bet you never sampled the boss's balls—well, I hold what there is of them in my hand."

Adrienne was incapable of speech.

"My name is on everything, Miss Adrienne. Every bank account, every savings account, and just to be thorough, every business account. I made sure Duncan added me to them all. I co own Quantum Engineering. So don't ever tell me what to do again. I'll do *what I want, I'll* go *where I want, I'll* spend *what I want."*

Monica sauntered to the door, turning to smile sweetly.

"And there's not a damn thing you can do about it."

Oh, but there was . . .

52

Duncan had to all but push Ethan into Lewis Taylor's office. Lewis Taylor, Attorney at Law with Grisham, Taylor, and Poe, was a gym-fit man in his early fifties, groomed and polished to a sharp edge as behooved a partner in one of the most prestigious law firms in town. He came around from behind his desk to greet them, clasping first Duncan's hand and forearm in a double grip, then Ethan's.

Duncan thanked him for seeing them on such short notice. Ethan mumbled something incoherent, looking like he might puke his chili up at any moment. They sat down in the two chairs opposite.

Tyler returned to his seat, leaned back, steepled his hands, and said, "Okay, as we discussed over the phone, my calendar is very full right now, so this must be a compelling case in order for me to take it on. I'd like to hear from Ethan what kind of trouble he is in. If I feel I can help, we'll move forward from there. I've had my assistant block out the time we agreed to on the phone."

At this he swiveled toward Ethan.

Fixing him with a laser beam look, he said, "You have my undivided attention. Go ahead, Ethan. What brings you here?"

Ethan stumbled through the basics. His stepmother's murder, his fingerprint being found on the gun and how it got there, target shooting with Nick, and finally, the police showing up at his school to talk with him, presumably about all of the above.

True to his word, Lewis didn't interrupt except to ask a few questions here and there. When Ethan was done, he asked if Duncan had anything to add. Duncan did, but most of what he had to say was how wonderful Ethan was and how he could never have done anything like that. He really had nothing substantial to contribute to Ethan's defense.

Lewis asked about whatever alibi Ethan might have for the window of time the police had established for time of death. He didn't have much. Nothing firm.

Lewis sat for a moment quietly.

"Here's the thing," he said. "The police have a solid piece of evidence linking you to the murder weapon. You have no solid alibi. You were on and off the stage, in and out working scene changes, but not all acts needed those, so you weren't visible each time. Your advisor, Mr. Le, can't back up your story because he didn't have eyes on you the whole time, right?"

"Right," Ethan said miserably.

***

"How did you feel about your stepmother, Ethan?" he asked.

Ethan's face reddened and turned dark, "What does that have to do with anything? Does that matter?" he asked. "It doesn't matter how I felt about Monica. I didn't kill her! And neither did Dad!" he shouted.

Lewis let that sit for a minute.

"Funny you should mention your father, Ethan. What about you, Mr. LeGrange?" the attorney asked calmly, turning his gaze on Duncan. "How was your relationship with your wife? And please don't be shy, these are all questions the police and opposing council will ask."

"Look," Duncan said, his voice rising slightly. "We just want to get someone who can handle this fingerprint thing—explain to the police how Ethan's one fingerprint got onto Nick's gun. The target shooting. That's all. There's no reason for them to go after him. He's just a kid."

"That's not how it works, Mr. LeGrange," Lewis said. "If you want me to represent Ethan, I need to have the whole story. I need to be ready for whatever the police ask Ethan. No surprises. All the skeletons in your closets are going to come out. And Ethan turns eighteen in three months. Hardly a kid.

"The good news," he added brightly, "is that if you retain me, I'm sworn to secrecy. I can't reveal anything you tell me to the police. My job will simply be to take all of the information and craft the best defense possible for your son."

"Does that mean you're taking the case?" Duncan asked.

"Of course, I am," Lewis smiled. "We'll set up an appointment down at the station. By the time I'm done with those hick detectives, they'll not only leave Ethan alone, but pay for an Uber to get him out of there. I doubt they'll arrest him on just this one piece of evidence alone. But first . . . let's get the paperwork end of things out of the way, then we can get down to business. We have a lot of ground to cover tonight.

"I'll have Cassie bring in some forms for you to sign. She can also take your check. You want anything, Ethan? We've got Coke, juice, whatever. And give Cassie your order. We've got Thai, Mexican, sushi, Vietnamese—whatever you want. Portland is a foodie paradise! Just sit tight. I'll be right back."

Ethan looked at his dad and smiled weakly. Duncan reached out and gave him an awkward sideways hug. "It's going to be okay, son," he said. "Everything's going to be okay."

Ethan wished his dad looked more confident than his words suggested. He had a worried look Ethan didn't understand. When the attorney had asked him what his relationship was with Monica was, he'd flinched.

The truth was going to come out. Part of Ethan couldn't wrap his head around the fact that his dad might have killed her when he realized she'd spent most of Ethan's college fund AND cheated on him.

Ever since the night of the big blowup, he kept waiting for his dad to sit him down and tell them they were divorcing, but that hadn't happened. Dad and Monica had simply co-existed, but Ethan had felt the undercurrent of loathing and bitterness rolling off his dad whenever she came strolling in late at night. Still, he said nothing. Was it all really about the money? Was that the power she had over him?

But Ethan didn't care about money. He didn't want his dad to stay in a rotten marriage for him. He needed to tell his dad that they'd be just fine! He was almost through with high school. He could get a job. If Dad had just divorced Monica, everything would be fine. But maybe he didn't see that. Maybe he thought he had to do something more drastic. Maybe he just couldn't put up with her sleeping around anymore.

Ethan shook his head to keep these thoughts from overwhelming him.

He looked around the office. He didn't know this lawyer. Could he really trust him?

He wished he could talk to his dad alone first, but what would he say? 'Hey, Dad, did you shoot Monica to get her out of our lives?' or even, 'Did you know where Nick kept his gun?' He just couldn't think how to ask the questions and find out what he really wanted to know. But inside, he thought he knew already.

If this lawyer was hired to defend him, would he be obligated to defend his dad, too? Or would he have to tell the police once he had the whole story? Ethan desperately wished he understood the law better. He had seen cop shows on TV where a lawyer could only defend one person at a time, he thought so, anyway.

How was he supposed to protect his dad? If the lawyer was only hired to protect Ethan, then his job would be to lay the blame at anyone else's door, including Dad's. He had to find a way, because if his dad really did it, he did it for both of them, not just himself. He had to find a way!

Before Ethan could figure out how to arrange his words, the lawyer's assistant, Cassie, came back in. She put a basket of sodas and snacks on the conference table, along with the paperwork, which his dad quickly flipped through and signed in all the indicated places marked with bright yellow tabs.

53

You have the right to remain silent. Anything you say can and will be used against you in a court of law. You have the right to an attorney. If you cannot afford an attorney, one will be appointed for you . . .

Nothing.

"Do you want to talk to me?" Wright asked.

"Lawyer."

***

Wright drove up to the box and punched in the code. The gate opened. He made a sharp left and fifty feet later rolled to a stop in front of the entrance to the jail. Leaving Nick in the back seat, he got out and went over to the lockers to secure his gun. Johnson did the same. Pocketing the key, he returned to the car to get their reluctant guest. Nick hadn't resisted arrest, but they'd cuffed him anyway. Standard procedure.

They walked him in and uncuffed him. They parked him on the bench and had him empty his pockets. He didn't have much, just his wallet and some Chapstick. He'd given a bunch of keys he had on his belt to Brittany before they took him in.

"""

Leaving Nick on the bench, Wright walked over to the cage and plopped his stuff on the counter. The jailer nodded, then proceeded to inventory the contents of Nick's wallet. Forty-two dollars, driver's license, phone.

When he was done, the jailer frisked Nick again, then took him back to be fingerprinted and parked. Nick kept asking for his lawyer but was told to pipe down. He'd get his phone call as soon as they were done, and not one minute before.

Wright should have felt better about this, but he didn't. Johnson seemed okay with it—at least resigned. He'd been doing this longer and understood how things worked.

After their fruitless foot pursuit of Carson and failed attempt at questioning Ethan—he'd already lawyered up—they'd returned to the station to find the DA waiting for them in Lieutenant Waters' office. The lieutenant pointed to a couple of waiting chairs. They sat. He then let the DA launch into his spiel. Within minutes, it became apparent the DA had no interest in the two loose ends the detectives were trying to nail down.

First, Ethan's attorney had called. Claimed he had a good explanation of how the kid's fingerprint got on the gun and said if they wanted to waste their time questioning the boy, he would be happy to make an appointment. And the fact that Ethan was seventeen and had never been in trouble before made him a tough target to try to pin a murder rap on.

As for their second 'lead'—the DA used air quotes to make his point—he pointed out there was no physical evidence tying Carson York to the crime. His fingerprints weren't on the gun. So he ran from the cops. So what? He was a drug addict. That's what drug addicts did. Besides, there were a zillion places to hide in Portland. Not worth the time and money it would take to hunt him down. Since Wright and Johnson had *screwed up* the only chance they had of catching him, they could scratch Carson off their list.

After this sarcastic summary, Wright looked over at his lieutenant for backup, but arms folded, Waters remained silent. No support coming from that quarter. He wondered why. Usually, the lieutenant stuck up for his guys.

But the DA was up for re-election and wanted this wrapped up. Nick was a slam dunk, he said. Totally guilty. He had motive, means, and opportunity. Between the email, the video, the calls, the threatening text message, and the fact that the murder weapon was his gun, and his prints were all over it . . . and only his wife could alibi him, the guy was going to be easy to put away.

A clean conviction for first degree murder meant another notch in the DA's belt and good press for the department. A win/win for everyone. In fact, they already had the warrant in process. All the two chastised detectives had to do was go bring him in. What were they waiting for?

The whole experience made Wright want to go home and take a shower. He spent what was left of the day writing up the arrest report, then headed home. When Suzie saw the look on his face, she went and made him a double scotch.

54

Logan pulled over the two chairs from the breakfast nook and nudged them in between the love seat and the overstuffed wingback in Glenda's living room, creating a small seating area around the fire. She fed in a few more sticks of kindling, leaning a larger piece of firewood against the stove to put in as soon as the smaller bits got going.

Glenda set a pot on the stove to boil and assembled a tea tray—cups, sugar, lemon, and milk—placing it on a low table in the center so everyone could help themselves. Carla arrived first, carrying a basket of freshly baked cookies covered by a red-and-white checkered kitchen towel.

"Oatmeal raisin or chocolate chip?" Logan asked, lifting the edge of the towel to peek inside.

"I had leftover dough, so made both," Carla said. "The oven was still hot from dinner, so Teresa said I could use it. It didn't take but a few minutes. They're still warm."

Logan verified this by taking one.

"How's Brittany?" Logan asked, between bites. "Has she heard from Nick, yet?"

"Don't know," Carla said. "I didn't want to bother her."

"I agree," Glenda said, bringing in spoons and napkins. "She'll let us know. No sense upsetting her unnecessarily."

Huey knocked and Logan went to let him in.

"Where's Joe?" she asked, looking behind him as if G.I. Joe was hiding in the shadows.

"Had to work," Huey said. "He's closing up the kitchen tonight." He removed his coat and neatly folded it on the back of one of the straight-backed chairs, then put his computer bag on the floor against one of the legs and sat down. "He said he really didn't have that much to contribute, anyway. Carson still hasn't contacted him."

Carla and Logan took the love seat, Glenda tucked into the wingback. Huey pulled his chair in a little closer. Since this gathering was mainly Logan's idea, once everyone got the treats they wanted, she started things off by just going around the room, having each person share what they knew or had learned that the rest of them may not know. Once they were all up to speed they could share ideas—if anybody had any. With Nick's arrest, the urgency to find answers was clear.

"The police are no longer looking for the real killer, so, scary as it may seem, we're it," Logan said. "We're the only hope Nick has. Us and his lawyer, of course. Glenda, you want to go first?"

Glenda started by reminding everyone that the encounters between Monica and Nick happened a long time ago, before he and Brittany were married. Then she reiterated what she'd already told Logan, about seeing Nick sneak in to spend the night with Monica in what was later Carson's room at the main house and his subsequent week off.

At the end, she emphasized the fact that this was a short-lived affair during a period of time when he and Brittany had been broken up. Nothing had happened since; she was sure of it.

Carla told Huey and Glenda about Logan noticing the poultry poop and mud on Carson's dress shoes when they went to clean his room and do his laundry, which indicated he had been out to the chicken coop that night after it rained. No one had a good explanation for that, and wouldn't, until he either turned himself in to the police, or at least called G.I. Joe. This made Logan wonder again how Rita would handle it if he ever did get back in touch.

Huey listened carefully, finished the last of his tea, and placed the cup back on the tray. Without sharing the explicit videos of Nick and Monica, he quickly summarized the gist of their contents and then pulled out his computer.

"Do you want to go first?" he asked Logan.

"No," she said, "That's okay. You first."

Huey proceeded to list the various personal, business, and tax accounts for Duncan and Monica as well as Quantum Engineering's. Realizing he was giving too much detail and not explaining with the figures meant, he got to the bottom line, "What all of this means is that Monica was bleeding Quantum Engineering, and therefore, Duncan LeGrange, dry."

"Well, then, why didn't he kick her to the curb?" Carla asked, outraged. Carla had been a doormat for years in her first marriage, but no more. Once she found her backbone, Carla did not suffer fools gladly. She'd kicked her former husband to the curb and saw no reason why Duncan shouldn't do the same.

"Because her name's on everything," Huey said. "If he tried to divorce her, she would take half of everything they owned, business and personal, and just walk away."

"But from what you just said about the accounts, if she kept spending like she was, there wouldn't be much left of the company to split."

"Exactly," said Logan. "The only way to stop her was to kill her."

Glenda spoke up, "Is this enough for the police to let Nick go? I mean, if the lawyer could find what you found through official search warrants and everything, they'd have to look at Duncan, right?"

"It wouldn't be that easy," Logan said. "Nick's lawyer would have to provide a reason to go digging through their financial records. He may or may not find a sympathetic judge to give him a warrant to do so."

"Which brings me to my news, such as it is," she added. "I enjoyed a gourmet lunch of chili and hotdogs with Ethan today."

She told them what Ethan had said to her and Huey earlier about target shooting with Nick and not wanting to get him in trouble for letting him shoot his gun, as well as revealing just how awful Monica was.

"The thing is, when I talked to him today, Ethan was upset for all those reasons, but what he's really worried about is that his dad may have done it. He thinks Duncan may have killed her. He admitted he sort of lied to the police—at least by omission—when he told them his dad never left his seat during the show. In reality, he can't vouch for him for the entire time. He's not sure of the exact time he left his seat and then returned, but it was empty during the window of time Monica was murdered. He could have done it."

"Wow," said Carla.

"Yeah," Logan said. "I also stopped by Quantum Engineering for a little while. I was hoping to talk with Duncan, but he was out. I did get to talk with Adrienne for a few minutes. Everything she said verifies the dirt you dug up, Huey. She really didn't like Monica. Felt she was running the company into the ground. Didn't like me much, either. All but handed me my hat and said, 'What's your hurry?'

Glenda laughed.

"So, where does this leave us?" Carla asked.

After reviewing all the information, everyone agreed Duncan was the most likely candidate, but the thought of him being the killer saddened them all. What Ethan would do with his mother dead, his stepmother murdered, and his father in jail was nothing any of them wanted to contemplate.

55

The darkened street held a thin, deserted air. Duncan parked right in front. Looking in through the glass doors, he could see Lindsey had long since left for whatever it was twenty-somethings did after work. Probably meet up with friends for a drink. Or maybe she cared for an elderly mother. Duncan didn't know. He used his key card to let himself and Ethan in.

The office officially closed at four-thirty, so everyone else had already gone home, too, except Adrienne. The light was still on in her office. Good old Adrienne. He'd have to give that woman a bonus. Or maybe just a gift certificate for her and a friend to a nice restaurant. He wondered if she had anyone to take. He'd never thought much about his office manager's personal life.

Wrung out from the hours-long session with the attorney, he reassured Ethan he was just stopping by long enough to pick up his messages and a few files. He planned on working from home again tomorrow. By Monday, the lawyer promised Ethan should be able to return to school.

"How about we get chimichangas from Mazatlán's?" he said, knowing it was one of Ethan's favorites. "We can pass right by there on the way home."

The attorney, Lewis Taylor, said he'd handle the police business from here on, which was a great relief. Now, all they had to do was get through the next few days. This nightmare would be over soon.

He flipped on a few lights in the hallway. Adrienne must have heard them come in. She emerged from her office with a stack of papers in hand, as if it were entirely normal for her to still be there at almost six thirty at night.

"Mr. LeGrange," she said, "I didn't expect you today, but I have your messages right here . . . Oh, and Ethan, one of your teachers stopped by with some schoolwork for you. I printed them off for you," she said, handing him the stack of assignments she'd printed out and neatly stapled.

"Thanks," Ethan said, taking them from her.

"I printed off enough for the rest of the week. Why don't you take these down to your dad's office and look them over? I was just organizing your dad's messages for him. As soon as he has everything, I'll send you two home.

"You both look like you could use some rest," she added with a warm smile.

Duncan sighed. The woman really was a gem.

Adrienne waved Ethan on his way and Duncan allowed himself to be ushered into her office.

Once Ethan was out of earshot, Adrienne turned to him, her whole face shining with excitement. She invited him to take a seat, but he reminded her that he really was very tired and just wanted to get home. If she could just give him his messages, he'd get out of her hair. In fact, he insisted that she go home, too. Whatever other business they needed to go over could wait until tomorrow.

"Why don't you set up a Zoom call for after lunch, Adrienne?" he said. "Unless there's something really urgent, it can keep, right?"

"No, it can't," she said, her face taking on a slightly panicked look.

In all the years they'd worked together Adrienne had never contradicted him or refused to carry out even a suggestion of an order from him.

"What?" he said.

Sticking her head out of the door in the direction Ethan had gone, she pulled back inside and said, "I've been trying to find some time to talk with you, Mr. LeGrange."

Well, if it was that important, he might as well hear her out. A few more minutes wouldn't matter.

"Okay, Adrienne," he said. "Talk to me about what?"

"I want you to know everything is *okay*," she said, leaning forward slightly.

What in the hell was she talking about?

"Everything. You know . . . everything! I took care of everything!" she said. "I just wanted you to know."

She looked very pleased with herself.

When Duncan's expression remained blank, she seemed to chafe at his ignorance. Arms held stiffly by her sides, she clasped and unclasped her fists. After checking the hallway one more time, she continued in a stage whisper.

"Monica!" she said. "I took care of Monica for you . . . and no one will know!"

Duncan backed into the chair in front of Adrienne's desk and sat down before he fell down. He thought he might pass out. A look of pure horror on his face, he just stared at the woman standing in front of him as if he'd never seen her before.

"What? It was you? You couldn't have, you weren't even there that night!" he stuttered.

Adrienne's eyes glittered, lit with a strange excitement he'd never seen before.

Clapping her hands together like little penguin flippers, she said, "Oh, but I was! I was! But no one saw me."

"How?" Duncan asked, feeling dazed.

56

The events of that night and all that led up to it reeled through his mind, frame by frame.

At first, everything had gone according to plan. The talent show had provided the perfect opportunity. Monica always went out for a smoke break. That was a given. All he had to do was slip out just after she did, go into Nick's office behind the kitchen and get his gun. He knew Nick had one because he'd seen it one day when he picked up Ethan.

He had been waiting in the dining hall because Ethan was still out helping in the garden. Nick didn't know he was there, but Duncan could see him in his office through the service window, putting a hand gun in a lockbox up on a shelf above his desk. That's when everything began to fall into place.

The situation with Monica had become unbearable. He knew he had to do something to stop her from ruining him and siphoning off all of Ethan's inheritance. But when he'd gone to get Nick's gun, the lockbox was empty. How had Adrienne gotten it? How did she even know it was there?

***

"It was you? You got Nick's gun?" he said. "How did you even know he had one?"

"Yes," she whispered. "It was simple, really. Monica was always late or forgetting to pick up Ethan from school. He had a dentist's appointment, I think. I went out to get him and they sent me back to the dining hall to pick him up. I saw him and Nick coming in from outside. They didn't see me, but I heard him give Ethan a little speech about gun safety and always making sure there were no bullets in it and locking it up. City slickers—what use is an unloaded gun? We always kept a loaded rifle near the front door. It's not like you can tell an intruder 'Excuse me! Could you wait here a minute? I need to get my gun and load it. I'll be right back!"

She shook her head, chuckling.

"But, why?" he asked. "I don't understand, Adrienne."

"To protect you, of course," she said. "I couldn't let you shoot her."

"But I wasn't going to shoot her! I was just going to scare her, make her sign the papers, then go away and leave Ethan and me alone," Duncan said.

"Don't be silly," she said, dismissing his explanation. "Monica was a horrible woman. I don't blame you a bit! I saw what she was doing to you and to the business. I knew she had pushed you into a corner. You were absolutely right to plan to get rid of her, but I know you, Duncan. I couldn't let you do that. You're a good man, and a terrible liar. You would have been caught.

"She made it easy, actually," speaking now as if Duncan wasn't even there. "The drugs, the men, she was so blatant about things after a while; didn't even bother covering her tracks since she got her name on all the accounts."

She patted Duncan's hand, which he was too stunned to remove.

"That was foolish of you, Mr. LeGrange. Oh, I don't blame you. You trusted her; of course, you did. You didn't know. Men never do. But I've dealt with filthy creatures like Monica all my life. She's no different than the rats and foxes in the henhouse I used to shoot. That's where I got the idea! Luring her back there. It was brilliant, if I do say so myself."

"But how?" Duncan asked, trying to understand what she was telling him.

"Oh, that's the good part!" she said. "All I had to do was use Monica's sordid habits and greed against her. I sent her a text message that night and asked her to meet me in the chicken coop!"

"But why would Monica agree to meet you—anywhere?" Duncan asked.

"Oh, that," Adrienne said, looking very pleased with herself. "She didn't know it was from me. I made the text look like it came from Nick's phone. There's an app for everything these days! So easy to do. Monica wanted attention. Oh, I knew all about women like her. She couldn't stand that he dropped her. I knew she'd nibble!"

Duncan just stared at her.

"And the beauty of it is that it will all be blamed on Nick!" Adrienne said. "His gun, that message . . . they'll find out about their affair—all the evidence will point to him. The police will have to convict him!"

"But he didn't do it," Duncan said, stating a simple truth. Whatever anger he had toward Nick didn't justify his being accused of murder.

"I know!" Adrienne said, completely missing his point.

She stopped to take a breath.

"The important thing is, it's over. You're okay. Quantum Engineering is okay."

"And," she added, reaching her hand out to touch Duncan's arm, her eyes softening, "We're okay."

Coming out of his stupor, Duncan visibly recoiled, yanking his arm away as if her touch were radioactive. He got up so fast he almost knocked over the chair.

"I never asked you to . . . ," he said. "I never gave you any reason to think that I . . . that we . . ."

Lurching into the hallway, he called out to Ethan, hoping his voice sounded something resembling normal, "Ethan, let's go. It's getting late."

"But, Duncan!" Adrienne said, stepping toward him, bringing her voice back to whisper level. "What about us?"

"There is no us, Adrienne," he said, stepping into the hallway, leaving her behind. "I don't know where you ever got that idea!"

Seconds later, Ethan slouched up next to his dad, assignments in hand, with a questioning look. Duncan hustled him out of the building, not even bothering to lock the front door. He'd have to go to the police, but for now, his only desire was to put as much distance as possible between them and the very crazy woman staring after them as they drove away.

No one heard her whisper, "But, I love you."

57

Adrienne watched as Duncan's taillights disappeared around the corner and the street again became dark.

She blinked her eyes several times, causing a few hot tears to spill out and roll down her cheeks. Quickly wiping them away with the back of her hand, she made her way back to her office and sat down at her desk, ramrod straight, staring into space.

This couldn't be happening. This wasn't supposed to be how it all worked out. She wanted to kick herself. She should have waited. Of course, Duncan wasn't ready. It was too soon. There hadn't been enough time for her to explain everything. He didn't mean what he said. He wouldn't have said those things if he understood all she had done for him. All that they had together!

She had been the one who helped him launch Quantum Engineering and helped it grow. She was the one who found this location. She knew it would be good for business and it was. She was the one who'd stood by him all these years. She'd cut her own pay when things were tough in the beginning. He never knew that. She'd never told him. He just didn't understand.

She had to give him a chance. There was still time for him to see the truth, to see how much she loved him and recognize that he loved her, too! He had been faithful to Virginia, of course, and even to that slut, Monica, but she knew. She saw the small things that showed his true feelings for her, even if he didn't recognize them himself. The smiles in the morning, that time he had put his arm around her shoulders for the group picture. His hand so warm and solid.

And the Christmas cards! Yes, he had Lindsey send one to each employee, but in one, he had written something just for her, 'Thanks for all your work, Adrienne!' She'd kept that one in her drawer. She knew he meant to write more but couldn't show his true feelings at the office.

She had to talk to him. Tonight. Straighten this whole mess out.

Reaching into the bottom drawer of her desk, behind the personnel files she kept locked, she took out her gun. Unlike that idiot, Nick, she kept hers loaded and ready at all times. It would be foolish for her to work late and walk to her car alone without keeping protection at the ready. She carried it back and forth every day.

She lifted her wool coat from the hat tree in the corner, removed the warm gloves from her pocket, and replaced them with the gun. Rooting around in the other pocket, she found her thick, wool beanie. It was an oatmeal color, so it went with everything. She pulled it on, making sure it covered her ears, then tugged her hair in place to add an extra layer of insulation.

Unlocking her car with the clicker, Adrienne got inside and started up the car, then turned the heater up on high, directing the blast of hot air to her feet, which were always cold. Once the engine had warmed up, she wove her way through the downtown streets. Once she was on I-5, she pointed her car southwest, toward Middleton. An older model, her car didn't have GPS. She could have used her phone, but she didn't need it. She knew the way.

Adrienne glanced at the clock. They'd probably stop at Mazatlán's on the way home to pick up some dinner. Mazatlán's was one of Ethan's favorites. See? Look how much she knew about them.

Feeling a small rush of excitement, she pressed her foot down a little harder on the gas. She couldn't wait to get there. This was all just a misunderstanding. Even with their stopover to pick up dinner, they'd probably get to the house at the same time. After she explained things, they'd sit down, share some chips and guacamole, and plan for the future. Duncan would see.

They needed her! She would help Ethan in his last year of school and then he'd be off to college! She and Duncan would have time then—time to do all the things they'd dreamed of doing—well, that she had dreamed of, and she was sure he would, too. Of course, they'd have to wait a decent amount of time before they got married, but she would be the wife Duncan deserved. No one could replace Virginia, of course, but Virginia was gone, and she knew Duncan even better. She'd worked side by side with him in the office, spent more time with him than any other woman, alive or dead!

Yes, Duncan needed her.

When she pulled into the driveway, Adrienne saw that the boys—that's how she'd started thinking of them—her boys— had beat her home. The garage door was closed, but there were lights on inside. She parked in the driveway, looking at the handsome, suburban house with new eyes. *Her* home. This would be her home, too, as soon as she could straighten all this out. With renewed confidence, she got out of her car, walked up to the door and rang the bell.

Ethan answered.

"Ms. Thorley," he said, his mouth full of chips.

Swallowing as quickly as he could, he added, "What are you doing here?"

"Hello, Ethan," Adrienne said, stepping into the hallway as if she lived there.

"I just need to talk with your dad for a minute. Is he back here?" she said, walking toward the kitchen.

"Uh, yeah . . . he's warming up the beans," Ethan said, closing the front door before following her back.

When they arrived, Duncan was punching in the time on the microwave, a spoon in his right hand.

"Ethan! Who was at the door?" he yelled, not having seen them come in.

When he turned around, he dropped the spoon and gripped the edge of the counter.

"Go upstairs, Ethan," he said, not taking his eyes off Adrienne.

"But Dad . . . ," Ethan protested.

"Now."

Ethan slowly eased back into the hallway and took the stairs two at a time.

58

As soon as Duncan heard Ethan's bedroom door close, he said, "You need to leave, Adrienne. I have nothing more to say to you."

"Of course," Adrienne said, "but not until I clear up our misunderstanding at the office."

"No, Adrienne," he said. "You need to go."

Adrienne tried again.

"This is just silly, Duncan," she said. "If you'll just listen to me, I know you'll understand. Just give me five minutes and I promise you you'll see things differently. You have entirely the wrong impression!"

Duncan hesitated for a split second and that was all the opening Adrienne needed. She sat down at one of the bar stools at the counter.

"Pour me a glass of wine, won't you, dear?" she said, smiling up at him. "I know you like red, but I like white. Chardonnay if you have any. You'll get to know these things about me soon, Duncan. All husbands know what their wives like to drink."

Adrienne hadn't picked up on it yet, but Duncan was biding his time, trying to figure out how to get out of this mess—how to get her out of the house so he could call the cops. He had planned on calling them after he got some dinner into Ethan and sent him to bed. Now he wished he hadn't waited. All Adrienne noticed was that he was pouring her a glass of wine.

"Sorry, red is all I have," he said, placing the glass carefully in front of her.

"That's okay, dear," she said, taking a healthy swallow. "Red will do in a pinch."

"Now," she said, settling onto the stool, "let's pick up where we left off, shall we?"

Duncan grimly nodded.

A glimmer of insecurity flashed across Adrienne's face, "I know I threw a lot at you all at once. Much too much to absorb right away, but I can explain it all better, now. I just need you to listen—to hear me out."

***

Ethan cracked the door open and tried to hear what Adrienne and his dad were saying, but they'd moved into the family room, and he couldn't make out all the words. Snippets of their conversation drifted up the stairs . . . 'always been there for you' . . . 'I know you feel the same way!' . . . and his dad's voice saying, 'We were never' . . . 'didn't ask you to' . . . 'how did you.'

But the most chilling of all was Adrienne's voice, loud and clear, saying 'She deserved to die!' and then '. . . I did this for *you*, Duncan! That should count for . . .'

Hands shaking, Ethan grabbed his cell phone, found the number, and stabbed Call. He hoped beyond hope that Ms. McKenna picked up. In two rings, she did.

"Ethan?" Logan said. "Is everything okay? Did everything go okay at the lawyer's?"

He'd almost forgotten about the attorney's office. All that had seemed so important a couple of hours ago. A lot had happened since then.

"I'm sorry," he said. "I know it's late, but you said I could call," he said, not knowing how to explain what was happening.

"Yes, of course, Ethan. You can call me anytime. What's going on?" Logan asked.

Dropping his voice to a whisper, Ethan said, "It's Ms. Thorley, my dad's office manager. She's downstairs and . . ."

"Okay," Logan said. "Is that unusual? Oh, that's right, she's probably there to give you your homework assignments. I stopped by your dad's office to give them to her today."

"No," Ethan said, cutting her off. "That's not it. We already went by the office. We stopped on the way back from the attorney's and she gave them to me then. No, it's something else . . ."

"Okay, I'm listening, Ethan," Logan said, all attention now. "Go ahead. What are you concerned about?"

"Everyone's acting weird," Ethan said, pacing in front of his bed. "At the office, Ms. Thorley said she had some business to talk about with Dad, so he sent me down to his office to get started on my homework, but then, just a few minutes later, he's calling for me to get in the car. He was upset, Ms. Thorley was upset. First, she was looking all googly-eyed at him and then, she looked like she'd been hit by a truck. When we got in the car, he peeled out of there, which he never does.

"Go on," Logan said. "So, do you know why she is there, now?"

"Not really," Ethan said. "Dad sent me upstairs and I can't hear everything they're saying . . . but from what I can hear . . . they're talking about Monica . . . I think . . ."

"You think what, Ethan? What do you think?" Logan asked.

"I think she's in love with my dad! She was talking about shooting Monica, I think. Maybe he's involved somehow . . . I just don't know!"

"Wait a minute . . . ," he said, going over to the window, peeking out through the shutters. "No, I thought I heard the door open, but her car's still out there."

"Okay, Ethan, do you feel that you or your dad are in danger? If you do, I want you to hang up and call 911 . . ." Logan said. "Or I can do it for you . . ."

"No," Ethan said. "I don't know. What if I'm wrong? My dad would kill me if I made a big deal about nothing. I just don't know what to do."

There was a moment of silence, then Ethan's voice came thinly over the phone, "Can you come out?"

Logan tried to think.

"Now? What reason could I give your dad for dropping by at your house at seven-thirty at night?" she said.

More silence as Ethan struggled to maintain his composure. Then he released a suppressed, strangled cry.

That was it. Logan couldn't leave this kid in the lurch. His imagination was probably running away with him. There was a very large possibility of her looking like a fool if she went out there, but she couldn't take that chance.

"I'll be right there, Ethan," she said. "I'll think of something on the way. In the meantime, lock your door and stay in your room, just in case. And if things escalate, please, promise me you'll call 911."

Tiptoeing out of the cabin so as not to wake Glenda, Logan pulled her boots on outside and bundled up in her North Face jacket, beanie, and gloves. Her breath curled away from her in the porch light. This was probably a wild goose chase. She'd go out there, there'd be some logical explanation for what Ethan had overheard, and she'd look like a fool. Oh, well. She'd certainly been there before.

But if what Ethan had heard was anywhere near on target, she'd be walking into an enclosed space with at least one murderer. Duncan or Adrienne? Until Ethan's call, she'd have put her money on Duncan being the killer, but everything Ethan said dovetailed with what she'd observed and learned while talking with Duncan's office manager at Quantum Engineering earlier today.

Just because Adrienne may have been in love with her boss didn't make her a killer. Her prints weren't on the gun. And Duncan had so many more reasons to kill his wife. He stood to gain the most by getting rid of her. So was she going in to protect a frumpy, lovesick middle-aged woman from a stone-cold killer, or would Duncan soon be the hapless victim of a woman scorned? Or were they in it together?

Until she knew more, she wouldn't know who to trust.

59

Logan stamped her feet on the front mat and knocked. There was no moon and dark clouds shrouded the sky. The only illumination came from a single porch light and one second story window to her left. Each home was set back from the road and separated by large trees. The neighborhood was quiet—everyone inside at this hour—and the house was still as a stone.

She'd come up with something of a cover story on the way over. She just hoped it was good enough to get her in the door. She needn't have worried. Ethan was the one who let her in.

"They're in there," he whispered, motioning to the back of the house.

He started to walk back with her, but she pointed to the stairs, insisting he wait in his room. Reluctantly, Ethan obeyed.

Putting on her happy face, Logan picked up her pace and breezily strode down the hall, calling as she went, "Hello? Mr. LeGrange?"

She rounded the entrance to the kitchen and saw Duncan first. He was seated in a lounger on the left. He turned to stare at her as if she were an apparition.

"Mr. LeGrange, sorry to startle you," Logan said. "Ethan let me in."

She walked briskly through the kitchen. Adrienne, who was seated on the right end of the couch, turned to look at the intruder. Her coat was slung over the back of the couch.

"Oh, hello, Adrienne,' she said. "I didn't see you there."

Turning to Duncan, she said, "I'm so sorry to intrude like this, but I'm afraid I may have left my computer here. I dropped by earlier today to go over Ethan's assignments with him and it's the only place I can think of that it might be. I had it at your office, Adrienne, but I know I put it in my car after that, so . . ."

Duncan came out of his stunned state, stood up and said, "This really isn't a good time, Logan . . ."

"Normally I wouldn't ask or barge in here this late, but I have an important meeting tomorrow at OSU and my Power-Point is on there. I should have backed it up . . ."

Adrienne was looking at her funny. She interrupted her midsentence.

"I told you I'd give Ethan his assignments and go over every-thing with Mr. LeGrange. Why would you need to come here and go over anything with him? Can't you see Mr. LeGrange is busy?" Her voice began to rise, "Why do you keep butting in where you're not wanted?"

"It's okay, Adrienne," Duncan said, walking into the kitchen. "She just needs to get her computer."

Turning to Logan, he said, "Where did you work with Ethan today? It shouldn't be too hard to find your computer if it's here. Do you remember what room you were in?"

"We were just in here," Logan said. "Ethan generously shared his lunch with me. We were working at the table over there."

She bent down to look for the imaginary lost computer, which of course, wasn't there.

"I'm sorry, Ms. McKenna, but your computer doesn't seem to be here," Duncan said, escorting her toward the front door. Within seconds, Logan found herself back on the doorstep, put out like a puppy who'd peed on the rug.

Fresh out of ideas, she started back to her car. Fine rescue squad she turned out to be.

She'd call Ethan when she got in the car and remind him to call 911 if his dad and Adrienne started arguing again and it got out of hand. Other than that, she was done for the night. Barring breaking down the door and dragging Adrienne and/ or Duncan out of the house, she couldn't think of anything else she could do.

Trotting down the short stairs off the porch, she was almost to her car when she heard a muffled scream from inside the house.

"No-o-o!"

Acting on pure adrenaline, Logan raced back, leaped onto the porch, and burst into the house. When she got to the kitchen, Ethan was standing there. Her heart sank. Why hadn't he stayed upstairs like she'd asked? How was she supposed to find out what was going on and protect him at the same time?

Logan's brain rushed to make sense of the frozen tableau in front of her. Duncan stood at the edge of the family room, Ethan right behind him. But it was Adrienne who held their attention. Standing in front of the fire, she held a gun, and it was trained on Duncan.

"You again!" she said. Then, shifting her aim briefly, she used the muzzle of her gun to point to one of the kitchen chairs on Ethan's right. "Sit! There! You just can't leave well enough alone, can you?"

Logan obeyed. Ethan looked over at her. She silently willed him to stay still.

Adrienne was talking to Duncan now.

"You lied to me," she said, "All those years. You knew how I felt. You let me do this for you. You counted on me doing this . . ."

Duncan's voice was pleading now, "No, Adrienne," he said softly, "I never did. I had no idea . . ."

"Shut up!" she yelled. "Just . . . shut . . . up!"

She scratched her forehead with the tip of her gun. "I need to think," she said. "Just give me a minute to think."

Duncan took a tentative step forward, "We'll get you some help, Adrienne," he said, "Please, you're frightening Ethan."

"No!" she said, "Don't use Ethan against me—to soften me up! You didn't care about Ethan when you married that whore! Monica made his life miserable—couldn't you see that? No, don't tell me it's my fault. All of this is *your* fault, Duncan! None of this would have happened if you hadn't brought that woman into our lives. *She* destroyed our lives, Duncan! I was trying to *save* us! Why can't you see that?"

Then suddenly, she became very quiet. Her body grew still, and her arm drifted down to her side. Even her facial muscles relaxed and a new expression dawned across her face.

"What a fool I was. You aren't worth any of this. It's *your* fault, Duncan. And you need to be held accountable. I'll take care of Ethan. He deserves better than you," she said calmly. Raising her arm, she aimed carefully at his chest.

Everything that happened next happened fast and Logan would only be able to recall the events later in ragged fragments. Just as Adrienne squeezed the trigger, Ethan threw himself sideways to shove his dad out of the way. Logan launched off her chair and vaulted into the family room, clumsily tackling Adrienne roughly at the legs. The gun flew from Adrienne's hand, but not before she got off one shot.

Just as her shoulder made contact with Adrienne's left knee, Logan saw Ethan falter and twist midair, then fall to the floor with a thud.

Logan's brain took all this in, but she could not go back to help. Adrienne may have been down, but she wasn't out. Fighting like a she-cat, she punched, kicked, and scratched. Logan grappled with her the best she could, forgetting everything her brother had ever taught her about self-defense. All she wanted to do was stop her before she reached her weapon.

Logan scrabbled forward, grabbing at Adrienne's ankles, dodging her feet, trying to work her way past Adrienne as she crab-walked frantically back to get to her gun before Logan could. Out of the corner of her eye, Logan saw Duncan bending over his son. He'd taken his jacket off and was pressing it to Ethan's side. There was blood.

Just then, Adrienne got in a sharp kick to the side of Logan's face, snapping her head back painfully. A brief smattering of stars shot across the back of her eyelids, then everything went black.

60

An EMT efficiently shone a light in each of her eyes and took her vitals. Logan was seated in one of the kitchen chairs, but wasn't sure how she got there. When she could see again, she looked around.

The LeGrange home was a very different place. A brightly lit, busy, confusing place, and all the players had changed. Ethan and Duncan were nowhere to be seen. Adrienne either. A rolling gurney was clanking down the hallway toward the front door. She hoped whoever was on it was going to the hospital and not the morgue.

Crime scene techs scurried around. A few feet away, one was taking pictures from different angles of the pool of blood on the floor—Ethan's blood—careful not to step in it.

Wrapping a blanket around her shoulders, the EMT told her to stay put and she'd be right back. *No problem.* She couldn't stand up if she wanted to. Her legs felt like lead or jelly . . . or both. She wasn't going to test them just yet to find out.

In the family room, she could make out the back of Detective Wright's head and shoulders, on the other side of the couch, crouched down, examining something or someone on the floor in front of the fireplace. A uniformed officer walked past the kitchen window, unspooling yellow crime scene tape as he went. Someone had turned on every indoor and outside light until it was bright as day. Eventually, she became aware of the audio portion of the scene around her and the low buzzing became distinguishable, human voices.

Wright's partner, Johnson, the older of the two detectives, appeared at her elbow with a bottle of cranberry juice.

"Here, you look like you could use this," he said, twisting off the top before he handed it to her. "Sorry it's nothing stronger."

She wondered if he took it from their fridge, or if they simply had well-supplied squad cars here. And yes, she wished it were something stronger, too. A double shot of vodka would not be out of order. With lime.

"Thanks," she said, taking a long drink before resting it on the table. Even this small movement seemed to take a lot out of her.

"What happened?" she asked. "How'd you guys get here? Did Ethan call you?"

Then she asked what she really wanted to know, but was afraid to ask . . . "Is Ethan okay? Was that him on the gurney? Did they get here in time? She shot him, Adrienne. I saw her do it . . . did you get her? Did she get away? I tried to stop her, but it all happened so fast . . ."

Logan realized she was rambling and shut up, giving Johnson time to answer.

"He's lost a lot of blood, but yes, Ethan's alive. His dad's with him. They're taking him to OSH now. And yes, he called us before all hell broke loose here. He said you told him to stay put. We did, too, but he obviously didn't wait."

Logan digested this information. Ethan must have heard the argument escalating and dialed 911 before he came downstairs.

He probably thought he could help in some way. Poor kid.

The last she'd seen of him Duncan had been pressing his suit jacket against Ethan's side. Rick always told her wounds to the torso were never good. Who knows what internal organs had been hit when Adrienne shot him. She could only imagine what Duncan was going through. How awful to know your child took a bullet that was intended for you.

So if Ethan was in the ambulance and his dad was with him, where was Adrienne? Logan looked over to where the crime scene tech with the camera was now snapping away at whatever lay on the floor between the couch and the fireplace.

In answer to her unasked question, Johnson nodded in that direction. "Yeah. Ethan said his dad's office manager was the woman arguing with his dad. Adrienne. We'll verify, but that's her, I assume. Suicide," he said. "At least it looks that way."

Logan tried to remember what Adrienne said just before she raised her arm to shoot Duncan. The rage toward Duncan as she squeezed the trigger, but then, when she hit Ethan, the complete look of shock on her face. The second she did, she must have realized that any chance she had with Duncan was gone. Suicide must have seemed like the only course left to take.

"You're lucky," Johnson said, "the shooter usually takes everyone else out before they do themselves in."

Something to be grateful for at least.

Johnson took a brief statement and said they'd follow up at the hospital. The EMT insisted she be seen by a doctor. They wouldn't let her drive, so she left her car there and accepted a ride in the ambulance.

The doctor said she'd had quite a kick to the head. He didn't think she had a concussion, but ordered her to stay overnight for observation. For once, Logan allowed herself to be rolled upstairs, given some lovely pain medication, and tucked into bed. Wright and Johnson stopped by her room, but when they saw how loopy she was, said they'd come back in the morning.

After the night nurse left, Logan called Glenda. She hated to wake her up, she but didn't want her to worry when she woke up and found her missing in the morning. She gave her the Reader's Digest version of events—including what hospital Ethan was at—the same one she was at, OSH. She wasn't family, so no one would tell her how Ethan was doing. All the nurse would say was that he was in surgery. That was several hours ago.

Glenda wanted to drive up to Portland, but Logan reassured her she was fine. She was going to be asleep in five minutes, and they could figure out how to get her back to pick up her car tomorrow.

Maybe it was the medication, maybe it was the culmination of a very long day and a very scary night, but Logan found herself crying, which was something she rarely did. It wasn't a full-on sob session, just a normal cry, but it surprised her. Since no one was around, she let the tears roll down her cheeks, washing away her pent-up emotions, without trying to suppress them. They were right. A good cry *did* make you feel better.

Finally, she called Ben.

This time, after hearing all she'd been through, he brooked no argument from her. He'd be on the next plane.

Her last thought before sleep was of her beautiful, emerald engagement ring, sitting all alone in its little, velvet box in her dresser drawer. She'd have to call Glenda in the morning and make sure she brought it with her. Time to let the cat out of the bag. It was time to put it on her finger, where it belonged.

61

As promised, Glenda arrived bright and early. With the velvet box. An orderly was just delivering breakfast and the new nurse was checking her chart. Everyone oohed and ahhed over the sparkling, emerald ring.

Then, with more emotion than Logan had ever seen the pragmatic woman express, Glenda leaned over, gave her a huge hug and whispered in her ear, "You deserve this, Love. Don't you ever forget it."

Glenda had known Logan's late husband, Jack, and hadn't approved.

When they were told the doctor wouldn't be able to release her until after lunch, Logan got dressed and checked herself out. Since Glenda was a nurse, this wasn't as risky at it sounded. She drove Logan to pick up her car at Ethan's house, then followed her to The New School, insisting she rest in the cabin until Ben got there.

More tired than she expected to be, Logan fell asleep within minutes. When she woke up, she found herself enveloped in one of Ben's huge bear hugs. Breathing in his scent, her whole body relaxed.

After some suitable physical therapy—Glenda had vacated the premises, pointedly saying she had some work to catch up on—and another long nap, Logan all but jumped out of bed.

"Let's go, lazy bones," she said. "I'm hungry and I've got a ring to show off."

When they arrived at the dining hall for dinner, a dozen confetti canons were released and Nicole started playing the wedding march on the piano. Every staff member was there. Ben and Logan were quickly surrounded. Someone pushed two champagne flutes into their hands and Carla, after making sure everyone else had theirs, raised her glass.

"To Logan and Ben," she began, then she got all choked up. "I had a longer speech, but I can't remember any of it now. I'm just so happy for you both. May all of your days be as happy as this one!"

Logan thought that about covered it. Well said! It certainly summed up the way she felt.

During dinner, which was another culinary success—Nick pulled all the stops out on this one—Carla and Huey caught her up.

After a four-hour surgery, Ethan was now home with his dad, recuperating. Everyone at The New School was turning themselves inside out to help. There would be special tutoring sessions over the summer to make up for the academic instruction time he lost and make sure he stayed on track for graduation with the rest of his class.

Logan noticed Carson was sitting with G.I. Joe at one of the tables.

"I'm so glad he's back, but where was he? Is everything okay?" she asked, taking a bite of Ben's mashed potatoes. She'd finished hers already.

"He called Joe, yesterday," Carla said. "Since he hadn't fallen off the wagon and had committed no crime, Rita's giving him another chance. He's on probation for leaving, but Joe is over the moon. He really got attached. I think he sees a lot of himself in that kid."

"But what about the chicken poop on his shoes?" she asked. "How did he explain that?"

"Oh, he was there, at the chicken coop. He knew Monica from Portland, when he was still using. He was her dealer. She wanted him to get her some stuff, but he refused. She threatened to plant some drugs on him, get him kicked out of the program here, maybe thrown in jail."

"Busy girl," Ben said.

'Yeah. Carson said he only met her that night to tell her to her face that he wasn't going to give in to her demands. She was alive when he left," Carla said. "Since the police now know Adrienne was the killer, they didn't really need his explanation, anyway. But it helped his case with Rita."

Nick and Brittany stopped by to congratulate Logan again and thank her for all she did.

Logan deflected the praise, giving most of the credit to Carla and Huey. She didn't mention that she and Huey had seen the videos Monica had made of them and didn't plan to. That door was permanently sealed.

Stuffed and sated, she and Ben were about to say their goodnights when Brittany rolled out a freshly-baked batch of wedding-themed cupcakes and the hot fudge sundae cart.

"Hope you saved room for dessert!"

Well, maybe just a little piece . . . and one scoop of ice cream . . .

62

Dimebox pushed the side of his face into Logan's legs, then rubbed against her ankles, weaving in and out between her legs, purring for all he was worth.

"Aww . . . ," Logan said. "I missed you, too, buddy!"

Usually, the fifteen-pound calico made a point of stiffly stalking by, head held high in the air, full of disdain, totally ignoring her when she returned from one of her trips to Oregon. Either he was getting used to her absences, or his loving, kitten personality overrode his cool tomcat persona. Either way, she was glad she'd been forgiven.

He certainly hadn't suffered while she was away. Tilly insisted on providing him with only the most expensive, healthiest cat food she could find. Logan didn't have the heart to tell her it was useless, the whole neighborhood fed Dimebox and none of his treats were dietetic. This week Tilly was away visiting her sister, so she and Dimebox had the place to themselves for a few more days.

Speaking of food . . . Logan remembered her mission and set off down Killer Hill toward Tava'e's, the coffee shop on the corner, for one of Jean's gigantic cinnamon rolls. Tava'e's was a local institution and a hub for all things chess. When they met, Tava'e had insisted she learn the game. She had yet to beat the Samoan woman at a game, but her losses were getting less embarrassing. She'd been home almost a week, but they'd been so busy, this was the first chance she'd had to make it down.

"Let me see, let me see!" Tava'e's rich voice boomed, calling her over to her custom booth in the corner, near the windows.

Logan obliged, waggling the fingers on her left hand so the emerald in her ring would catch the light.

"Very nice!" Tava'e said. "Ben has good taste. Meg would approve."

That was the ultimate seal of approval. The former owner of Logan's house, a local writer and independent spirit, Meg had been a close friend of both Ben and Tava'e.

Logan took her usual seat opposite the massive woman in the booth. Epiphany, barista extraordinaire, appeared at her elbow, cinnamon roll and coffee in hand. Logan noted she had fewer piercings, but her hair was still jet black and spiked and her octopus tattoo had some added color.

"Welcome back, Logan," she said, before disappearing behind the counter to help another customer.

"Now," Tava'e said as she set up the chess pieces for a game. "I hear you managed to get yourself in the middle of another murder up in Oregon."

For the next half hour, between moves, Tava'e asked questions and Logan told her what she knew, including how it all ended.

"It is always sad when someone takes their own life," Tava'e said. "But, in this woman's case, this Adrienne, she would have suffered perhaps more if she had lived."

Logan wasn't sure what she believed. She'd never known anyone who'd killed themselves. She was glad Adrienne was no longer able to hurt anyone else, but the woman had been a person, a human being. That little girl in the photo, grinning from ear to ear, so proud and happy, beaming with innocence and joy at having bagged her first turkey—that little girl had been in there somewhere. How she got from there to the twisted soul she became . . . no one would ever know.

If there was an afterlife, Logan doubted suicide had solved Adrienne's problems. If her soul was floating around out there somewhere, it would almost certainly continue to suffer.

Leaving these morbid thoughts behind, the two women caught up on family and friends. Epiphany and Danny were still going strong. Danny, a mentally-challenged young man, had more or less been adopted by Tava'e and Jean when his father kicked him out. When he displayed a natural talent for baking, Jean took him on as an apprentice in the kitchen.

With a little help from Tava'e and Jean, he and Epiphany bought a small house and were fixing it up together. Danny was painting the entire inside by himself. Each room a different color. He beamed with pride whenever he talked about it.

The Southern California Marine Mammal Rescue and Education Center had changed its name to the much more manageable Sea Otter Center and was a huge success. Thanks to Amy, every school-aged child in the county had been able to tour the facility and see the otters up close.

Speaking of Amy, Logan needed to get back and make some deviled eggs for tomorrow's picnic. They were Liam's favorite. Ian wasn't yet sure about them. 'Making' deviled eggs was kind of a stretch. All Logan did was boil and peel them. Ben didn't trust her to mix the right proportions of mayonnaise, his special brand of Maille Dijon mustard, and horseradish with the yolks, whip it all together until there were no lumps, and spoon them in just so before adding the finishing touch—a sprinkle of Hungarian smoked paprika.

Logan didn't mind that he was the culinary talent in the family. As long as she got to enjoy the food!

Ben was already part of the family, but they were making it official on June 28th. Nothing fancy. Just a backyard wedding with the kids, Rick and Paula, Ben's sister and nephews, Taylor and Iona, Tava'e's crew, their neighbors, a few friends, and of course, Bonnie and Mike. Bonnie was going to be Logan's one and only wedding attendant. Rick was going to serve as Ben's best man. He'd already threatened to throw him a bachelor party to be remembered. Even with just friends and family, when you included her New School friends and Huey's sister, Than, well, it was a good thing Tava'e and Jean again offered their ocean-front home and catering to boot.

They hadn't decided on a honeymoon location yet, but they wouldn't have to worry about paying for it. Logan finally told Ben about the music video going viral and the influx of cash. He was absolutely fine with it. Turns out, he had a little stash of his own he hadn't wanted to brag about. Between the two of them, Ben's nephews and Logan's grandson, Ian, had their college funds secured.

As belated Christmas gifts, without fanfare, they also helped Amy and Liam with their house, and paid off Ben's sister's medical bills which she'd incurred while undergoing extensive breast cancer treatments. She was in remission now and doing well.

After the eggs were done and cooling in her little domed fridge, Logan grabbed Bella, and trotted up to the roof. It had been one of those gorgeous winter days in Southern California. Bright and warm, followed by a cool night.

She couldn't remember when she'd been so happy. She had so much. An amazing family, a home, creative work she couldn't wait to do every morning when she woke up, and financial security she'd never expected. And love. She'd never really expected that either, but there it was. Ben was real and wasn't going away. What a glorious feeling! She only hoped she could add to his life as he had added to hers.

As the traffic thinned on the 101 and the soft, winter night descended, Logan picked up her violin. Bella never disappointed. She was like an extension of her arms, her body. Logan's whole soul swelled as she pulled her bow across the strings.

C-E-G-A-flat . . . yes, definitely A-flat . . . the notes coalesced in her mind and the composition she'd been working on before she left became clear. All the love imbued into every atom of the Appalachian wood from which this instrument was created poured out, overflowing past the artificial boundaries of houses, property, and roads, to the ocean, from whence all life came.

Later, when Ben came over, they sat together quietly, wrapped together in a wool blanket, listening to the ocean's lullaby.

A great horned owl's easily recognizable call—hoo-hoo-HOO-hoo-hoo—surprisingly close, punctured the silence. Logan looked out at the ocean, hoping to see a spout. She knew it wasn't time yet, but the gray whales would soon be out there, returning from Baja with their calves, passing by on their way back to Oregon and beyond, to their feeding grounds in Alaska.

Not all of the calves would make it. Killer whales were waiting for them. No one could guarantee the safety of their children. But most did, and killer whales had to feed their babies, too. All in all, life was a risky business, but an exhilarating one.

Having weathered her own storms, Logan laughed. Ben pulled her close and kissed the top of her head. She loved that she didn't have to explain everything to him.

She felt good. Strong! Able to handle whatever life threw at her. A shiver of happiness ran up her spine. And snuggling against Ben's chest, she was also glad she had a partner—a true partner at her side, to share the journey.

THE END

NOTE

1   *Reluctance* is a poem written by the author, Valerie Davisson, and previously published in *Tilting Windmills,* in 1991..

ACKNOWLEDGMENTS

When I began Logan McKenna's journey seven years ago, I was a fledgling mystery/thriller author. Creating characters and plots was the easy part. Understanding police departments, homicide investigations, ballistics and the many ways and technical aspects of how a human being can die . . . that was all new and required a ton of research. Since I wanted my books to portray these details and professions accurately, I reached out to law enforcement, first responders, and medical professionals for help. Each and every police officer, detective, investigator, doctor, ME, EMT, and dispatcher I contacted gave generously of their time and expertise to help make each book better than the last. I can't thank them all enough. There isn't room to list them all here, but please refer to previous books and consider them thanked twice!

In addition, I enjoy exploring a wide array of topics in the series—glassblowing, sea otters, Vietnamese culture, violin making, spousal abuse, Native American culture, geology, knife knapping, mineral rights, probate, urban parks, charter fishing boats, 1930s rum running, the homeless, education, music, and more. Again, people opened up their hearts and shared their passions with me and subsequently, you, my readers.

In Whisper Creek, I drew on many prior interviews and as always, Googled my way through unfamiliar topics such as the nuts and bolts of viral videos and how people make money from them. And, as always, my husband John, who served as a reserve police officer in Pomona for several years, helps me keep it real when I'm writing cop dialogue or want to know what kind of bullets to have my killer use.

When writing the part of Carla and her Golden Retriever, Freya, who is in training to become a volunteer search and rescue dog, I was fortunate to be put in contact with Ryan Simmons, K9 Officer and Supervisor of the K9 Team for the Newberg-Dundee Police Department. His knowledge of what a K9 may be capable of finding was essential to the story. As many of you know, the fictional New School I introduced in Forest Park is located in the Dundee hills, so it was fun to revisit this area.

Kudos and big boxes of chocolates to Beta Readers Extraordinaire Alisha Henri, Maurice Davisson, Sue Levy, and of course, my husband, John Davisson. Cover design and editing credit go to the talented Kim Peticolas, my partner in crime, so to speak, and everyone in Val's Reading Pals.

Due to Covid, some of my in-person interviews had to be put off, but between phone, Zoom and email, we got the job done! As always, in spite of the heartbreak and challenges so many people faced during this last year, people have come through. I continue to be heartened by so many who reach out to help others vs focusing on their own struggles.

Special thanks are reserved for my readers, reviewers, fellow authors, and family who lifted my spirits after the death of my sister and kept me going by telling me how much they enjoyed Bella, Vanishing Day, Safe Harbor, Lies That Bind or any of the other books and can't wait for the next one to come out. This one's for you!

Last, but not least, I'd like to thank the Director of the Cascade Raptor Center, Louise Shimmel, for allowing me a behind-the-scenes glimpse into the fascinating world of raptors and those who work with them, including master Bird Curator, Kit Lacy, and my tour guide, Partnership Coordinator, Julie Collins. Be forewarned . . . a certain, elusive raptor is making its way into Logan's world in Book 8!

ABOUT THE AUTHOR

A self-admitted book addict, Valerie Davisson was the kid with the flashlight under her pillow, reading long after lights out. After a life of travel, she now lives on the Oregon coast with her husband, John, and their new puppy, Finn. When not working on her latest book, she's probably in the kitchen, cooking up a storm for family and friends.

Enjoyed the Book?

If you enjoyed *Whisper Creek*, please consider leaving a review on Amazon or Goodreads. And be sure to check out the rest of the Logan McKenna series.

Shattered (Book 1)

Forest Park (Book 2)

Devil's Claw (Book 3)

Vanishing Day (Book 4)

Safe Harbor (Book 5)

Lies That Bind (Book 6)

Whisper Creek (Book 7)

Want to know more about Valerie Davisson or her next book? Make sure to visit www.valeriedavisson.com and sign up for her newsletter.

www.ingramcontent.com/pod-product-compliance
Lightning Source LLC
Chambersburg PA
CBHW071411200726
48294CB00002B/353